Thump thump! Thump thump! Thump thump!

It was the baby's heartbeat—the most miraculous sound Becca had ever heard. *Thump thump! Thump thump!*

"It's so fast!" she choked out. She giggled, then burst into tears. She looked from the doctor's smiling face to Will's, as though the three of them had, then and there, created the little life whose heart was beating inside her.

Taking off her own headpiece, Dr. Anderson handed it to Will. "Here," she said, "try this."

Will moved in closer, leaned down and placed the stethoscope over his ears. Becca couldn't take her eyes off his, waiting for him to hear that first sound.

She wasn't disappointed when he did. His eyes, so closed to her lately, were filled with the same awe, the same wonder and joy, she was feeling herself.

We did this, his glowing face seemed to say.

For that moment, she felt as perfect in his eyes as the day they'd first fallen in love.

Becca's Baby
Tara Taylor Quinn

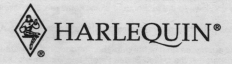

TORONTO • NEW YORK • LONDON
AMSTERDAM • PARIS • SYDNEY • HAMBURG
STOCKHOLM • ATHENS • TOKYO • MILAN • MADRID
PRAGUE • WARSAW • BUDAPEST • AUCKLAND

For Kevin.
Again and again. I've grown with you, changed with you
and love you more than ever.
Now and for eternity.

ISBN 0-373-70943-9

BECCA'S BABY

This edition published by arrangement with Harlequin Books S.A.

® and TM are trademarks of the publisher. Trademarks indicated with
® are registered in the United States Patent and Trademark Office, the
Canadian Trade Marks Office and in other countries.

Visit us at www.eHarlequin.com

Printed in U.S.A.

Dear Reader,

I'm so happy you decided to join me in Shelter Valley. The weather's great here—a paradise—and living expenses are low. The desert landscape is a little barren at first glance...but only until you've been in Arizona long enough to see the wildness, the freedom and the incredible beauty in this terrain. Besides, if it's more color you desire, all you have to do is look up. You'll be amazed by the bluest skies you've ever seen and a sun that just keeps on shining.

I hope you'll find the townspeople of Shelter Valley warm, hospitable and friendly. They tend to welcome strangers with open arms. Maybe—like a lot of small-town people—they know a little too much about each other's business, but it's not just nosiness. It's genuine caring. They're some of the best folks I've ever met and, if you let them, they'll touch your hearts, as well.

Becca Parsons is one woman you'll want to meet. Energetic and beautiful, she's a doer, a giver. People in town rely on her—but that's because they know they can. She's like the coolest girl in school, although she's forty-two years old and has been out of school a long time. Her husband, Will, is the president of the local university, so it's not as though she's left school behind altogether. Becca has a lot of friends, people who consider themselves lucky to be included in her life, but you, dear reader, are in an even more fortunate and unique situation. In this first book, *Becca's Baby*, you get to climb right into Becca's head—into her heart—and find out what really makes this woman who she is. I hope you'll find something of lasting benefit, something to remember.

Becca's story was a tough one to tell. It required brutal honesty and a good hard look at what life is meant to be. But also at what life *can* be if we're strong enough to endure and to give it a chance. I have to admit the story was fun to write, too. I love Becca's house. Will is to die for. I got to play a part in helping Becca make a dream come true. And I got to hang out in Shelter Valley!

I have to be honest with you. Wonderful though it is, Shelter Valley has its problems. The people here deal with difficult and hard-hitting issues, just like they do everywhere else. But they prove that you *can* deal with them. With solid values and big hearts they make life manageable, well worth living—and fun!

So, I hope you enjoy your stay with us. Be sure to visit Weber's Department store for a step back in time. The Valley Diner serves fabulous home-cooked meals. And don't miss a stop at Montford University—the town's core means of support. Some people call it "the Harvard of the West"; it may be small compared to other universities (only six to seven thousand students), but it attracts the best of the best—in students and in faculty. Montford has turned out some of the nation's most promising scientists, businessmen, educators and leaders of the future. The women's basketball team is number one in its division and hoping to win the championship for the second time running, if you care to get in on that action. The cactus jelly plant just outside of town is fun to tour. There's so much more, so many great people to meet, but I'll leave all that for you to discover....

Happy Exploring!

Tara Taylor Quinn

I love to hear from readers. You can reach me at P.O. Box 15065, Scottsdale, Arizona 85267-5065 or on line at http://members.home.net/ttquinn.

Shelter Valley Stories:

Becca's Baby (Superromance #943)
My Sister, Myself (Superromance #949)
White Picket Fences (Superromance #954)

And in May 2001, watch for a special Shelter Valley story coming from Harlequin Books: *Sheltered in His Arms*

CHAPTER ONE

THE STICK HAD TURNED blue. Another mistake in a day that seemed to be full of them. The stupid thing wasn't *supposed* to turn blue.

At forty-two, Rebecca Parsons had firmly believed she was on her way into early menopause. A welcome relief from the monthly inconvenience she'd endured for thirty years. For many, many of those months, the inconvenience had been accompanied by bitter disappointment—*not pregnant*—until she'd eventually given up hope. She'd accepted a life without motherhood. A life with other compensations. And now...

She'd only bought the dumb test to prove to herself that she did indeed have cause to celebrate the departure of monthly cramps, weight gain and irritability. To prove that she'd missed her period because she was menopausal.

"Dammit, don't you know anything?" she swore at the stick. She tossed it into the bathroom trash and proceeded out to the kitchen to prepare Friday night's dinner. She'd been in committee meetings all day and Will would be home soon with only half an hour for his evening meal. Becca intended to make sure he enjoyed it.

No idiot stick was going to get in her way.

HIS THICK DARK HAIR silvered at the temples, Will looked as handsome as ever when he strode through the door a little while later, depositing his briefcase on the counter before he came over and gave her a kiss. Becca deepened the kiss.

"Mmm," he murmured, the sound vibrating against her lips. Beginning an intimately familiar dance, his tongue met hers, mingled. His arms went around her and he pressed his hips to hers.

Becca moaned, and begged with her body, suddenly desperate to be lost in Will's lovemaking.

"Hold that thought," he said, giving her one last kiss before he stepped away. "I have to be back at the U in twenty minutes."

Becca wished she could go with him. Not because she had any interest whatsoever in the Friday-night National Honor Society awards ceremony he, as president of Montford University, had to attend, but because she wasn't looking forward to an evening at home with her own thoughts, her own pile of work to get through.

Oh, yes, it had been a bad day.

Pulling a casserole, one of Will's favorites, from the oven, she joined him at the table. They were both still dressed in their sleek business suits, Becca's shoulder-length dark hair styled as though she'd just stepped from a fashion magazine, Will's looking as though he'd run his fingers through it more than once. They were the epitome of the successful, happy couple.

"How'd things go with Mayor Smith today?" Will

asked. He barely glanced over at her as he devoured two helpings of the casserole.

"Worse than we expected," she said. "The guy's a butt."

Stopping in midbite, Will raised his eyes. Her less-than-flattering description brought a frown of commiseration to his face. It touched her familiarly. Warmed her up a bit.

"That bad, huh?" he asked.

"Everyone who voted for me, everyone in town, knew I was running for city council to see this Save the Youth program born," Becca said, putting down her fork as she stopped pretending to eat. "Now that I'm elected, our dear mayor tells me he doesn't intend to part with one dime of city money to help fund the program."

Will swore. Checked his watch. And swore again. "So you'll fight him, honey," he said, standing. "You've got a lot of strong supporters."

Yeah. She did. But... "Do you think I'm thinking with my emotions, Will? That I'm being illogical?"

"Hell, no!" He carried his plate to the sink, rinsed it and dropped it in the dishwasher. "The town of Shelter Valley *owes* it to its teenagers, dammit. We have to educate our youth about the dangers of alcohol and drug use, give them other options, provide them with support. To continue pretending that teenage pregnancy and drug abuse don't exist here is ludicrous. Don't let that weasel make you second-guess yourself, Bec."

"He claimed that I'm only fighting this battle because of Tanya.'' Becca almost teared up when she thought of her young beautiful niece—her sister's only child. The promising life cut cruelly and senselessly short by a teenage drunk driver.

Will leaned against the counter, drawing her attention to thighs visibly muscular even in the dress slacks he wore. Distracting her again. At forty-two, Will's body was still as lean and virile as it had been at twenty-two. And still had the power to make her forget everything but making love with him.

''Tanya's death certainly opened your eyes to the need for the type of program you're proposing,'' Will said. ''But don't forget that's how most great programs get started. Because someone saw the need. And unfortunately that often requires a tragedy.''

He was right, of course. Will usually was. Which was why she valued his judgment so much.

Glancing at his watch again, he pushed away from the counter, grabbed his briefcase, then approached the table. ''Gotta run, honey. See you tonight.''

Lifting her mouth for his goodbye kiss, Becca wished she could entice him to stay.

When they were twenty-two, she would've been able to.

OUT ON THE GOLF COURSE the following Wednesday afternoon, Will was feeling pretty pleased with himself. Mid-March, and the Arizona afternoon was near perfect. Clear, seventy degrees, the desert air so fresh he'd be richer than Bill Gates if he could bottle it.

The morning's business had been good, productive

beyond his tentative hopes. As an architect, John Strickland was the best. The plans he'd drawn up for Montford University's new "signature" building were downright impressive. A brick exterior that would blend with the hundred-year-old buildings surrounding it and an interior that made superb use of space and offered a calm atmosphere conducive to learning.

As a golfer, John Strickland was better than average, but Will, even with a good five years on the other man, could still beat him. Will's shot was on, his putting accurate. Life was good.

"We've never done a college building before," Strickland said, aiming up for a difficult putt on the eleventh green.

Will watched the other man prepare, admiring his slow controlled movements as he stepped up to the ball, pulled back on the club, and then gently tapped the ball at enough of an angle to take the roll.

"That's an asset in my book," Will said, watching it fall in the hole. Maybe his easy win wasn't going to be quite so easy, after all.

"You mean the putt?" Strickland asked, rubbing in his expertise with a grin.

"No—your inexperience," Will grunted. Strickland's experience was legendary. The man was one of the leading commercial architects in the country. Will considered himself fortunate to have snagged him for the project that was so important to Montford's future.

Lining up for his own putt, one just as challenging

as Strickland's and a little farther from the hole, Will said, "We need a fresh vision if we're going to stand out above the rest." He tapped the ball. Felt a thrill of satisfaction as it disappeared into the hole.

"And why is that so important?" Strickland asked.

"In today's world, university enrollments are market-driven. That's just a reality—all academic institutions have to face it. If we want to attract the best students, we have to be able to compete with the best schools. And image, unfortunately, still remains more important than it should. All the big schools have their signature buildings. Their library or auditorium that proclaims innovation, success, money." Will fished his ball out of the hole. "Montford needs to look just as good."

"So why not build a new library or auditorium?" Strickland asked, picking up his bag as he followed Will to the twelfth tee.

"Because we have a beautiful old library that will still be standing long after we're dust. The auditorium is only ten years old. And we need more classrooms."

Strickland nodded, glanced up the comparatively short fairway. "What do you think, a seven iron?"

"Sure." Will nodded, then pulled out a five for himself. Let John try to make it with a seven.

Watching him, John Strickland let his seven iron fall back into his leather golf bag, taking out a five, instead.

Eighteen holes of golf, a round with one stroke between the winner and the loser, and Dr. Will Parsons figured he might just have found himself a new friend. Which was kind of a rare occurrence in a town the size of Shelter Valley.

He noticed the wedding band on the other man's hand as John raised a juicy steakburger to his mouth in the club's popular grill. "What's your wife think of you traveling so much?" he asked, curious. John designed buildings all over the country. He'd been places Will hadn't even heard of.

Other than vacations with Becca, Will had spent his entire life in Shelter Valley.

And was happy to have it that way.

"She'd hate it if she were still alive," John said. His eyes clouded briefly, then quickly cleared. "She was killed in a car accident three years ago."

"I'm sorry." There was nothing more Will could say.

But he meant it in the deepest sense. He couldn't imagine a life without Becca. Turned cold just trying to do so.

And John was a genuinely decent guy. He deserved to be happy.

"You have any kids?" Will's question dropped quietly into the silence that had fallen. Both men were holding their half-eaten burgers. Neither was eating.

John shook his head. "We were both too busy with our careers," he said softly, looking out the wall of windows to the golf course beyond. Following his gaze, Will couldn't help but think that Arizona's perennially blue skies and bright sunshine suddenly seemed out of place.

"Meredith was a stockbroker."

"Commercial or independent?" Will asked.

"Independent." John smiled. "She was damned good, too."

Even after such a short acquaintance with John, Will would have figured that much.

"We were waiting until we were more established before starting a family. Meredith wanted to be a stay-at-home mom, working out of our house, and she needed enough steady clients to be able to do that." John paused, his gaze returning to the bright green lawns, surrounded by desert. "We waited too long."

John's heartache, his regret, was almost tangible. "Life loses something without kids," Will said, commiserating with the other man. He still had a hard time accepting that he was going to grow old without ever having known the joys—and trials—of parenthood.

"You don't have any children, either?" John asked, glancing over in surprise. "Considering your education background, I figured you had a houseful of them. Seems to be the thing to do here in Shelter Valley."

If the reminder wasn't still a painful one, Will would have smiled at how quickly John had picked up on Shelter Valley culture. Of course, Will had sent him a demographic study of the town when he'd first approached him for a bid on the Montford project. And then there was their breakfast conversation with the expansion committee this morning, which had revealed that three of the four other members came from large families and had gone on to have their own.

"Becca and I spent twenty years trying. Just never succeeded," Will admitted. It was something he rarely talked about.

Something he tried not even to think about any more. At least not any more than he could help.

IN THE FIVE DAYS since she'd taken the pregnancy test, Becca had managed to get herself firmly in hand. Anxiety attacks were unacceptable. Worrying, while unavoidable in the dark of the night, could be curtailed by keeping shorter nights and longer days. She worked like a madwoman, researching funding alternatives for her Save the Youth program. Spent so many hours at the library she'd missed the pastor-parish-relations committee meeting at church.

But she didn't miss her weekly lunch at the Valley Diner with her sisters—Sari, Betty and Janice—and her mother. She might have herself under control, but she still hadn't wanted to risk their barrage of questions if she missed Wednesday's lunch. Sari, her younger sister by a year, would worry. Betty, the oldest sister and organized to the point of driving them all insane, would insist on either an explanation that suited her or an overhaul of Becca's schedule—which would no doubt include more pressure on Becca to quit her volunteer work at the day-care center. Janice, the second-oldest sister, would be avidly curious. Only their mother would have let Becca get away with it. Rose Naylor was so scatterbrained the girls sometimes wondered if she even noticed that the house had been minus Mr. Naylor—who'd died suddenly of a heart attack—for almost ten years.

Becca could have handled the questions, fielded them without making any of her family suspicious. There was nothing to be suspicious about, she reminded herself frequently, since those home pregnancy tests weren't as reliable as a doctor's visit…were they? The sticks lied now and then…didn't they? Things went awry. For all she knew, she'd stuck the wrong end in the cup.

But there was no point in raising any questions in their minds, putting herself under the family microscope, having them all on the lookout for any changes in her. She just didn't need that right now. Not if she wanted to keep panic at bay.

Lunch had been the usual pleasant couple of hours, she reflected later that afternoon. It was a constant in her life, that once-in-a-week exchange of news and views. Being with her mother, her sisters, joining in the familiar, funny, irritating and completely wonderful conversation, had helped her more than they'd ever know. She'd needed them and, as always, they'd been there for her. They always were. She and her sisters and her mom, no matter how well they knew one another, how irritated they got, how different they were, could always be counted on to offer support.

Besides, they were all helping her with another project that was very dear to her. A civic project that was long overdue. They were researching the biography of Samuel Montford, the founder not only of Mont-

ford University, but of Shelter Valley itself. Some of
the basic information about their founder was general
knowledge, like the fact that he was originally from
Boston, that he came from a wealthy family. That
he'd lived with some Southwestern Indian tribes for
a time. That he'd founded the town almost a hundred
and fifty years before. But there was so much more
they didn't know. Like why he'd left Boston to begin
with. Where he'd met his wife. Why he'd chosen
Shelter Valley as his home.

The man had been an enigma, protecting some as-
pects of his past with a vengeance that nearly equaled
the intense love he felt for his family. But as the future descended on Shelter Valley with frightening
speed, Becca felt a desperate urge to remind the
town's residents of their roots.

Before they'd left for an extended stay in Europe,
the current Montford heirs—parents to Samuel Montford the fourth—had lifted the family's ban on the
personal details of the first Samuel Montford's life,
allowing Becca to pursue a more thorough knowledge
of the man and his town. They even turned over some
journals that had been locked in a vault in their private library.

Shelter Valley meant everything to Becca. Home.
Family. Security. Love. Everything that mattered was
right there in that town. She was planning to reaffirm
Shelter Valley's sense of itself and its history with a
big Fourth of July celebration that would culminate
in the unveiling of Samuel Montford's statue.

And thinking of the celebration, she had to start

tracking down the founder's namesake, Samuel Montford IV. He'd left town in disgrace almost ten years
before, but surely by now everyone would be willing
to accept him back. She knew his parents would be
overjoyed—might even come home themselves if
Sam was here. In any case, the man should be there
for the unveiling of his great-grandfather's statue. If
she—

"You can get dressed now, Mrs. Parsons. I'll see
you in my office in a couple of minutes."

Becca was brought back to her present surround-
ings, ones she'd been trying to avoid, with a jolt. The
words were the first the doctor had spoken since she'd
asked Becca a battery of questions before the exam.
The lunch Becca had shared with her mother and sisters several hours before had settled like a rock in her
stomach.

Well-versed in the techniques of not panicking,
Becca remembered to breathe, slowly and deeply. She
nodded and slid off the examining table. Early menopause was all it was. She knew that. So why was
she feeling so much anxiety where there was no need
for it?

Not for the first time that Wednesday afternoon, she
wished her husband was with her.

He would have been, too, if she'd told him she'd
made this appointment with a Tucson gynecologist.

She'd decided not to go to her own doctor in Phoenix. There hadn't seemed any point in involving anyone who knew her—or her medical history. Anyone

who might not understand that early menopause could be a good thing.

Changing quickly into the red business suit she'd worn for a meeting at the city offices that morning, Becca shivered. Everyone was saying the weather was unseasonably warm for mid-March, but everyone was wrong. Becca was cold.

Pulling on her jacket, she freed her hair from the collar, glancing around for a mirror. Tongue depressors, cotton swabs, innumerable scary-looking things, but no mirror.

"Menopause is nothing to get worked up about," she muttered when she found herself hesitating to open the examining-room door. "Nothing to bother Will about, either."

She was lucky, actually, that Will was so busy with the new signature building at Montford. She could have her little midlife crisis without involving him.

With one last reassuring pat to her flat stomach, she yanked open the door, marched down the hall to the doctor's office and settled herself in a chair across from Dr. Hall's desk.

"You're forty-two, Mrs. Parsons?" the woman asked, frowning down at Becca's chart.

"Yes." So it was a little young for menopause; Becca wasn't complaining. As a matter of fact, she thought the early onset a blessing, cause for celebration. She'd pick up a bottle of Dom Perignon on the way home.

And maybe some steaks, too, if the doctor would

just quit frowning. At the moment Becca's stomach didn't want Becca to think about steaks.

"It says here that you've never been pregnant?" the woman asked, still reading the chart.

Becca shook her head. She didn't like Dr. Hall's glasses. They were just a bit too chic for someone who frowned so much. And who wore her hair in that old-fashioned twist that made her look more like a spinster schoolmarm than a compassionate caregiver.

The doctor raised her head, pinning Becca with an expectant stare.

"*Have* you ever been pregnant, Mrs. Parsons?" Dr. Hall asked.

"No. No, I haven't."

"You didn't want children?" The woman's lips were pursed, her brow still puckered, but at least her gaze was back on the chart in front of her.

Becca couldn't help wondering what it was the woman saw there that was so interesting. "A long time ago I wanted children, yes," she answered slowly. She hated having to tell this clinical woman about one of her greatest heartaches. Hated having to explain something that her regular gynecologist in Phoenix knew so well. "My husband, Will, and I tried for years, went to fertility specialists, spent far more money than we should have trying every way we could to have a family, but it just wasn't meant to be."

"Not then, apparently." The doctor nodded, her finger tapping her lower lip as she continued to study a chart she must have memorized by that point.

"Not ever," Becca said adamantly. "We've made a good life for ourselves, Will and I. We both have careers, hobbies, a lifestyle that suits us. We're happy."

Most importantly, they had each other.

Becca had finally come to emotional peace with her childless state. She was all through with feeling sorry for herself. And through with other people feeling sorry for her, too. Early menopause was really and truly a blessing.

Apparently satisfied with Becca's answer, the doctor closed the chart and, hands folded on top of it, looked across her desk at Becca.

"Mrs. Parsons, the test you took at home last week wasn't wrong. You *are* pregnant."

"No," Becca said, or meant to say. The word was little more than a strangled whisper. "I can't have children."

How many times over the years had she had to explain?

"Yes, well, that's what we need to talk about," the doctor said. She leaned forward, her elbows on her desk.

"From what you're telling me, you and your husband are unprepared for this pregnancy."

Numb, Becca nodded. She had no idea what the doctor was talking about. The dark nights of the past week were taunting her—telling her that those worries hadn't been pointless, the panic not unreasonable. Her life as she knew it was ending. And she had no idea where to find the beginning of a new one.

She *couldn't* be pregnant. There had to be some other explanation.

"You're forty-two years old, Mrs. Parsons."

"Yes." Becca was fairly certain of that fact. It was familiar. Something that she could grasp. "Yes." She nodded vigorously. "I'm forty-two."

"Having a baby at forty-two, while not uncommon anymore, is still a risk…" The doctor's gaze was serious, though not unkind. Becca clung to that look, the woman's actual words fading in and out. She heard something about weak placentas.

"…your blood pressure is a little high, which makes me additionally concerned…"

Feeling that something was expected of her, Becca nodded again. The doctor was right. Her blood pressure did have a tendency to run a bit above average when she was stressed out. And Lord knows, it had been a stressful week. What with Mayor Smith's financial bombshell and all. As a paid—and elected—official of Shelter Valley's town council, Becca should have some say in how the town's money was spent. She ran her fingers through her hair, comforted by the familiar feel of the stylishly mussed strands.

"…there are also the hormonal considerations."

Becca tuned in again. "Many women giving birth at your age," Dr. Hall went on, "experience some rather alarming postpartum hormonal imbalances. Women who've had children before. With this being your first, you're even more susceptible to these types of things."

Her first.

Paralyzed with shock, Becca tuned out again. If she could only clear the fog surrounding her...

Why couldn't she get rid of the fog?

Or the terrible churning in her stomach?

She needed Will.

She wanted to be out of here, on the road, driving her Thunderbird.

"...birth defects."

Becca heard only the two words, but the doctor was finally finished. She'd stopped speaking, her eyes filled with sympathy.

Becca hated that. More than just about anything, she hated pity.

She couldn't seem to do a damn thing to take control of the situation. To show the doctor that there was absolutely no reason in the world to feel sorry for Rebecca Parsons.

Having heard very little of what the doctor had said and comprehending even less, she didn't really know what the situation was. She only knew that it had to be happening to someone else.

"You'll need some time to discuss this with your husband, of course." Dr. Hall finally broke the silence that had fallen. "Though I wouldn't recommend taking more than a few days."

"Yes," Becca agreed. She needed her husband. It was another of those things, like her age, that she didn't question.

"I'll speak to him, too, if you'd like," the woman added softly.

"Thank you."

The doctor stood, so Becca did, too, taking the doctor's hand as it was extended.

"As soon as you decide to go forward as I've recommended, I can perform the operation right here at the hospital as an outpatient procedure."

"Procedure?" Becca asked. The blankness that had overtaken her mind was scaring her.

"The pregnancy termination," Dr. Hall said. "I'd like to give you all the time you need, but as I've already explained, you're at least two months along, which doesn't leave us more than a few weeks to do this as safely as possible. The sooner we can get it done, the better."

Termination? Becca started to panic. Dr. Hall said that so matter-of-factly. As if there really was something within Becca to terminate.

"Thank you," Becca said once more. She had no idea why, but it seemed appropriate. And if she had nothing else, she always had her manners.

Somehow she made it out of the office. Into the mild March day, lifting her face to the sun's warming rays. Arizona sunshine. It felt so good. So warm and enveloping. So strong and reassuring. So normal.

How could anything feel normal when everything inside Becca, everything she'd ever been, had changed?

And how could she just get in her car as if the world hadn't permanently altered, shifted completely off its axis?

"You okay, lady?"

Focusing on the young man who'd stopped his bicycle beside her in the parking lot, Becca tried to smile. ''Fine, thank you.''

And then, because he seemed to expect it, she unlocked her car, opened the driver's door and slid inside.

No, she wasn't okay.

She was pregnant.

CHAPTER TWO

THE SLEEK MIDNIGHT-BLUE Thunderbird swallowed the miles, traveling highways, city streets, even, for a brief turn, a desert track. Becca was tempted to just let the beautiful car rest out there in the middle of nowhere, cacti and skillfully concealed roadrunners its only company. She was going nowhere. Might as well be out here, where human reality hadn't reached yet.

She was pregnant. Finally. A baby of her own was growing inside her. The sudden elation took her breath away. And then brought it back in a whoosh of nervous excitement.

Which was followed almost immediately by an incredible rush of fear.

Her stomach lurched. She had a major problem. Spurred by thoughts she had to keep at bay, she jerked the car into gear and drove off again, leaving a huge cloud of dust in her wake. The two-hour trip from Tucson to Shelter Valley had taken four and she wasn't even close to home.

Despite an entire town of family and friends ahead of her, she'd never felt so alone in her life. This was her body. Her problem.

Her prayers of more than twenty years had been answered. But answered too late?

Becca knew one thing for sure. She was scared to death.

Finding the freeway that led to Shelter Valley, she turned her powerful car toward the town that had everything she needed—security, happiness, love. Home. And picked up her cell phone.

Her chances of getting anyone were slim, which might have been why she was finally ready to try.

"Tucson Women's Health Clinic. May I help you?"

Becca's stomach protested again. "Is Dr. Hall still there?"

"One moment, please."

As it turned out, the doctor hadn't left yet. She was quite willing to repeat what she'd told Becca earlier, in her office. This time, Becca heard every word.

Fifteen minutes later Becca dropped her cell phone into the console beside her. She put her foot on the gas and took the next ten miles at more than a hundred miles an hour. She was the dean's wife. The town matron. The one other people came to when they had problems. The one who usually managed to solve those problems.

And she was losing it.

Whatever fates had thought her capable of handling this day were wrong. She couldn't do this.

It was dark by the time she turned off at the Shelter Valley exit. Will would be home, wondering where she was. Hungry. Worried.

The first time they'd thought she was pregnant, Will had brought home a beautiful little antique table box he'd spent their grocery money on, with an inscription carved in its frosted glass top. It had read Mommy's Treasures.

Inside she'd found a tiny square card on which he'd written, "I'm thankful you're going to be the mother of my children, but more than that, I'm thankful you're my wife."

The box had remained on a shelf in a closet after that first disappointment. And after the second and third, as well. Becca wasn't quite sure when it had disappeared. She only knew that one day, when she was looking for something in that closet, she'd noticed it missing.

Although they'd never talked about it, Becca knew Will had disposed of it for her. For both of them. The precious box had been too painful a reminder of broken dreams.

Becca couldn't face him. Couldn't see to his needs. Couldn't even see to her own.

So where did she go now?

Her mother? Unequivocally no. Her mother lived in the past. She always had, but Rose's preoccupation had grown much worse since Becca's father's fatal heart attack a decade ago.

And she couldn't go to Sari. Though she'd always been closest to her younger-by-a-year sister, Sari was still grieving for the daughter, her only child, she'd lost two years before. Becca's problem couldn't help but remind Sari of Tanya, would only be a catalyst for more pain.

And as she'd never confided in her two older sisters in her life, now probably wasn't the time to start.

Mentally running through everyone she knew in town, Becca had reasons for avoiding all of them. Her friends were married, had families they'd be sitting down to dinner with. Her colleagues would be doing the same. Not that she had that kind of relationship with them, anyway. You didn't show up on their doorsteps with a personal problem. Shelter Valley residents were close enough to know everyone else's business, but they still respected one another's privacy.

She thought of the minister at church, but other than the one committee she still served on, she and Will weren't too active anymore—didn't even always attend church. She'd grown somewhat distant from Reverend Creighton.

Randi. Driving by Shining Way, the street where Will's sister Miranda, younger by twelve years, had just moved six months before, Becca suddenly knew where she had to go. She hung a U-turn in the middle of the road and was in front of Randi's new house in seconds.

"Please be home," she begged aloud, searching the pretty house for signs of life.

There was a light on in the back—the kitchen—but that didn't mean anything. Randi always left lights on.

She rang the bell with shaking fingers. And waited.

Tapping her foot, counting, blowing the bangs off her forehead, she tried to think where Randi might be if she wasn't home. Did she have a game tonight? Becca couldn't remember her having said so when they'd had dinner with Will's parents and Randi at his brother Greg's house on Sunday.

Could Becca show up at the field dressed in a suit, looking for her?

"Becca! What a nice— What's wrong?" Randi stood framed in the doorway, wearing a pair of tight-fitting gym shorts and a T-shirt.

Relieved that her sister-in-law was there, after all, Becca opened her mouth to make light of the day she'd had. To practice on Randi before going home.

She burst into tears, instead.

FUNNY HOW LIFE could be so fickle, Will thought without humor. What had been a great day, from this morning's discussion, through the golf game and lunch to the late financial meeting, had turned into a nightmare. Becca was missing.

Carrying the portable phone with him, he strode through the house again, looking for the note he must have missed. Becca never went anywhere without leaving him a note. He lifted his briefcase off the kitchen counter, in spite of the fact that he'd already checked there twice since arriving home more than an hour before. And he racked his brain for someone else to call.

There was no council meeting tonight, or any other type of meeting he could think of that she could possibly be attending. She hadn't said anything about being gone that evening, and she always told him her schedule. He'd already called someone from every one of Becca's committees, anyway. The Women's League. The Fine Arts Council. Church. He'd called her mother and Sari, though he was careful not to alarm either of them. Her friends were all eating dinner with their families and hadn't heard from her. His only comfort was that neither had the hospital nor the police department.

His mind raced ahead, concocting a scenario worse than an accident. Becca was strikingly beautiful. Could she have caught the attention of some sick bastard? Surely not here in Shelter Valley. There hadn't been a rape in years. And she hadn't mentioned anything about making the one-hour trip into Phoenix.

Cold in spite the day's warm temperature, he moved on, studying her desk again for clues. More thorough this time, he went through the drawers and then, the notepad she kept by the answering machine. There were names he didn't recognize, but that was nothing unusual. Becca dealt with a lot of people outside Shelter Valley in the course of performing her various charitable and civic duties. And she'd been looking furiously for a funding source for her newest project, Save the Youth.

The red suit she'd put on that morning wasn't in the closet, so she hadn't changed. Had she told him about a meeting out of town and he'd forgotten? Not likely. He was always aware of Becca. Came from almost thirty years of loving her, he supposed. And close to twenty of worrying about her as they struggled through attempt after futile attempt to have a family. There'd been a time or two in years past that he'd been afraid the disappointment was going to kill her.

A time or two when it had nearly killed him.

Will jerked sharply when the phone in his hand pealed.

"Hello!" he said roughly. "Becca, is that you?"

"Will, it's Randi."

Randi. Biting back the crushing disappointment, he pinched the bridge of his nose. He was probably just overreacting. Strickland's tragic story had been lingering in his mind all afternoon. Becca was fine.

"How ya doin', sis?" he asked. A gifted athlete and his athletic director at the university, Randi held a very special place in his heart. He was glad he was the brother she kept in touch with the most.

"Fine." She sounded a little subdued. "Listen, Becca was just here."

His heart stopped, then started to pound. Thank God. "What was she doing there?" he asked, grinning with relief as he sank down on the side of the garden tub in their bathroom.

"She's on her way home," Randi said, not answering his question. Her tone of voice sent warning signals Will couldn't miss.

"What's wrong?"

"She just needs to talk to you, Will," Randi said in a hurry. "But listen, you need to be nice to her, okay?"

"I'm always nice to her." He stood up. "Tell me what's wrong, Randi."

"I...can't, Will."

"Is she hurt? Ill? Tell me, dammit!" he, who never raised his voice, yelled into the phone.

"Calm down," Randi said, not the least bit intimidated. Which, ironically enough, relieved him somewhat. "She's not ill and she's not hurt and you'd better be patient with her, you hear me?"

His baby sister was yelling at *him?* Will looked around the huge bathroom, the double sinks, the Persian rug Becca had been so excited about finding. Was he in the right house? The right life?

"Have you ever known me not to be patient with her?" he asked slowly, deliberately, all the while sorting through myriad possibilities to explain this strange phone call. This strange night.

"No," Randi conceded. "It's just...she's upset, Will. I've never seen her like this."

He could have cheerfully strangled his sister. "Is there someone else?" He choked out the question. Becca had certainly had her share of male admirers over the years.

And he'd never felt the least bit threatened by any of them.

"Of course not," Randi said, her voice sympathetic. "You know Becca's only interested in you."

Yeah. He did know.

"I can't say anything more, Will. This is Becca's to tell."

"Come on, Randi," Will muttered. "At least give me a hint."

"She'll be there soon, so I'm going to go. Just be nice, okay?"

Confused, with traces of fear still clouding his thoughts, Will gave up. "Sure."

"I love you."

"Love you, too," he answered automatically. He hung up the phone and ran downstairs to wait for his wife. Whatever her problem was, they'd deal with it together.

THE KITCHEN LOOKED exactly as it had when she'd left that morning, startling her with its sameness when her life had changed so completely.

Will was standing at the door when she came in from the garage. She walked straight into his arms. Held on.

"I was worried about you," he said, his words muffled against her ear.

"I know."

He smelled good, familiar, a combination of the shampoo they used and his musky aftershave. He was still in his suit.

"What's wrong, Bec?" he asked gently. He pulled back to look at her. "What's wrong?"

Becca met his gaze bravely for a second and then broke away. She'd gained a little strength from Randi. Was a little clearer about this whole mess. She just hadn't come to grips with any of it yet.

"Let's go into the other room," she said. Will tried

to keep hold of her hand, but Becca, pretending not to notice, slipped away from him. In their windowed sitting room, she took her usual seat on the leather sofa, staring out the glass to the desert behind their house.

Will sat beside her, taking her hand again as he turned toward her.

"Tell me."

"I went to the doctor today," she started, and realized her mistake immediately. His eyes filled with horror. And fear.

Becca's heart cried for him. For both of them. Her being ill might have been better news.

"Randi said you weren't sick," he said. His lips were thinned, his face grim.

"I'm not." She took a deep breath. Forced herself to look at him. "Will, I'm pregnant."

She'd have given anything to spare him the shock, the fear, the trapped feeling she'd been experiencing on and off for most of the past week. And to spare him the heartache of what was to come. But the child was his, too. He had a right to know.

And she needed him. She wouldn't make it through this without him.

Emotions crossed his face so quickly she had a hard time keeping up with them. She recognized shock, which she'd expected. But the happiness...

"Did you say pregnant?" he asked, his voice filled with disbelief. His whole body seemed to be smiling as he anticipated her answer, awaited her confirmation.

No, Will, don't do this to yourself. This isn't good news.

Becca nodded.

"We're pregnant?" He scooped her right up off the couch, swinging around in circles, laughing with pure unadulterated happiness.

Becca gave a small knowing smile. A shrug. Reality was going to set in. And with it the terrible weight of depression, of panic, that she'd been fighting all day.

Looking up at the man she adored, the man she'd spare pain at any cost, she was surprised to see tears of joy matting his lashes. Will never cried. In the twenty years they'd been married, she'd never once seen him cry. Not even during all those disappointments. He took one after another with a strong back and dry eyes. Becca had shed enough tears for both of them.

"We're pregnant!" he suddenly hollered at the top of his voice.

Becca started to cry again. And waited for his reaction. He'd catch up with her soon enough.

And somehow they were going to support each other when it happened.

"You told Randi?" he asked, gazing down at her as he still held her in his arms.

Becca nodded and continued to wait. Surely he was going to see the pitfalls. The difficulties of even attempting to have a baby at their age. She'd already known—and then discovered the problems were worse than she'd thought when the doctor had described them all in exhaustive detail. Randi had shown concern, too, even before Becca had told her what the doctor had said.

But Will didn't seem to understand. Not yet, anyway.

"Have you told anyone else?" Will asked. He finally set her down, but didn't let go of her. Taking both her hands in his, he swung them, looking down at her belly. "We have to call your mother. And mine, too."

Will's parents and three brothers, as well as Randi, all lived in Shelter Valley.

She didn't think they should call anyone.

She wouldn't even have told Randi if she'd had any other choice, if she'd been capable of pulling herself together without help.

Will frowned. Their clasped hands lay still against their thighs. "You aren't with me here," he said. "What's wrong, Becca? Is...is there something wrong with the baby?"

Becca shook her head. "We're forty-two years old, Will," she said softly, looking up at him through teary eyes as she attempted, gently, to help him along. "The risk of birth defects is so much higher now, at my age—it's scary." She shook her head. "And we're far too old to be coping with midnight feedings and chasing a toddler around the house."

"We'll manage," he said just as gently, his voice coaxing. "Others have done it."

Pointing at the glass walls surrounding them, Becca tried again. "This house isn't meant for a child, Will.

It's accidents waiting to happen. And our careers aren't conducive to child-rearing, either. We're out late more nights than not.''

''The house can be made baby-proof, Bec. We just never had reason to worry about it before now. And if it can't, we'll move. A house is a small thing.''

''And is your job or mine a small thing? The dean of a top university unable to meet his social obligations because he was home changing diapers?''

Will frowned. ''You're looking for problems, Becca,'' he said. ''Sure, we're going to have adjustments to make, and no, it's not all going to be easy, but certainly our baby will be worth every effort.''

Becca wished he wouldn't make this so hard. Wished he wouldn't give her even a glimmer of hope when she knew deep inside that there was none at all.

''The doctor's concerned about my blood pressure. It's too high.''

''We'll watch it closely,'' he said, nodding.

If only it was that easy.

''There's the risk of a weak placenta, which could not only cause me to lose the child but would then probably lead to hemorrhaging, as well, which puts my life further at risk.''

His jaw tight, Will dropped her hands.

''And like I said, the chance of birth defects in pregnancies over forty is much higher, and for a first pregnancy all the risks multiply.'' This, she thought, was perhaps the most compelling argument of all. The greatest fear.

The words came pouring out of her, almost verbatim from her telephone conversation with Dr. Hall. Becca wished for a return of the numbness she'd felt during her meeting with the doctor. It was far preferable to the weight of depression pulling her down now.

"I could develop kidney or bladder problems, and chances of a severe hormonal imbalance are greater."

Will's expression was impassive.

"All that aside, how fair is it to bring a child into the world whose parents will be retiring before he starts college?"

"Do we have any other choice?" he asked, but the question was clearly rhetorical.

Muscles in his jaw worked. Nothing else about him moved.

Swallowing, Becca knew that a day she'd thought couldn't get any worse just had.

"Dr. Hall says that I'm high-risk, Will. She assumes we're going to terminate the pregnancy."

The words sounded worse out loud than they did in her head. Worse in her own home than they had in Randi's.

"Did you tell her that?" His eyes were like stones, flat and hard.

"Of course not! I didn't do anything but listen. This was all her idea." Which made it so much worse. A medical professional had just told her she shouldn't give birth to her baby.

"Then we'll go to another doctor. And I thought your doctor's name was Anderson."

"It is," she said. Her head hurt. Her face hurt. Her

whole body hurt. "I went to a woman's clinic in Tucson today."

Still frowning, immobile, Will asked, "Why'd you do that?"

As if it really mattered.

"I wanted the anonymity."

"Why?"

She didn't know why. She'd just somehow felt that if she'd gone to her own doctor in Phoenix, a doctor who knew her, the answer could have been even harder to take. Not that going somewhere else had done any good on that score.

Or had it?

Becca didn't know where the thought had come from, but was there another reason she'd chosen to go to Tucson, a place where no one knew her? Had she maybe, in the back of her mind, chosen the clinic because she knew they did abortions?

Sick to her stomach, Becca sank to the couch.

She didn't *want* to terminate her pregnancy. She honestly, soul-deep, didn't want to do that.

But she didn't want to be pregnant, either. Not at forty-two. Not with all the risks. To her. To the baby.

Pregnancy at twenty-two or at thirty-two was wonderful. At forty-two it was petrifying. She was middle-aged. Fighting high blood pressure.

People her age didn't have babies. They had grand-babies.

Will joined her on the couch. Took her hands again. "Talk to me, Becca," he pleaded softly.

His eyes, when she met them, glowed with the love

she'd taken for granted since she'd been in junior high. It gave her the strength to be honest with him.

"I don't want to have a baby," she whispered.

Giving her hands a little squeeze, Will smiled gently. "Of course you do. You love babies. This is our dream come true, Bec."

"No, Will, not anymore." She stopped briefly when she saw the remoteness that came over his face. But she had to continue. "I'm too old. I'm scared to death, afraid of the risks."

Understanding, love, lit his eyes again. "I'll be right here with you every step of the way," he tried again earnestly. "Together we can do anything."

"No, we can't." She shook her head. "We couldn't make a baby twenty years ago, and we can't make one now. The chances of Down Syndrome, of other defects..." Her voice trailed off.

He sat back, stared at her almost as if he'd never seen her before. "You aren't actually suggesting that we do what that quack doctor recommended, are you?"

Dr. Hall was not a quack. But Will knew that. He knew Becca would never have gone to a doctor who wasn't completely and properly certified.

"She didn't recommend an abortion, Will, she just assumed it was the only course to take. And—" Becca paused "—I'm thinking about it." The last words were whispered, and ended in tears. She hated herself. Hated her body and its aging. Hated a fate that was so cruel it granted her life's wish when it was too late to let the seed bear fruit. This was far worse than never having been pregnant at all.

Will didn't say a word. He wouldn't look at her, either. His face was that of a stranger. Because she'd known him all her life, he'd never been a stranger to her. She got scared all over again.

"I don't know what else to do." She sniffled, thought about getting up to find a tissue.

"I can't stop you, of course," Will said, his voice devoid not only of warmth but of any familiarity at all. "But I would at least ask that, before you do anything, you get another opinion. Preferably from your own doctor, because she knows you, knows your history."

"Okay." She nodded through her tears. And then said, "Thanks," when Will handed her the box of tissues from the end table.

Heading toward the door, he turned back. "You'll call tomorrow?"

Beyond speech, Becca nodded—watched as her husband walked out of the room. And felt as if he'd just walked out of her life.

CHAPTER THREE

THE NAYLOR WOMEN, Becca's sisters and mother, met at the Valley Diner for lunch the following Wednesday. Without Becca.

"What's up with her, Ma?" Betty, the oldest, asked when Sari delivered Becca's apologies.

Smiling to herself, Sari listened while her mother assured her two eldest sisters that Becca was extremely busy with her new city-council position. In a flowered circa-1945 dress, cinched in tight at the waist, Rose Naylor held court—as charming and as self-involved as usual. It hardly mattered that she didn't know what she was talking about. After years of not being heard, Becca had stopped telling her mother any details about her life, and Rose, being Rose, didn't realize that.

Becca was in Phoenix. But she'd rather skillfully avoided telling Sari why she was there.

"Is Mayor Smith still giving her a hard time about the money for Save the Youth?" Janice asked, frowning.

"I'm sure he is," Rose said. Shoulders back and chest held high, showing off beautifully the vintage cameo brooch she wore, Rose sounded like quite the authority. "You know, that boy never did have a thought for himself. His old granddad leads him around by the nose. Always has.''

Sari could have told them that Becca had left George Smith, Jr., in the dust two weeks ago, that she'd already located two possible funding sources. But she didn't. She was the baby in the family. Nobody had ever listened to her. Except Becca.

Betty and Janice nodded in unison. At forty-five and forty-six, the women were both striking to look at, with the big brown eyes and chocolate-colored hair all four Naylor girls had been born with. Sari had always thought Betty and Janice were more like twins than merely sisters. Each seemed to know what the other was thinking. They had the long Naylor legs, too, though Janice had never lost the weight she'd gained with her third child.

Taking a notebook from her purse, Betty looked around the table expectantly. ''We might as well go ahead, even though Becca isn't here,'' she said. ''We have a schedule to keep if we're to get this finished in time for Becca's Fourth of July celebration. So, what did everyone find out?''

''Samuel Montford never actually earned a college degree,'' Janice reported, pulling a folded sheaf of papers from her purse.

''Sure he did,'' Rose interjected. ''He had several of them. They're still hanging in the student-union building at the university.''

''That's what I thought, too,'' Janice said, leaning forward as she met each of their gazes in turn, her eyes wide with surprise. ''But they were all honorary.

He was a student at Harvard, some say he wanted to be a professor, but then his father died and he had to take over managing the family fortune.''

"How old was he?" Sari asked. She couldn't explain her unusual interest in this project they'd all taken on for Becca, researching Shelter Valley's founder for the dedication ceremony of Samuel Montford's statue in the town square on the Fourth of July.

"He'd just turned twenty."

Everyone knew that Samuel Montford had settled Shelter Valley in the early 1870s, and they knew a few other facts—for instance, that Montford University's famous code of ethics was the result of values he'd learned while living with various Southwestern tribes. But much of the man's life had been kept private until now, a hundred and fifty years later.

Becca, who loved Shelter Valley more than just about anyone did, was setting out to fix that. She'd lobbied for the monument made in Montford's likeness, and held fund-raisers for almost five years to commission the statue. She was also chairing the committee in charge of this year's Independence Day celebration.

Becca believed that by preserving the town's heritage, they could preserve the town's character, even though the world was growing so much smaller—and Shelter Valley so much bigger—with the advent of all the new communication technology over the past ten years.

As usual, the rest of the Naylor women were right beside her.

"He was originally from Boston, as we all know," Janice continued. Her assignment had been the early years of Montford's life. She'd found much of her information in the newly released journals, but had been corresponding with some descendants she'd located in Boston, as well.

"He moved to the Arizona territories in the late 1860s," Sari said. "He was only twenty-four at the time." Her assignment had been the later years.

"He had several offspring," Rose piped up. "And he was married when he settled in Shelter Valley. Did he bring his wife with him from the East?" She was in charge of the descendants. She'd visited a family history center in Phoenix and discovered a lot of information in their archives.

"No." Janice frowned. "That part's really sad."

"He came out here alone with kids?" Betty asked. Sari couldn't tell if her eldest sister was impressed by that possibility or thought the man was out of his mind.

Shaking her head, Janice was solemn. "He fell in love with a black woman who was the housekeeper for one of his scholarly acquaintances from Harvard. He married her, too."

"White men usually didn't do that in those days," Rose told them, as if they didn't all know that segregation was alive and well in the mid-1800s.

"Well, he did," Janice said. "Although from one of the journals I got from the Montfords, she wasn't all that eager for the wedding."

"She didn't love him?" Sari was unhappy to hear

that. She'd grown quite fond of the man during the weeks she'd been putting together the pieces of his life in Shelter Valley.

"She loved him," Janice said. "She just knew that the marriage wouldn't be accepted, especially not in his society. The Montfords were one of the big Boston families. They were quite prominent and very wealthy."

"Then what was he doing out here?" Betty asked, taking notes furiously, in spite of the fact that Janice had her facts written down.

Over-organized as usual, Betty was their team captain. She was compiling all the information and would be writing the actual biography that was going to be printed in a special edition of Shelter Valley's newspaper. One of Becca's friends would use Betty's compilation to write a play about Montford's life that was going to be performed—they hoped by Becca's Save the Youth kids—during the Fourth of July celebration.

"As I said, he married Clara, and brought her to the Montford mansion to live. But she was right. The family and their friends refused to accept her." Janice was reciting by rote, not even looking down at the typed pages in front of her. "And when she got pregnant, the family and close friends really went through the roof. They couldn't stand what they called 'the dilution of Montford blood.'"

"So he brought her out here?" Rose asked, completely attentive for once.

"No." Janice shook her head, glanced down at her

page, then back up again. "Shortly after she had her baby, a little boy, she and the baby were attacked while out on a stroll. They both died."

"Oh, God," Betty said, her pen suspended above the pad of paper.

Sari had known something pretty bad must have driven Samuel out west. But she'd never guessed it was anything this heartbreaking.

"His family did that to him?" Rose asked, shocked.

Watching her, Sari was flooded with warmth, with love, for her sweet, zany, busybody mother. Regardless of her idiosyncrasies and preoccupations, family was everything to Rose.

And because of her, it was everything to her daughters, as well.

"According to his journal, Samuel couldn't bring himself to believe that a Montford was responsible. He blamed their deaths on a society that just wasn't ready for interracial marriage. But he was devastated by his family's lack of grief or even sympathy for his loss. Only he and a few of his university friends attended the burials. That was the last day he wrote in that journal."

"No wonder he wanted to escape," Sari murmured, linking the man she'd come to know with the story she'd just heard.

Choked up, she felt the familiar grief slide over her and wished Becca was there to help pull her out. Sari could feel Samuel's pain as though it was her own.

She knew only too well how devastating it was to lose a child.

Excusing herself, she made a beeline for the bathroom and a cold compress. She'd had enough history for one day. But unlike other days when the darkness was debilitating, it took only minutes for Sari to start feeling strong again. Strong enough to march out and tell her sisters that she had an appointment to keep and get herself out into the healing Arizona sunshine.

They barely noticed her departure.

She wasn't coming to another Wednesday meeting without Becca.

Whatever was bothering her absent sister would either come out tonight when Sari visited and called her on her lame excuse for missing lunch, or Sari was going to Will. Though no one else seemed to have a clue, she knew something was wrong with Becca. And that frightened her.

AFTER HER SECOND physical exam in a week, Becca was beginning to feel as though her body wasn't hers anymore. Pulling into the driveway on Wednesday evening, she couldn't seem to work up any real steam over the loss.

She'd seen her doctor, as Will had asked. Though Will didn't know it yet, she also had another appointment at the clinic in Tucson on Friday.

But for now, for tonight and tomorrow, she was a free woman. Free not to think about the problems facing her. The heartache could wait. She'd done all she could do until the end of the week.

There was a note from Will on the refrigerator. He was grabbing something to eat at the university before his board meeting that evening. Becca was okay with that, too, especially since he'd barely spoken to her in the past week. Having the house to herself for one night would be a relief.

Besides, Sari was coming over.

Becca had already changed into a pair of jeans and T-shirt and had just popped a frozen dinner into the microwave when she heard Sari's knock at the back door.

"Just in time for cabbage rolls," she greeted her younger sister.

"You look good!" Sari said, sounding surprised. She kissed Becca's cheek as she passed by.

"I feel good," Becca answered, amazing herself with the truth. After weeks of anguish, she'd called a truce. She wasn't going to think about Will. She wasn't going to think about the other problem facing her. She needed some distance, a complete break, or she'd fall apart.

"You look wonderful!" Becca said, studying her sister for the first time. Sari had gotten her hair cut, short and sassy, the way she used to wear it. She was in jeans and a black angora sweater, loose enough to hide the fact that Sari had lost way too much weight.

"I had my hair done this afternoon," Sari said, shrugging. The microwave beeped and Sari followed Becca, peering over her sister's shoulder.

They decided together that the cabbage rolls were ready.

"Mmm, they smell delicious," Sari said, dipping her finger into the tomato sauce.

"Have you had dinner?"

"Yeah, but I can eat again. I left lunch before we ate today."

Instantly defensive on Sari's behalf, Becca readied herself to say something scathing about whichever sister had been insensitive to Sari.

"What happened?"

"Nothing happened," Sari said. "Janice found some great stuff on Samuel Montford. But it was so sad I just needed to get out for a while."

"I'm sorry, Sar."

Sari shrugged. "It didn't last long," she said, then grinned. "And it gave me an excuse to cut out early on Mom. She wore that hideous flowered thing again. She was so busy telling Janice and Betty about some talk show she'd seen on TV I don't think she even knew I left."

Becca believed her. Their mother loved them all dearly, but she was more than a little absent most of the time.

"Are we going to eat that or just smell it to death?" Sari looked pointedly at the carton Becca still held.

"Guess we'd better eat it. Want to grab some plates and forks?"

Becca was glad to share her meal. Dinner was the hardest one to keep down, so the less she sent down in the first place, the better.

"So where were you today?" Sari asked, helping herself to one of the cabbage rolls.

"I had an appointment," Becca said. It felt strange not confiding in Sari; they'd always told each other everything. But she knew Sari would anguish right along with her, and Sari didn't need that. She was just starting to rejoin the world.

Sari chewed, swallowed. "Same place you had an appointment last week?" she asked.

Startled by the challenging tone in her sister's voice, Becca stared at her, fork raised halfway to her mouth. It had been so long since she'd heard that tone she'd almost forgotten it.

"No," she said slowly.

Sari took another bite. "Were both of your appointments in Phoenix?"

"No."

"Where was the other one?"

"Tucson. Why?" Becca asked, exasperated by all the questions, especially since she already felt uncomfortable about keeping something so important from her sister. But she was just a bit thrilled, too, that Sari was taking such an interest. She'd missed that so much these past two years, Sari's interest.

"Because I want to know what's wrong."

Sari had finished her cabbage roll. Becca had barely started hers. Her stomach was roiling.

"Nothing's wrong," Becca said, getting up to take their dishes to the sink.

Following her, Sari dropped her hand over Becca's on the faucet. "You forget I know you, Bec. You

were vague last week and you even missed lunch today. That means something's wrong.''

Becca met Sari's worried gaze and was tempted to
spill it all right then and there. She'd needed Sari so
desperately these past couple of weeks. Especially
since Will had stopped talking to her.

How could she reach her husband if he never gave
her a chance to speak?

And how long could this go on before permanent
damage was done to their marriage?

But as she looked at her sister—and saw the resid-
ual sadness lurking in Sari's big brown eyes—she
knew she couldn't ask for Sari's help.

''I'm just busier than I expected with the city-
council job,'' she said, instead.

''The funding, I know.'' Sari nodded. She still held
Becca's hand captive. ''But your eyes are telling me
what your words won't, Becca. Something's wrong
and I'm not leaving here until I find out what it is.''

''Sari, I'm telling you—''

''I'll wait for Will to get home if I have to.''

Shoulders sagging, Becca turned, put their plates in
the dishwasher. ''You have enough to deal with.''

''Stop it!''

Becca stared as her sister crossed back to the table
and sat down. She couldn't believe Sari had just
yelled at her.

''Stop what?'' she asked.

''Coddling me, treating me like I'm some kind of
emotional invalid. I can't stand it anymore.''

"I don't do that!" Becca might have felt hurt if she wasn't so astonished. She joined Sari at the table.

"Yeah," Sari said softly, "you do."

Becca didn't know what to say.

"I'm not blaming you," Sari said. "For a while there, I needed to be coddled. But I have to get back to living, Bec, or I may as well die."

"You are living! You're on three of my committees."

"That's existing, not living." Sari's expression was pleading and adamant at the same time. "I need to be able to contribute something meaningful if my life's going to mean anything. I'm ready, Becca. I want to live again."

"Have you told Bob?" There'd been a time when Sari's husband had been afraid he'd never have his wife back again.

Becca had shared his fears.

"We've talked," Sari said. "He's still skeptical, but I know I'm ready. I feel strong now." She smiled. "I was so irritated at Mom today I wanted to scream."

With tears in her eyes, Becca took Sari's hand. "Welcome back," she whispered. And thanked God for what had just been returned to her.

"So, you gonna tell me what's wrong?" Sari asked again, so gently Becca started to cry in earnest, but she was smiling through her tears.

"I've missed you," she said, pulling her sister around the table for a hug.

But when they broke apart, Sari still had the look

of a pit bull working on a side of beef. "Tell me what's wrong, Bec. Maybe I can help."

Becca shook her head. "There's nothing you can do. Nothing anyone can do."

"You're scaring me."

"Don't worry," Becca said automatically. She'd been protecting Sari for a long time. It wasn't a role she was comfortable relinquishing, no matter how badly she needed to do so. "Everything's going to be fine. I promise."

Sari sank back into her chair. "Who's sick?"

"Nobody's sick." Becca sat down, too. For not being sick, she had a stomach that was sure giving a convincing imitation.

Sari looked her directly in the eye. Becca held her ground.

"What do you want to do while we wait for Will?" her sister finally asked.

"Sari." Becca drew out the name, begging her sister to let it go.

"We could play cards. Or figure out what to do with that empty alcove in your foyer."

"We already decided to tile it, and don't do this. You don't want to know."

"Yeah." Sari's eyes filled. "I do. I want to help if I can."

The tears in her sister's eyes were Becca's undoing. "Oh, Sari, it's all such a mess. Please just let me take care of things. Let me get…this out of my life."

Her own words made her cry again. How in hell was she ever going to do it?

"What are you taking care of, Bec?"

Becca sighed, shaking. "I'm pregnant."

Sari's eyes lit up, and the sadness that had become part of her was, for a moment, completely erased.

"Wait, I'm—" Becca stopped, unable to continue. Unable to kill that happiness in her sister's eyes. The same happiness that, when wiped out of Will's eyes, had been replaced with emptiness.

Concern—and fear—lining her face, Sari leaned forward and placed her hands just above Becca's lap. "There's something wrong with the baby, isn't there?"

"I don't know," Becca shook her head. Attempted a smile. "It's too early to be sure. So far, they think it's okay, but…"

"Then what—"

"I can't have it, Sari! I have to terminate the pregnancy."

"Have an abortion?"

Becca didn't know who'd been more horrified, Sari or Will. She only knew she'd never felt so isolated in her entire life. She didn't bother answering her sister's question. There was no need. And no point, either.

"Why?" Sari asked.

For the third time Becca listed all the reasons. Her age. The risk of birth defects. Her high blood pressure. The potential hormonal problems. The other health issues. After an entire week of hearing them in her mind every waking moment of every day, they were almost like old friends—or bitter enemies.

They'd become as familiar as her own name. She hated them, these words, these reasons.

"You said you went to two different places, one in Phoenix and one in Tucson," Sari said when Becca fell silent. "I hope that means you got a second opinion."

Nodding, Becca tried to swallow the lump that was forming in her throat again. She had to be strong. Deal with this. Get through it so life could go on.

Somehow it was going to *have* to go on.

"And?"

"Dr. Anderson knows how hard Will and I tried to get pregnant. She'd never have the heart to tell me I couldn't have this baby."

"She would if she was certain your life or the life of your baby was in danger."

"She said there were risks."

"Insurmountable ones?"

Becca didn't want to think about it. Couldn't handle the *hope*. Or the fear.

"What did she say, Bec?"

"That she'd have to watch me closely, but there was a chance I could deliver a healthy baby."

"What kind of chance?"

"She said it's too early to tell for sure, but right now, other than my blood pressure, things look fine."

"Is your blood pressure really high?" Sari was obviously worried. But she was handling this much better than Becca had expected.

She shook her head. "No higher than usual. Not yet. But it could climb."

"Did she put you on medication?"

"It wasn't that high."

And dammit, the report had been enough to make Becca give herself these two days to dream. To wonder. To hope.

Just a couple of days was all she wanted. A couple of days to pretend that after a lifetime of trying, she really was pregnant. To pretend that she really might be able to have the baby that was growing inside her.

Just a couple of days.

And then she'd consider doing what Dr. Hall had insisted was her only choice.

Thinking about that, Becca felt the nausea rising. She barely made it to the bathroom in time for her nightly ritual. But tonight, when her stomach was finished with its usual protest, she wasn't alone to face the emptiness.

A cold compress was pressed gently across the back of her neck. Then Sari wiped her mouth, her cheeks, her forehead. Sitting on the bathroom floor, Becca leaned into her sister's ministrations, soaking up the care she'd needed so badly.

"Whatever you decide to do, Bec, I'm with you, okay? I know you wouldn't even think about terminating unless you had no other option. I mean, the doctor wouldn't recommend it otherwise."

Becca nodded, feeling better than she had since she'd first suspected she might be pregnant. It felt so damn good to have someone else take care of her, even if only for a minute.

She could hardly believe she was getting Sari back.

She'd been too preoccupied to see that Sari was ready to come back, but now—besides the overwhelming regret at her own situation—she also felt a sense of relief.

Sari rinsed the washcloth, hung it on the rack and slid down beside Becca. "How long do you have to make this decision?"

"I made an appointment at the clinic in Tucson for Friday."

Before the words were even completely out of her mouth, Becca wished she could take them back.

Will was standing in the bathroom doorway. She'd been so busy retching she hadn't heard him come home.

But there was no doubting what he'd just heard.

And no mistaking the rejection she saw in his eyes.

CHAPTER FOUR

"WE HAVE TO TALK."

Will turned as Becca walked into his home office late Wednesday night. Still in the shirt and slacks he'd worn to work that morning, he'd gone straight to his office after hearing Becca's announcement from the bathroom doorway. It was long past midnight now. Sari must have left hours ago. He'd hoped Becca was in bed asleep, leaving him to stumble around the chaos of his feelings in peace.

She looked lovely in the long white silk nightgown he'd bought her for Christmas the year before. As she stood there, perched on the brink of he knew not what, he had to admit she looked fragile, too.

Dammit.

"Apparently there's nothing left to say," he said, using every bit of self-control he had. What he wanted to do, *needed* to do, was shout. To tell her what he thought of her and her decision. To tell her how unfair the whole thing was, how helpless he felt. That the baby she was killing was his too.

Just the thought of what she planned to do made him burn with anger and with grief.

And yet, because the body that carried his baby was hers, because he believed in a woman's right over her own body, and because she believed this damn doctor, he held his tongue. Or tried to. The body might be hers. But that baby was *his*.

"I was going to tell you about it."

"Oh?" he asked, pushing back from his desk to replace some books on the wall of shelves behind him. "When?"

"I don't know." She paused. He could hear her moving farther into the room. His room. "Before I went."

"So you're going to do this." Just clarifying. Making certain of his facts.

"I..." She was behind him, too close. "Will, please look at me."

He couldn't.

His back still to her, he asked, "Have you decided for sure?" He had to know exactly how bad it was. Had to hide how much he hated her at this moment.

"I feel I don't have any other choice." Her voice broke.

Right along with his aching heart.

"You always have choices, Becca," he said. God, he sounded like some pompous school official. Surely, as her husband, he should be supporting her in whatever she felt she had to do.

But there was no way he could support her on this. She was killing their child.

She sniffed, twisting his heart a little more.

"I need you to talk to me about this," she begged.

Against his will, he turned around, cringing inside when he read the despair on her face.

Was it for herself, for their marriage? Or was she suffering, as he was, for the baby they'd tried for twenty years to conceive—the baby she no longer wanted?

Staring silently, Will couldn't hold back his frustration and disbelief—his hurt—enough to be civil. Who was she, this woman who looked like his Becca, but didn't want the baby they'd spent half a lifetime mourning the absence of?

"Why won't you talk to me, Will? You can't ignore me forever."

He wasn't so sure about that. "I can try."

"So that's it?" Her eyes, while filling with tears, were also angry. "You crucify me because I have to do something you obviously don't agree with?"

"No!"

"Then what?"

He turned back to his bookcase. "This is about far more than you doing something I don't agree with," he bit out. "You're talking about a life here."

"You think I don't know that?"

"I don't understand how you can know that and still plan to keep that appointment on Friday."

"Then talk to me!" she cried. "Maybe we can help each other here, Will. That's how we work, isn't it?"

Her words struck a familiar chord. Finally, something that was Becca.

"And," he continued, unable to stop the flow now that he'd started, "I don't understand why, the physical risks aside, you don't want this baby."

"I never said—" She stopped.

Will turned to face her, his eyes shooting the accusation his mouth wouldn't say. "You didn't need to." The words were soft, but still conveyed the anger he was struggling with.

"Doesn't it scare you at all?" she asked. "The thought of raising a baby at our age? Of keeping up with midnight feedings? Of having the energy to lug paraphernalia everywhere we go? What if we no longer have the patience to deal with inopportune crying, constant demands and the stress of teaching a child all the things we take for granted? A baby deserves to learn and grow in a loving environment."

She'd obviously given this a lot of thought. Perhaps more than he had. Still...

"We were given this chance." He told her what he'd been repeating to himself over and over this past week. "I believe that if we're meant to be parents, we'll also be granted the strength and wisdom to handle the responsibility."

That sounded more than pompous, even to his own ears. And yet, he stood by every word.

"Perhaps."

Becca fell onto the sofa along the opposite wall, tucking her bare feet underneath her. Will joined her there because he was exhausted, not because he felt any need to be closer to her.

"Did you call Dr. Anderson?" he asked.

She nodded. "I went to see her today."

Will's heart sank. He'd been hoping the doctor would build Becca's confidence. Help change her mind about this godawful thing she was considering.

"And?"

Winding the bottom of her gown around her finger, Becca stared at the ankle she'd just exposed. He'd always loved her ankles. Didn't matter where they were, a meeting, out to dinner, church in days gone by, if she was wearing a dress and hose, all he had to do was look at those delicate ankles to get turned on. They were even better at home. Naked.

"What did the doctor say, Becca?" he pressed. He didn't want to think about Becca and nakedness. Getting her naked was what had gotten them into this mess in the first place.

"That I'm higher risk now than when I was twenty."

That was to be expected.

"Did she advise against carrying the baby to term?"

Not quite meeting his eyes, Becca shook her head. "But she wouldn't, Will, not knowing how hard we've tried."

"She would if your life was at risk."

Shrugging, she returned her attention to the hem of her gown. "She said I might very possibly miscarry. And if I don't, we can expect problems with my blood pressure."

"Abnormal problems?" He knew a lot of women dealt with blood pressure concerns during pregnancy. Knew, too, that most could be treated simply and safely with medication.

She glanced up and back down quickly. "Maybe. Maybe not."

"What else did she say?" He wanted the facts. All of them. If Becca's life was truly in danger, there was no decision to make.

"That I'd have to slow down."

He refrained from telling her they could accommodate her there. She knew that already.

"There's an increased risk of birth defects."

"There's always a risk of birth defects," he acknowledged, turning cold at the thought. "Even for women in their twenties. But there are tests they can do to determine a lot of these things fairly early on, ways to prevent some of them."

He couldn't deny the frightening possibility that he and Becca might not have a normal child, but there was also every possibility that they *would*. Women in their forties were having babies—healthy babies—all the time now.

And if they were meant to be parents, they'd have to take whatever they were given. That was how life worked. He wished they could be guaranteed a perfect baby; who wouldn't? But nothing in life came with guarantees, not even the certainty of life itself.

"I'd be willing to bet that if you asked the parents of handicapped children if they'd rather they'd terminated the pregnancy than had that child, most of them would tell you no."

She didn't respond.

"There's a chance of kidney or bladder stress, as Dr. Hall said," Becca's voice, falling into the silence a minute or two later, jarred him out of his thoughts.

"A serious chance?" he asked.

Becca shook her head slightly. "Dr. Anderson didn't seem overly concerned. It was more that she felt it her duty to warn me, I think."

Confused, frustrated beyond anything he'd ever known before, Will stared at his wife, wishing he had access to more wisdom than he possessed. Were they dealing with a normal over-forty birth, or was there a greater risk, something she wasn't telling him?

And was a normal over-forty birth really too risky?

But then, why were so many over-forty women having babies? And doing just fine?

"It sounds to me like Dr. Anderson thinks we could go ahead with this."

Becca shrugged, making Will angry all over again.

"So why is it that you insist on trusting the advice of a doctor you just met rather than the advice of a doctor you've been seeing for almost twenty years?"

"Because maybe, in this case, it took a complete stranger to tell the truth."

"Dr. Anderson wouldn't lie to you."

"No." Becca paused. "But she might be more willing to look for positives."

"And that's bad?" He didn't understand. No matter how hard he tried, he wasn't with her at all.

"I need the bald truth, Will, not a truth messed up with emotions and hopes and dreams."

"So...what are you going to do?"

Her eyes were red rimmed. She'd removed her makeup, and while she still looked beautiful, her fatigue was evident.

"What do you think I should do?" she asked.

She knew what he thought. He hadn't heard anything that made him think having an abortion was necessary. So why did he feel like the bad guy? He was trying to preserve a life here. A very precious, long-awaited life.

It was an unfair move, turning the tables on him when they were dealing with *her* body. *Her* health.

"What do you *want* to do?" he countered.

"I don't know," she whispered. A tear dripped slowly down her cheek. "I'm frightened, Will."

His heart, even bruised as it was, went out to her. He was tempted to pull her into his arms, to press the advantage she'd just given him and convince her to have the baby he so desperately wanted. But he remained still, his arms at his sides.

"Do you want the baby?" That was the crux of the matter, he believed. In more ways than one. If she wanted this child, they could investigate the health issues, pursue all the options, assure themselves that the risk was no greater for Becca than for any other woman her age. Hell, pregnancy was a risk for women at any age, but that didn't stop women from having babies.

But if she didn't *want* it...

"I don't know what I want."

The words were blunt, honest, ugly—and filled with anguish.

"I don't think I'd be a good mother now. I don't have the patience."

"Patience can be acquired." He was counting on that, certain he had some acquiring to do himself if

his middle-aged household was to be taken over by a
child. "And you'd be a great mom, Bec. The best.
Because you've got enough love for at least ten kids.
Look how much you enjoy volunteering at the day
care. And how much those kids love you."

A small tremulous smile spread on her lips, but was
quickly gone.

"Tell me what you're thinking," he said. He was
clutching at one hope: that the connection that had
been between them since childhood still existed. That
they could reach each other—and an answer that was
right for both of them. That he could somehow understand.

"I feel so trapped." Her words weren't reassuring.
In fact, just the opposite. Will's heart grew heavier
with every word.

"I don't want to have this baby. I'm afraid something will be wrong with it. And…I'm afraid of dying." She paused, looked him in the eye, leaving no
doubt about the truth of her words. "And I don't want
to *not* have it, either."

"Why?"

"Doesn't seem right."

"Don't make this a moral issue, Bec."

"How can I not?"

He was still working on that one himself. "You
have to be logical about it." He prevaricated with the
only thing he knew—sound reasoning. "Instead of an
abstract issue of right and wrong or things that can't
be weighed or proved, you've got to focus on the

factual pros and cons and come up with an answer from there.''

''I've spent more than half my life wanting a baby,'' she whispered. ''If I were thirty, even thirty-five, I'd be ecstatic.''

''There hasn't been that much change in the last six or seven years, Bec,'' he said. ''We're active, we eat well. We've kept ourselves in shape.''

Becca nodded. And then sat silently beside him for a while longer. She had another whole day before she had to make her decision. He had another day of standing at the precipice of a nightmare from which he couldn't seem to save either one of them.

''You coming to bed?'' she asked when the wee hours of the morning were firmly in place.

Because he couldn't think of a better alternative, Will walked her down the hall to their bedroom, quietly undressed and slid between the sheets. Any other time he would have reached for her, fitting his body snugly around hers, but now he found himself lying flat, instead, staring up at the ceiling. He couldn't turn his back, but he couldn't move close to her, either.

Despite an exhaustion that went much deeper than the mere need for sleep, one fact remained constant in his mind. No matter what Becca decided, a certain amount of damage had already been done. At some point, without his even noticing it, he and Becca had grown apart.

Not just a little apart. Not something that could be fixed with a bit of attention. He and his wife of twenty years weren't even living in the same world anymore.

"MRS. PARSONS! Mrs. Parsons! Sit over here!"

"No! It's my turn, Brian! She said she'd sit by me this time. Didn't she say that, Miss Bonnie?"

"Yes, Lillie, it's your turn," Bonnie Nielson told the precocious four-year-old who not only never forgot a thing, but felt it was her duty to make sure nobody else did, either.

"She's gonna wanna hold the babies again. Everyone wants to hold the babies."

That was from Brenda. Only four years old and her glass was already half-empty, instead of half-full.

"We ain't got none today," Mick told her pompously.

"Uh-huh," little Gwen nodded, her sweet fat cheeks puffed out more than usual with her certainty. "Funny Bo is here. They just brung him in."

Becca's heart skipped a beat at the mention of the Down Syndrome infant who was a regular at the day care where she volunteered on Thursday mornings. Only three months old, Bo was clearly a Down's baby, but it was too early to tell how severely he'd been affected. She, like almost everyone in town who knew the Roberts, hoped that Bo's case wasn't severe at all. His parents were just out of high school and were hardly ready to cope with having a first child, let alone a *handicapped* first child.

And yet, as Becca finished reading to the four-year-olds and made her way to the nursery to take a peek at Bo, she had to admit that never had a baby been more loved than this one. He was always clean, neatly dressed and almost always smiling. His bag, full of everything a baby could possibly need and then some, was packed fresh every day.

"He's a cutie, isn't he?" Sharlyn, the nursery "teacher," came over to stand beside her.

"Yeah." But how heartbreaking to think of the life that awaited him. Watching him in the crib, his eyes skewed as they tried to focus on the colorful mobile swinging gaily above his head, Becca knew that her decision had been made. How could she possibly bring a baby into the world knowing that she had a better chance than Bo's mother of having a baby with serious birth defects? How could she knowingly do that to a child?

"Wanna help with finger-painting?" asked Alice, teacher of the three-year-olds, poking her head in the door of the nursery.

"Sure!" Turning, relieved, Becca followed the young woman into the loudest room. She needed the noise. And loved the children.

When it had become obvious, at least to her, several years ago that she wouldn't be having any babies of her own, Becca had made up her mind to find other ways to bring children into her life. She'd been volunteering at the day care ever since. There, her mothering was lavished on young children whose own mothers had to go out to work, to earn a living to support their offspring. She liked to describe the arrangement as a kind of partnership parenting. Other volunteers she knew felt the same way. She got to be a parent, and the parents of those children got mater-

nal love and care for their children during the hours
they themselves couldn't provide it.

And the children—they got the best of both.

Maybe if Will understood that, he'd understand
why Becca was no longer so desperate to have a child
of her own.

BAD KARMA seemed to be following Will. Which was
a damn clever feat, since he didn't believe in it. Problems at home weren't enough; now he had a potential
disaster waiting for him at work, as well. He'd received a couple of reports from different sources, and
while he didn't want to believe there might be any
truth to them, he didn't dare assume their lack of va-
lidity; he had to verify it. And then he had to figure
out how to kill the rumors before they hurt his colleague and good friend.

"Todd, have a seat," he said warmly early Friday
morning as Todd Moore, dressed in his usual khakis
and polo shirt, approached. Will had deliberately set
up this meeting in the diner downtown before classes
started for the day. He didn't want anyone, including
Todd, to think this was official.

Besides, the earlier his meetings, the sooner he
could get out of the house and away from Becca.
He'd had to leave before she awoke that morning or
risk saying something he'd not only regret, but knew
would make this day even more difficult for both of
them.

He needed to get out of his house and not think

about what today meant. He'd been a father for a brief agonizing week. What a cruel twist of fate.

He couldn't believe Becca was doing this to them. He'd tried to put himself in her position, to understand the feelings she was experiencing. So far he'd failed.

Shaking hands with him, Todd slid his bulk into the bench across the booth from Will. Todd had played football in high school and still worked out a couple of times a week.

"How's Martha?" Will asked, perusing the menu even though he always ordered exactly the same thing when he came to the Valley Diner for breakfast.

"Good. Busy with the kids. Ellen's going to her first dance next weekend, and Martha's sewing her a nice dress."

Will nodded. He was used to all the references his friends made to their kids, the peek at a life he'd wanted but wasn't destined, apparently, to have. This morning he felt more of a pang than usual. Might his child have been a little girl? A girl who'd be attending *her* first dance fifteen years from now?

"I hear Becca's having some problems with Mayor Smith." Todd resumed the conversation after they'd each given their orders for *huevos rancheros* and toast to the college student who'd come to wait on them.

"You know Becca," Will replied, taking a strange comfort in being able to say that—at least about some parts of her life. "She's already found a couple of other possible sources for funding."

"Damn good thing," Todd said. "A bunch of us

plan to take up a collection ourselves, if something else doesn't come through.'' Todd sipped his coffee, pursing his lips in the funny way he'd been doing since the two of them had been college roommates right there at Montford. Back in those days they'd both been forced to turn to coffee for the caffeine boost it gave them. ''The Save the Youth program can't get up and running soon enough to suit me, I'll tell ya. Having a teenager—or being a teenager—isn't the piece of cake it was when we were young.''

Will smiled, remembering the pranks they'd all pulled as teenagers. He had a feeling it hadn't been a piece of cake thirty years ago, either. But it was true that the temptations kids faced today were much more dangerous than the back seat of a car or a lake made for skinny-dipping. Hell, Shelter Valley had been dry back then. They hadn't even had the occasional beer to experiment with.

Breakfast came and went, and Will still hadn't broached the subject of his meeting with Todd. He'd handled many delicate situations during his tenure as president of Montford University, but couldn't remember encountering one quite this awkward.

Nor one he felt so unprepared to handle. If it turned out that Todd was guilty of a serious ethical breach—involving a student—Will didn't want to know. Not today.

''So, you got any promising students this term?'' He decided to take the outside-in approach. A noted professor of psychology, Todd Moore was well-known for a couple of startling articles he'd written on the genius within. Todd believed that there were many more highly intelligent people in the world than anyone knew. He claimed that socially learned behaviors taught kids at a very early age to camouflage their abilities in order to fit in. The studies he'd done over the years, the statistics he'd compiled, were pretty conclusive.

But right now, Todd had just declined a refill on his coffee. Will didn't have much time left.

"Sure," Todd said in answer to Will's question. "With our market-driven enrollment, how could I not have promising students?"

Will conceded that with a nod. He was proud of Montford's enrollment, was partly responsible for the high level of academic achievement to which they could hold their applicants. Because of the strict standards his administrators and faculty maintained, a Montford education was highly sought after.

It was also one of the main reasons that Will was so certain the rumors about Todd, which he'd come to put to rest, were just that. Rumors. Todd's career, his reputation, were just too important to him. Not only that, he valued his family and community too much to risk it all on some…some liaison with a student.

"So what's up with Stacy Truitt?" he asked—nonchalantly, he hoped.

"You've met her?" Todd looked up, surprised.

Will shook his head. "Just heard of her."

"As well you might. She's one of the most promising students I've ever had the pleasure to teach." It wasn't so much Todd's words that made Will uncomfortable, but something about his tone—the way his old friend seemed to come to life when he spoke of this girl.

But then, to an educator, finding a student who was going to change the world was a life-giving experience.

Todd continued to tell Will about Stacy's accomplishments, her goals. "No matter what I give her, she comes back for more," he said, referring to an independent study course he was administering for Stacy.

Was that all it was, then? Todd and Stacy had been seen off-campus together a couple of times. Perhaps it had something to do with the independent study. Perhaps it really was that simple, Will thought with relief.

"What's her project?" he asked.

"Medical-personnel rating of peers who care for AIDS patients in comparison with those who care for patients with other infectious diseases."

Heavy-duty stuff. Running a quick mental overview of what such a project would entail—surveys, lots of math, some interviews—Will was having a hard time figuring out what would require Todd and Stacy to meet off-campus.

"It's amazing," Todd went on, his eyes alight with interest, but whether that interest was in the project or the student, Will wasn't sure. "The preliminary findings sustain the idea that nurses think nurses who tend to AIDS patients receive less respect from their peers.''

''You've been pretty involved in the project?''

''No.'' Todd shook his head like a proud papa. ''She's done the whole thing on her own. From conception to conclusion.''

Will cringed at Todd's choice of word. Conception. That was all he needed. And on top of that, his long-time friend had just shot his ''Todd and Stacy together for the independent study'' theory all to hell.

Looking at Todd, the new lines on his face, the graying at his temples, the other changes time had made, Will felt damn sad. And sorry. There was no way in hell he wanted to ask his friend if he was having an affair. Todd deserved his trust.

Besides, if Todd was doing something so crazy, so foolish, Will just plain didn't want to know. Not right now, anyway. Todd had been his friend long before he'd been his colleague.

And Will needed a break. At least for a day or two. Long enough to get through the fact that his wife could be, at that very moment, on her way to Tucson to kill their baby.

Then he thought of Martha, home sewing a dress for Ellen, Todd's daughter, who was only five years younger than Stacy Truitt. Anger started slowly, but came quickly to a boil. How dared Todd do this to his family? To his children? He had it all. A job he loved. A beautiful wife. And a strong healthy family. He had the children Will would never have. Children Will would've given anything to have.

And he was willing to throw it all away? On a co-ed? Surely there was some other explanation. Will had known Todd since they were kids. Shared life's ups and downs with him. And Todd would never do what he was accused of doing. He would never have an affair with a student. He wouldn't be unfaithful to Martha, period. Todd was a decent honorable man. He loved his wife. Hell, Will had stood up for them when they'd gotten married.

"Does Stacy live on campus?" Will asked, aware that she had an apartment downtown.

"No." Todd shook his head. "She didn't want the distraction of dorm life."

"She lives with a relative, someone she knows in town?"

"She's got an apartment, lives alone," Todd said, though he seemed to be choosing his words a little more carefully. His glance was furtive, and Will liked that least of all. "But you already knew that, didn't you?" Todd asked softly, looking at Will from beneath lowered lids.

Will nodded.

CHAPTER FIVE

TODD'S SILENCE was virtually an admission of guilt, and Will couldn't stand it. He felt physically ill.

He wasn't sufficiently equipped at the moment to deal with the personal ramifications of this particular disaster. He settled for the professional, instead. Montford had very clear standards. And ironclad policies that enforced them.

"How far has it gone?" he asked.

Todd didn't answer, just gazed at the pattern he was tracing with one finger on the tabletop.

"Yeah." Will pushed his empty coffee cup away. "Maybe it'd be best if you told me nothing."

He knew he should ask outright. Because if Todd was indeed guilty, as he seemed to be, Will would have to take action against him.

But he didn't have to ask today. He could do the research first. He'd have to do it, anyway, to build a case before any action was taken. He could pretend for a little while longer that his entire life wasn't careening out of control.

Ignorance was sounding more and more like bliss. He sure as hell wouldn't be suffering so much if Becca had kept her news to herself.

"Does Martha know?"

Todd glanced up. "Know what?"

Todd hadn't told her, either. Now, why didn't that surprise him?

As angry as Will felt, as betrayed, he couldn't just hang his friend out to dry—for the same reason he'd gone home to Becca every night during the past week.

"There've been formal complaints," he said quietly, giving his friend a commiserating nod when Todd's head shot up. "There will have to be an investigation."

"On what grounds?"

Will could almost see his thoughts spinning. "You've been seen coming and going from her apartment. I've been told there are pictures."

Todd swore, the way they'd done as boys first testing their manhood. It sounded a lot worse at forty-two than it had at fourteen.

"I haven't seen any photos," Will told him. "They may not exist." Until half an hour ago, he'd been certain they hadn't. Damn.

"Where do we go from here?" Todd asked.

Good question. Will knew what he was required to do—but Todd was his friend and deserved whatever help Will *could* give him.

"Let me do some discreet checking, find out about this alleged proof." Will stood. "Why don't we meet again, in my office, next Tuesday morning?"

Todd nodded. He didn't rise.

He was still sitting exactly as Will had left him, arms on the table in front of him, head bent, when Will drove by the diner five minutes later.

Stepping on the gas, Will wished, for the first time in his life, that he could just keep going, drive down Main Street to the freeway and out of this town. Shelter Valley didn't have any shelter to offer him anymore. Everything was changing. The people he'd always trusted and loved weren't the people he'd thought they were at all.

He didn't know who was to blame. If anyone was to blame. He just knew that all in all, it had been one hell of a bad week.

THE HUM of the Thunderbird speeding along the highway sounded like an impending death sentence, pronounced over and over, drawing her closer and closer to the chamber that would irrevocably end everything. Each breath a conscious struggle, Becca finally had to pull off the freeway, stopping the car on the shoulder of the road.

How could she do this?

Cradling her flat stomach with both hands, she stared down at it, confused to see it looking exactly the same as it had the year before. And the year before that. But it wasn't the same. A new life was growing in there now.

A direct product of the love she shared with Will.

How could she not do everything in her power to help that life?

Becca started to shiver. She stared out the windshield, at the unending expanse of brown landscape, dotted with pale green saguaro and desert brush and suddenly something became very clear. If she terminated this pregnancy, her own life would be exactly like that barren landscape. Alive, but solitary, dry. Existence without joy. Survival without meaning.

Without Will?

She was afraid of dying. Afraid this pregnancy could kill her. But what would her life be worth if she preserved it by killing the baby she carried? The baby she'd always wanted.

Once she saw it in such basic terms—that she had to choose between her own life and her baby's—there was no longer a choice.

There were other risks, other things to consider, but when compared to the ultimate question of life and death, they, too, paled in significance.

Her head seemed too heavy for her neck to support; it dropped to the steering wheel. Her entire body trembling, Becca hugged her arms around her middle and burst into tears.

She was going to have a baby.

WILL DIDN'T COME HOME for dinner Friday night. The steaks Becca had bought and grilled were like leather by the time she finally heard his car pull into the garage well after midnight. The candles she'd lit were wax puddles in their holders. The chilled wine had long since lost its chill.

Shoulders hunched, he walked slowly, quietly, into the darkened kitchen, setting his briefcase on the counter in its usual spot. He didn't notice her sitting there.

"Hi." It wasn't what she'd wanted to say or had

planned to say, but at the moment it was all she could manage.

He jumped, turned around. "I was trying not to wake you."

"I know."

"I didn't think you'd still be up."

Hoped she wouldn't be up, Becca translated.

"I made dinner," she said, as if that explained why she was still sitting, in her flowing white gown, at a dinner she'd put on the table hours before.

"I'm sorry," he said, his glance brushing the laden table. "I should've called."

Where were you? she yearned to holler at him. But somehow she'd lost that right. She wasn't sure how or when. She hadn't been unfaithful to him. But she knew right then that if she acted like a wife, he was going to walk out on her.

"Did you have dinner?" she asked, instead.

He shook his head. "I had a late lunch."

Oh? With whom? She knew better than to ask the question that would have been natural a week ago. What she didn't know was how to find her husband inside the stranger he'd become. She desperately needed to talk to her best friend. To lean on him. To gather strength from his strength.

She needed to be held.

"Would you like me to fix you something?" she asked.

Neither of them had moved since the moment she'd first spoken. They remained in the dark, barely able to see each other. And maybe that was best. Becca was afraid to see in Will's eyes the death of all she held dear.

"That's not necessary," he said, his voice weary.

She expected him to walk away from her, hole up in his study until he was sure she'd gone to bed, as he'd been doing all week. But he didn't move. He simply stood there, almost as though he didn't know what to do. Becca's heart went out to him. She longed to reassure him, to comfort him, to hold him and love him as she alone had ever done.

But she could no more approach this man than she could a stranger on the street.

"You went to Tucson?" The words, when he finally spoke again, were clipped.

Filled with a resurgence of the panic that had beset her on and off all afternoon, Becca swallowed. "Yes," she whispered.

His head fell, and then he raised it.

"You're okay?"

Depends on how you define okay.

Her body was fine. For now, anyway.

Looking up at him in the darkness, Becca wished he'd look back at her. Wished he'd take her hand, pull her into his arms. Love away the horror of the past week so recovery could begin.

She had to tell him.

She hadn't planned to do it like this. She'd had hopes of starting over. Of playing this out the way she'd always dreamed she would when she told Will the news they'd been waiting for all of their adult lives. She'd planned steak and candlelight, a negligee, soft smiles—love.

"I didn't do it, Will," she blurted to the stranger in her kitchen.

"You rescheduled?" He sounded almost angry. Fool that she was, Becca was thankful for that. She was desperately relieved to see any emotion in him at all.

"I called and cancelled. I decided to have the baby."

That, too, got a reaction—of sorts. He sank into the chair at the end of the table. A chair normally reserved for guests.

Unable to stand his silence, afraid of what might be going on in his mind, terrified that he'd continue to reject her even now, Becca filled the silence with babbling. "I never wanted to go at all, but I felt I had no choice, so I made myself make the appointment, made myself drive down there. I saw the little Roberts boy at day care yesterday and I told myself I was doing the right thing, sparing a child a cruel life like that and…and sparing us the possible heartbreak of having a handicapped child."

Becca paused, but Will didn't speak. Didn't move a muscle.

"On my way down there today, I started thinking about him again. And you know, the only thing I could remember was how happy he is. And how much his parents love him, how much joy he's added to their lives, how much they've grown from having him. And I thought about how he makes me smile and how fond all of the day-care workers are of him, and suddenly saw a great purpose in his life.''

She fell silent. She could hear every breath Will took in the darkened kitchen, reminding her of the hundreds of nights she'd lain awake over the years, mourning the child she couldn't have, listening to Will breathe. The nights she'd spent crying over the way her body was failing him.

''It was when I thought about that life, the fact that it *was* a life, that I had to turn around. Because I'd rather lose my own life than take the life of a child.''

And maybe she was overreacting on the health issues. Dr. Hall had scared the hell out of her. But Dr. Anderson hadn't seemed all that alarmed. And Becca had been trusting Dr. Anderson for almost twenty years.

She tried to chuckle, sort of choked, instead. ''I'm scared, Will.''

''I know.''

It wasn't much, but it was enough to give Becca hope.

''I'm afraid for my health, scared to death something's going to go wrong.''

''You'll have the best care,'' he said softly. ''With today's technology, the doctors know things about our bodies before we do. I wouldn't ever let your life be put at risk, Becca. We'll have all the tests, make sure you're carefully monitored—everything.''

The tension at the back of her neck eased just a bit.

''I'm afraid to let myself hope,'' she continued,

pouring her heart out to him. "What if we go through all this and something happens? What if I miscarry or the baby dies?"

He rubbed his eyes, pulling his fingers through his hair before allowing them to drop back to the table. "There's no life without hope, Becca," he said. His voice wasn't quite as cold, but it wasn't loving, either. "And in life, there are simply no guarantees, either. We just have to carry on as best we can and find ways to cope with whatever happens."

Despite his assurances, he still hadn't moved. He wasn't grabbing her up, whirling her around. He wasn't celebrating.

"I made another appointment with Dr. Anderson for Monday," she offered tentatively, trying to gauge his state of mind. Trying to figure out where she stood—and how to get closer to him. "I figured you'd want to be there, so I took the latest one she had."

Naming the time, Becca said a little prayer that her husband would go with her. She couldn't do this alone. No matter what anyone thought, she just couldn't. She'd waited too long. Been disappointed too many times.

"I do want to be there, thank you," he said. The shadowy shape across from her remained stiff, unyielding.

"She's already done the exam, but she wants to talk to us about maintenance over the next few months and put me on vitamin supplements."

"Good."

"I thought you'd be happy."

"Happy?" He said the word as though it was foreign to him.

"About the baby."

"I'm exceedingly relieved."

"But not happy?"

Coming around the table, he took her into his arms. Finally. Becca sank against him, waiting for Will to crush her to him—to squeeze the tension out of her and the fear.

He didn't. He held her loosely, his lower body not in contact with hers.

"I'm not sure what happy is anymore, Bec," he said. His tone, at least, intimate.

Becca's heart skidded. "What do you mean?"

He moved away from her, hands in his pockets. "I feel I don't know you anymore, for starters," he said.

She struggled to breathe. "Why not?" But she knew. If she was honest, she had to admit she'd barely recognized herself.

"The woman I married, the woman I've lived with through disappointment after disappointment, would never have considered aborting our child—not unless it was one hundred percent absolutely necessary. Probably not even then. The woman I thought I was married to would have *wanted* this baby, would have wanted the chance to experience midnight feedings and diaper changes—not worried about how they were going to change her life."

"I'm sorry."

"It's made me take a good hard look at things, at

us, our lives, and I begin to wonder if I ever knew you at all...."

"Of course you did!" she almost shouted. "It's been a bizarre few weeks." She ran her fingers down his arm, silently asking him to take her hand.

He didn't.

"I've been a little out of my head," she tried again, "but inside I'm still the person I've always been."

"Maybe I've just never really stopped to find out exactly who that is."

Stepping back, Becca wrapped her arms around herself, chilled in the white satin gown she was wearing. "What are you saying?"

"I'm not sure."

Becca, horrified and frightened beyond belief, didn't know what to do. Couldn't even think.

"Let's just get some rest." Will's voice sounded as weary as she felt. "We can talk about this later."

She couldn't go to bed, couldn't lie there alone in the dark, tormented by waking nightmares.

"Do you want a divorce?" She had no idea where the words came from. Or the strength to say them.

Her heart splintered when she heard his softly—painfully—uttered, "I don't know."

"And when do you think you'll know?" The sudden rush of anger was keeping her alive. Breathing. "Because I kind of need to know, seeing that *I've* got more than just me to think about."

"We both have more than just ourselves to think about, Becca."

She accepted the reprimand because she deserved

it. Will was the most responsible man she'd ever met. He'd never desert his child. Or her, if she needed him.

He'd never make an appointment to have his child aborted, either. Not without far more conclusive evidence than she'd had.

"Do you want me to leave?"

Her agonized heart found a moment's solace when Will's head jerked up, his eyes piercing her even through the darkness surrounding them. "Of course not!" he said.

He'd obviously never even considered the idea. She took courage from that. If Will's thoughts were turned toward divorce, they hadn't traveled very far along that road.

In the long run, it meant nothing, only that he hadn't reached the end of his soul-searching journey—which she'd already known. It changed nothing. She'd still done something, contemplated doing something, that had changed her in his eyes.

And maybe in her own, too.

"Let's just give this all some time to settle, eh, Bec?" Will drew his hand along the side of her face.

Unable to help herself, Becca leaned into the caress. She allowed him to gently dry her tears, too, when they began to spill silently down her cheeks.

AFTER ONE of the longest weekends of his life, Will discovered that Monday morning seemed even longer. He sat at his desk, in the presidential suite of offices at Montford University. He signed papers, talked to important people, dictated a day's worth of work for his secretary.

And watched the clock.

He spoke with John Strickland on the phone. The architect was going to be making a second trip to Arizona. Will invited him for another round of golf after they finished the work Strickland was coming to do.

And he watched the clock.

Montford had to hire a new English professor, and because of the university's mission to uphold only the highest standards, Will personally looked over each application before the department chairs began the interview process. Distracted though he was, one of them caught his attention. Dr. Christine Evans was overqualified for the entry-level professorship position. He couldn't help wondering why the woman was leaving a more prominent position in Boston to come to Montford.

But he couldn't find any reason not to grant her that chance. Her portfolio was impeccable. He'd be the final part of the interview process if, indeed, the department chose to hire Dr. Evans. If there was a problem, he'd be able to ferret it out then. Giving the application his approval, he glanced again at his watch.

It was only eleven o'clock. The day was crawling by.

Yet when three o'clock finally rolled around, it came far too soon. He stopped at home for Becca, waiting in the car. All the way to Phoenix he struggled to find something to say to his wife. Words, which usually flowed freely between them, seemed completely out of reach.

He wasn't the only one struggling. Other than hello, Becca hadn't said anything to him, either.

"How are you feeling?" he asked as he pulled into the parking lot of the doctor's office.

"Fine."

"No morning sickness today?" He'd been rather alarmed at the bout she'd had the night before. Too much retching like that and she was going to have bruised ribs.

And he'd been helpless to do anything about it.

"It only happens at night," she said, getting out of the car.

He hurried to catch up with her, holding the door open as they entered the building. "It's happened a lot, then?"

He should know these things.

"Pretty much every night."

"Damn." He'd been a self-absorbed fool to shut himself off, to keep himself distant, to stay out as often as he had. But no more. He'd be home by dinnertime from now on.

There wasn't time for further conversation. They were shown into Dr. Anderson's office, where a nurse weighed Becca, checked her blood pressure and led them to the waiting doctor.

Will caught Becca's eye just before they went in. He felt her excitement—and trepidation—mirrored inside him. With the silent communication of people who'd lived together forever, she told him she was glad he was there. He was glad, too.

And glad they could still share those silent messages.

"We'll be very careful, of course," the doctor said half an hour later. "I'll want to see you, Becca, biweekly, at least for the first trimester, but I see no reason why we won't get this done without a hitch."

After the long speech full of warnings and dangers that the doctor had just given them, Will was immensely relieved to know she wasn't really worried. He couldn't say the same for himself.

"By the next visit we might be able to hear your baby's heartbeat." Dr. Anderson smiled at them.

Will looked at Becca's stomach, hardly daring to believe this was really happening. His glance slid naturally up to meet hers. Full of pride, hope, excitement, her expression was every beautiful thing he'd ever imagined it would be when she finally came to him to tell him she was carrying his child.

"In the meantime, follow the diet I've given you…"

Clutching the pamphlet, Will made a mental note to stop at the grocery before heading home that night.

"…get plenty of rest…"

He'd make sure she made it to bed early every night, even if it meant going there with her and doing mental planning until the hour grew late enough for him to sleep.

Becca, listening intently to the doctor, nodded.

"...and feel free to continue with an active sex life...."

Will swallowed.

"As a matter of fact, please see that you do. New studies report that having intercourse, and orgasm, twice a week increases the production of prostaglandins, Becca, and..."

News that would ordinarily have turned him on, that would've been an instant source of humor and heat between him and Becca, was now only a source of further strain. Staring straight ahead, as if his wife wasn't there, he waited for the doctor to move on to a less volatile topic. Like vitamins.

He wasn't even sure he loved his wife. How could he possibly think about making love to her?

CHAPTER SIX

BECCA WAS QUIET as they left the doctor's office. Not at all the happy woman she should rightfully have been. With a pang of guilt, Will realized he had to take some blame for that.

"How about going out to dinner to celebrate before we drive home?" he asked, putting the past couple of weeks behind them, at least for now. This was a time in their lives they'd always remember. One for which they'd been waiting so many years. The moment deserved more than either of them was giving it.

Their future child deserved more.

"You're sure you want to?" Becca asked, her eyes vulnerable.

"Positive." Will opened the car door for her. "Don't you think the imminent arrival of little Kristen or Dennis warrants a party?"

She studied his expression for a moment longer— and then smiled. And in that smile he saw a trace of the woman he'd fallen in love with so long ago. The woman he'd married and lived with for more than half his life.

"Okay, Dad," she said, turning to slide into the car. "Let's go party."

THEY ATE. They drank—nonalcoholic daiquiris—and they talked. About the doctor's visit. Her warnings. About the things they'd missed in each other's lives during the previous two weeks. Will told her about Todd, his very real fear that he was having an affair with one of his students. And felt the burden lighten somewhat when Becca shared his shock and horror over their longtime friend's probable infidelity.

"Does Martha know?" she asked over the apple cobbler à la mode they'd been splitting for dessert.

Will shook his head.

"Have you seen her?"

He shook his head again.

"Should we call her?"

He met her eyes. "What do you think?"

"If it was my husband, I'd want to know."

"But wouldn't you rather hear something like that from me?"

She took a long time answering, her empty spoon poised in midair. "I'm not sure it would make much difference," she said, frowning. "The news would be so devastating in itself that how I received it would be secondary."

Reading the insecurity in her eyes, he wanted to take her hands, connect physically to the woman he'd become so distant from. He held his spoon, instead.

"You know you have nothing to worry about on that score, don't you?"

Becca, searching his eyes, smiled slowly and nodded. "Thank you."

Will was glad he could still make her smile.

CHRISTINE EVANS pored over available positions she'd collected that week from the Internet-academic-job-placement services she'd signed up with. Nervous excitement churned in her stomach, and with fingers that weren't quite steady, she weeded out all but the most hopeful possibilities. She was close to finding Tory. The detective hadn't been any more optimistic that Saturday afternoon than he'd been any other time in the three months Christine had been searching for her younger sister, but Christine *knew* they were close. She could feel Tory needing her.

And she had to have a new job in place, somewhere far away, when she found Tory. She couldn't risk Bruce finding Tory again, as he always did, beating her into submission so she wouldn't leave him, forcing Tory to run again. Someday he was going to hurt her so badly she couldn't run. And then, Christine knew, he'd kill her. Somehow she had to keep her twenty-six-year-old sister safe from the maniac she'd married—and divorced.

Somehow she had to break the chain of abuse that had bound both of them their entire lives. And hope to God that Tory's scars weren't as irreparably deep as her own.

Her best option was Montford University—a position teaching several undergraduate American literature classes. She already had an interview set up with them. Montford was looking for an English professor. The requirements were a little beneath her; the pay not as good as she was currently collecting, but that was indicative of the fact that this was an entry-level position; it had nothing to do with the school. Montford was a private college with impressive credentials. She'd be honored to be named on their faculty roster. And eventually she'd see her salary climb beyond anything she could make at Boston College.

What made Montford so perfect was its location. Shelter Valley, Arizona, was about as far from Boston as she could get.

She'd learned, however, never to count on anything. She had to have other interviews set up, just in case.

Christine jumped when the telephone rang, checked the caller ID, then picked up the phone.

"Phyllis! I thought you were gone until tomorrow night!" She greeted the woman who was the closest thing to a real friend Christine had ever allowed herself. Like Christine, Phyllis Langford was a professor at nearby Boston College. Her friend taught upper-level psychology classes and had left the previous afternoon for a seminar in Washington, D.C.

"I gave my workshop, discovered there wasn't anything else worth my while and took the train home."

"Brad was there," Christine guessed, playing with a lock of her long dark hair. After three years, Phyllis was still in love with the man who'd married her and then discovered that he didn't want to be married to a woman who was arguably smarter than he was.

"Yeah."

"You wanna come over?"

"Yeah."

"I'll put the wine in to chill."

"Teriyaki rice bowls sound okay?"

They sounded great. Sandpaper sounded great if it meant Christine didn't have to spend another Saturday night home alone—worrying. Remembering.

OTHER THAN SARI and Will's sister, Randi, Becca told no one about her pregnancy. She demanded a promise from Will that he do the same. At least until she was through her first trimester. Until they heard an actual heartbeat. Until she was a little more certain she'd carry the fetus to term.

And so, for the next two weeks she spent most of her time either immersed in committee work or with Randi or Sari. Her friends, her mother, nagged at her about how busy she was. Her younger sister and sister-in-law tended to her as if she was a helpless rag doll. And Will...

Just thinking about her husband hidden in his study—again—as she sat alone in the family room she used to love made Becca feel sick. And she'd thought, when they'd made it through the evening dishes without incident, that she was finally going to have a night free from the nausea that had been plaguing her for weeks.

She'd been wrong.

She made it to the bathroom, barely, and Will was there before her, the toilet seat up, holding a clean washcloth, running it under the tap.

She retched until her ribs hurt, and when it appeared she was finished, Will reached over to flush the toilet with one hand, rubbing her neck with the other.

Then he grabbed the cool wet cloth, passing it gently across her face.

"I hate it that you're suffering," he said almost to himself.

Not trusting herself to speak, Becca kept her head lowered, her neck exposed to his tender and soothing administrations.

"Hopefully we're nearing the end," he continued. "The sickness usually only lasts for the first trimester."

They'd been trading baby books. When he'd read his, he'd leave it on her nightstand. She'd leave hers on his.

Other than the dishes and the nausea, it was about all they shared.

"WHAT'S UP WITH YOU and Will?" Randi asked one Friday night almost two weeks after their visit to the doctor.

Becca pretended to be busy with the address list Randi was helping her prepare for a mass mailing seeking sponsors for the Save the Youth program. She'd had a couple of bites, but final confirmations took time, and she wasn't leaving anything to chance.

"Nothing's up," she said, studiously copying an address from the book of funding possibilities Will had brought her from Montford's library.

"I've been here three nights in the past two weeks," Randi said briskly, writing away. "He's come home, had dinner, said almost nothing and retreated to his study, from which he doesn't emerge until sometime after I'm gone. If at all.''

"He emerges." He was still sleeping with her. But that was all he was doing. Sleeping. And after their celebration dinner, she'd been so hopeful...

"He's not upset about the baby, is he? I thought he'd be ecstatic.''

So had Becca. Will had been one of the major reasons she'd worked up the courage to cancel her appointment in Tucson.

"He is thrilled. He's always wanted children.''

"For a man who's thrilled, he's sure giving an excellent imitation of one who's being eaten up inside.''

Randi knew her brother well. Becca wrote down another address.

"You don't seem particularly excited, either,'' Randi persisted. She'd pushed her book, pad and pen to the middle of the table. "I thought that when you got your second opinion and decided to have this baby, your dreams were finally coming true.''

"I gave up thinking about babies of my own years ago,'' Becca said, still copying from the grant book. "I'm not the same woman I used to be.''

"You're not a woman who loves children?'' Randi scoffed. "And this is why you volunteer at the day care every week?''

Of course she loved children, but... "Will and I are pretty set in our ways.'' She tried again to verbalize some of the reasons she felt so panicked. "We enjoy traveling more than just about anything. We've even begun to plan our retirement.''

"Which is a good twenty years down the road," Randi said gently. "Bec, you and Will were getting old before your time. Not having children was doing that to you."

Pen poised, Becca looked up. "You really think that?"

Didn't Randi see the gray strands in her hair? The passing years? She was closer to fifty than thirty.

"Look around you, Bec, at the friends you guys went to high school with. Are any of *them* joining adult tours of Europe for their summer vacations?"

"Of course not." Becca dropped her pen. "They have kids to—"

She stopped, staring at Randi but seeing the past ten years flash before her eyes.

"I understand your not wanting to vacation on the beach with a bunch of children," Randi continued. "Not the way you two were hurting for so many years. But instead of jet-setting or finding a cabin in the mountains to have wild and raucous sex, you two hooked up with a group of senior citizens."

"They're very nice." Becca had to defend some of their vacation buddies. "We've made some good friends."

"And not one of them is within two decades of you guys. I've seen the pictures, Becca. They're all old enough to be your parents."

"But—"

"And that's only *one* example."

There were more?

"You guys used to drive into Phoenix a lot, go out for dinner and dancing. Or fly to Vegas for the weekend."

She'd forgotten that. They'd had some great getaways in Vegas. When had they stopped going? Why?

"Now you work. Or stay home and read stuffy books."

"*The Seven Habits of Highly Effective People* isn't stuffy."

"But it couldn't possibly raise your blood pressure, either." Randi's earnest brown eyes pleaded with Becca to listen. "You're making yourselves old and it's not time yet."

Did she dare believe her young and energetic sister-in-law? Had she really created some of her own fears? Had she made the wrong assumptions? Because of a difficult fortieth birthday, perhaps. A birthday that had forced her to accept the end of her hopes and dreams.

Randi sat back. "I know so," she said emphatically. "My other brothers and I have all talked about it—several times."

Will's brothers had noticed, too? Becca was seeing the world from so many new perspectives lately it was frightening.

"Can you see me sitting in the park with the rest of the mothers?" she asked Randi. "I've changed most of *their* diapers."

"Well, you didn't change mine—and I'm thirty, but I'm not sitting there yet."

Becca thought about that, too. Giving her precocious sister-in-law a weary smile, she asked, "Who the hell made you so smart?"

Randi scrunched up her nose. "Hey, woman, I grew up with four older brothers. What chance did I have if I couldn't outsmart them?"

Returning to the task before them, the two women wrote silently.

"Do you think Will's open-minded?" Becca asked as she reached the bottom of the last page of potential patrons.

"To a point, sure," Randi answered slowly.

"And always seeking to understand?"

"Usually, yeah, that's Will."

"Usually?" Becca repeated. Asked the same question herself a month ago, she would've answered with an emphatic "Absolutely."

"It's easy to be understanding when your personal universe isn't involved."

"You're saying he doesn't care?"

"No! His life, his dedication to the students at Montford, is a tribute to how much he cares, but none of that affects his heart and soul. Not like you do."

"He's become so black-and-white," Becca murmured, remembering the conversation they'd had after his second meeting with Todd the previous week. Will wasn't willing to concede that if Todd was indeed guilty of having an affair with one of his students—which Todd still had not admitted—it didn't necessarily make Todd a bad person. A misguided one, certainly. An unhappy one. A man who'd made a serious mistake. But it didn't change the forty good years Todd had put in on this earth.

Randi rubbed the back of Becca's hand, a sad smile on her face. "He's not getting over the fact that you considered an abortion, is he."

"Nope."

And there was nothing Becca could do to change that. She'd had the thought. She couldn't not have it.

"Give him time, Bec. My brother's a fair man. And he loves you. He'll come around."

"I love him, too," she admitted. "But I don't think I can live with a man who only sees things his own way. When did he become so judgmental?" And how had she missed noticing it?

"The man you're describing may be the man who's holed up in that office in there," Randi said, gathering their papers in a neat pile as she stood up. "But he's not Will. Give him time," she said again.

At the moment Becca had few other choices. And time was something she had a lot of. Six months of it, to be exact.

WILL'S INTERVIEW with the prospective new English professor, Dr. Christine Evans, just happened to be on the same Monday as Becca's second doctor's appointment. He was glad of the diversion as he wondered what the doctor might tell them later that afternoon. He'd spent the past two weeks going over the warnings Dr. Anderson had laid out the last time they'd seen her. He'd done his research, knew which tests were necessary and which Becca could be spared. He also had several questions that needed answers.

He wouldn't allow himself to think that the doctor might find some negative change in Becca's condition, that the pregnancy wasn't progressing as it should. But somehow the fear crept in, in spite of his very forceful admonitions to the contrary.

The first thing he noticed about Christine Evans was the silky dark hair that hung all the way down to her hips. She had the thick tresses pulled back at the sides with a couple of pearled barrettes.

Just the way Becca had worn her hair twenty years ago. Back when she'd been all natural, before travel, education—life—had put a stylish veneer on her beauty.

The second thing he noticed was the quiet determination in Christine's shadowed blue eyes.

They reminded him of Becca, too. Shadows and all.

"Please, have a seat," he said as he shook her hand. He waited for her to settle in one of the maroon leather chairs in front of his desk before taking his own seat.

Her legs, when she sat, barely touched the floor. She was much shorter than Becca. But just as shapely. And slim.

"I've read your résumé," Will said. He'd read it more than once, actually. Christine Evans was a dedicated woman when it came to her career. According to her interviews, the only family she had was a younger sister. "You achieved your doctorate at twenty-six. That's impressive."

She shrugged, her eyes lowering briefly. "I always knew what I wanted."

Asking the standard questions the position required, ensuring that Dr. Evans was aware of—and supported—the standards of conduct demanded by Montford, Will completed his portion of the new-hire interview.

"So what do you like most about teaching English?" he asked, trying to ignore the twinge of conscience that told him he had no need to ask such a question. "Literature or writing?"

He'd read the reports from his colleagues, the unanimous recommendations that Dr. Evans be offered the position for which she'd applied. Normally this last interview was merely a formality, a handshake and an offer. But Will didn't want Dr. Evans to leave his office so quickly. He was curious about her, this woman with her downcast eyes who reminded him so much of his wife.

"Literature," she said after some thought. "Though I do a lot of personal writing, too."

Hands folded across his stomach, he leaned back in his chair and nodded. "Ever been published?"

She looked away. "Some, not a lot."

He found it hard to believe that someone with her credentials, her many impressive references, hadn't yet realized success in the journal-publishing arena. Scholarly journals usually snapped up people like her, regardless of whether they could actually write or not.

Judging by the two-page review she'd submitted on her views of education, she could write.

"You must be submitting to the wrong forums," he suggested.

Her eyes, when she turned them on him, struck him with an almost tangible sensation. Held him captive. So full were they of pride, of self-respect—and insecurity.

"What I've submitted has been published. I just don't submit a lot."

He'd have jumped on that instantly, encouraged her to submit as often as possible, offered to help her if he could, but she forestalled him.

"I write for myself," she said. "A form of catharsis. My work isn't intended for anyone else to see."

Will wanted to read what she'd written more than he could remember wanting anything in ages.

Christine Evans was having a strange effect on him. For the first time in weeks, he was starting to take a genuine interest in the world around him.

He hired her on the spot.

BECCA CHATTED all the way to the doctor's office. Through Shelter Valley, along the freeway, across the busy Phoenix streets, she kept up a string of comments and questions that prevented her thoughts from flaying her raw. After two weeks of virtual silence, she and Will once again got caught up on each other's lives.

So far, he'd been able to avoid the Todd issue. The alleged pictures were never produced. Stacy had been

questioned and had managed to avoid admitting anything that proved Todd had committed any ethics vi-
olations.

"So it all just goes away?" Becca asked, not sure
she agreed with that. It really sounded as though Todd
was involved with this girl. And if he was, something
should be done about it. A lot of people stood to get
hurt.

Will signaled to change lanes. "Not quite." Looking in his rearview mirror, he slid back into the right
lane. "I'm obligated to do some checking," he said.
"The complaint was filed officially and demands investigation."

"What are you going to do?" She didn't envy Will
his task. But she admired his ability to do what was
right, even in a situation as hard as this one. She'd
complained to Randi that he seemed uncompromising
these days, but as she watched him struggle with the
questions of Todd's guilt, she was no longer con-
vinced of that.

"I've hired an investigator from Phoenix to do
some simple surveillance," he said. "I don't expect
him to come up with anything." He glanced over at
her, his expression pained. "I hope to hell he doesn't,
that this is all some big mistake." His eyes were back
on the road. "But at least I'll have a paper trail to
prove that we did look into it to clear Todd's name
if this ever comes up again."

Becca settled herself more comfortably in the seat.
Her skirts were getting a little tighter than she liked.
"I saw Martha at the grocery the other day," she told

Will, glad to finally have a chance to speak with him about it. "The whole thing was really awkward. She was her usual cheerful self, asking about the Fourth of July script as if nothing was wrong. I felt horrible for her."

He loosened his tie. "Did you say anything?"

"I didn't." And she felt bad about that, too. She was weak. A coward. "I wanted to, though."

"I don't think we should. Not unless we have something substantial to give her." He glanced quickly at Becca again, then back at the road. Traffic was heavy. "Otherwise, we're just as bad as the old ladies in this town passing gossip that has little basis in truth."

"You're right," Becca said, feeling much better. This was why she needed Will. He was the sounding board for her thoughts, helping her see issues and concerns that remained hidden from her, giving her a second and immensely valuable viewpoint.

Which was what made this whole baby thing so much more devastating. She'd thought Will would be logical, fair, clear-minded, as always. She'd counted on him to help put her fears to rest, to give her some insight that would have made the decision, either way, feel like the right one.

Not only had he not done that, he'd removed himself from the position of sounding board altogether. He'd retreated into a kind of numbness.

"I'm hoping the entire mess will disintegrate," he said. It took Becca a second to realize that he was still discussing his friend. "With luck, Todd will take a heads-up from our conversations, and if he's been seeing more of the girl than he should, he'll heed the warning and stop.''

''No pun intended,'' Becca said. Considering the situation, Will's choice of words wasn't funny at all.

A NURSE ADJUSTED the lead weight as Becca stood on the scale. ''Same as you were last time.''

Frowning, Will looked over the nurse's shoulder. Becca could feel his heat along her back, could smell the aftershave she'd chosen for him more than two decades ago and still loved.

She couldn't help thinking, as they were ushered into a little examining room, that if the doctor's visits served no other purpose, at least they were an excuse for her and Will to be together.

The blood pressure cuff was tight on her upper arm. Becca tried to be calm, to will herself healthy. And just in case her best efforts weren't good enough, she prayed, too.

''Blood pressure's fine,'' Dr. Anderson said as she jotted numbers on Becca's chart.

''Thank God.'' Will's soft sigh warmed Becca. Despite the emotions and doubts churning inside him, despite his withdrawal, he was concerned about her. He wouldn't leave her to deal with this pregnancy by herself. That meant the world to her.

''Why don't you slide up here?'' the doctor said, patting the paper-covered examining table. Even dressed in her wool slacks and long-sleeved cotton blouse, Becca shivered, but did as she was told.

Feeling a little awkward all of a sudden, lying flat between her husband, who hadn't seen her naked since before their last visit, and the doctor, Becca stared straight up at the little dots patterning the ceiling. Everything was going to be fine. She'd promised herself it would be.

"She's still getting violently ill every night," Will reported as the doctor lifted Becca's blouse up past her ribs, exposing a belly that was actually a little bloated.

Dr. Anderson nodded silently.

"That doesn't worry you?" Will persisted.

"It's perfectly normal," the doctor murmured, feeling Becca's stomach. "She's at twelve weeks now, so it should pass soon."

Will was looming right above her beside the table. From her peripheral vision Becca could see him watching the doctor intently.

Hands resting on Becca's abdomen, the doctor met her eyes. "You're eating well throughout the day?"

Becca nodded.

"All the books recommend daily exercise," Will said. "But they don't say how much."

Becca had wondered about that. She'd had no idea Will was wondering, too. It was imperative that she do everything necessary to help this baby into the world and, equally, that she not do anything to weaken her chances of a successful delivery and a healthy child.

"We can go over that when we're through here,"

the doctor said, though she sounded distracted. "I've got some pamphlets...."

The room was silent as the doctor continued to probe gently, and Becca started to worry in earnest. She couldn't do this. She just couldn't bear it if something went wrong. She wasn't strong enough to cope. Her chest tightened, making each breath labored, a painful chore.

"Have you felt any cramping?" the doctor asked.

Becca shook her head, still gazing at the ceiling, enduring, doing everything she could to lie there calmly.

She almost jumped right off the table when Dr. Anderson pulled her stethoscope out of the big pocket in her white coat. Staring at the thing, which had two headpieces, feeling as though it was some big menacing needle, Becca sat up on her elbows, heart thundering. She wasn't ready for...whatever this meant.

"Lie back down," the doctor said, easing Becca's shoulders to the table again.

Longing for a return to the bliss of ignorance, of hope, of having moments when she actually allowed herself to believe it could all be real, Becca did as she was told.

The stethoscope was cold as the doctor moved it around on her belly. Becca held her breath, waiting, wishing the doctor would say something. Wishing Will would ask another question. She couldn't bear to look at her husband. Was afraid of what she might see on his face.

"Here we go." Dr. Anderson's voice was as soft

as always, but there was an odd note of satisfaction in it, too. "Who wants to listen first?"

Becca watched as Will picked up the second head-piece attached to the stethoscope, boosted her up with his free hand and placed the earpieces on her head.

Before she could even react, her entire being was consumed with the most miraculous sound she'd ever heard.

Thump-thump! Thump-thump! Thump-thump!

"It's so fast!" she choked out. She giggled, then burst into tears. She looked from the doctor's smiling face to Will's, as though the three of them had, then and there, created the little life whose heart was beating inside her.

Taking off her own headpiece, Dr. Anderson handed it to Will. "Here," she said, "try this."

Will moved in closer, leaned down and placed the stethoscope over his ears. Becca couldn't take her eyes off his, waiting for him to hear that first sound.

She wasn't disappointed when he did. His eyes, so closed to her lately, were filled with the same awe, the same wonder and joy that she was feeling herself.

We did this, his glowing face seemed to say.

For that moment, she felt as perfect in his eyes as the day they'd first fallen in love.

CHAPTER SEVEN

THE FOLLOWING WEDNESDAY, Becca had run out of excuses for skipping the weekly family lunch. She'd been avoiding her mother and older sisters for too long. Besides, they were all scheduled for another update on Samuel Montford, and Becca was eager to hear what they'd found out about Shelter Valley's founder.

She was hoping to have her Save the Youth kids enact Montford's life story on the Fourth of July. Her friend, Martha Moore—Todd's wife—had offered to write the script for them as soon as Becca's family had finished their research. Before the birth of her first child, Martha had been a drama major and through the years she'd been involved with the local community theater.

Becca was grasping at anything and everything in an effort to keep her thoughts occupied. And off Will. Or the baby they'd created. She'd made it through the first trimester.

Which meant she had a promise to fulfill. She'd told Will they'd only stay quiet about the baby until the end of the first trimester.

But first, Samuel Montford...

Sliding the Thunderbird into a spot along the curb

outside the Valley Diner, Becca looked for Sari's car and didn't see it. Her mother's was there, though. Betty and Janice—whose homes were on the same block—lived close enough to walk.

"Becca! Haven't seen you in a while," Nancy greeted her when she stepped through the door. Nancy had been Valley Diner's hostess since graduating from high school two years behind Becca.

"I've been busy." Becca smiled. The mother of six children, Nancy had blossomed by about forty pounds, but she was still pretty.

"Found any funding yet for the Save the Youth?" Nancy asked, her brow furrowed. "My Cara's fifteen now and could sure use something to do after school. She's spending far too much time watching MTV and on the Internet."

"I should have something within the next month," Becca said. "Keep your fingers crossed."

Nancy held up both hands, fingers crossed, then nodded toward the far window. "They're over there."

Becca thanked the hostess with a smile. She'd already seen her mother—could hardly miss her. Rose Naylor was wearing a tall, bright-red feathered hat that could have been worn by one of the Ziegfeld Follies girls back in the 1920s. And a bright-red, high-bodiced and very short dress to match.

Betty and Janice, sitting with her, were both wearing jeans—designer, of course—and stylish blouses. Dressed in her standard suit, with a skirt that had grown just a bit tighter around the waist, Becca envied them their comfort.

"Lenore's granddaughter, Kaitlin, came home from Phoenix last weekend with a tattoo on her shoulder," Rose was saying as Becca approached the table.

"It was painted on, Mom," Becca said, taking one of the two empty seats. "It washed right off."

"It's the thought that counts, that's what I told Lenore, and it *could* have been real. I once knew a girl during World War II, who walked into a men's tattoo parlor and had one done on her left cheek, and I don't mean her face."

Sharing a smile with her older sisters, Becca sat back and picked up the menu. She needn't have worried about explaining her absence these past weeks. As she suspected, her mother probably hadn't even noticed. Becca never supplied juicy gossip. Or created it, either.

"What's been so critical that you had to miss these lunches?" Betty asked, pen in hand.

Okay, so she'd been a little hasty in abandoning her worry.

"Not the day care." Becca chuckled, knowing that was the one activity of hers that drove Betty nuts. Her older sister saw no sense in Becca spending so much of her valuable time taking care of other people's kids when there were professionals being paid to do it.

She also knew that Betty had such a problem with her volunteering there because she thought Becca was rubbing salt in her own wounds. Betty had never understood that the little bit of mothering she'd been able to experience at the day care had been a balm, instead.

Janice leaned forward, her arms resting on the table. "Tell us what you've been doing!" she said. "Maybe there's something we can help you with."

Smiling at her sister, Becca shook her head. "It's all the usual stuff. I've just got more meetings, with the council thing being a paid position now, instead of volunteer committee work."

Janice would do anything for anyone; unfortunately she also wanted to climb right into your skin.

A couple of minutes later Sari joined them. "Where've you been?" Becca asked softly beneath Rose's chatter. Their mother was reaching a crescendo as she expounded her views about Mark Baxter's choice of wives. Mark was a widower, an old friend of their father's, and he'd chosen poorly in Rose's opinion.

"With Bob—he came home for something and we got...carried away," Sari whispered, her eyes glowing. Becca's stomach gave a happy little flip. Sari was looking better every day. Dressed in overalls, belted at the waist, and a figure-hugging black top, she didn't seem much older than the daughter she'd lost.

They ordered lunch, salads for everyone, before Betty pulled out her notebook. "Okay, Sari, you're up."

Rose glanced at her youngest daughter. "You look very nice today, sweetie."

So the change in Sari wasn't just Becca's wishful thinking. Even her mother had noticed.

"You do look good," Betty confirmed. Janice nodded agreement.

Sari blushed at all the attention, obviously ready to slide under the table.

"Before Sari starts, I just want to say that I've tried every avenue I can think of, but I still can't find any recent word on Sam Montford. The man sure travels a lot," Becca said, rescuing her.

"I heard he was in the Peace Corps," Janice said.

"Yeah, but that was a few years ago," Betty added.

"Has anyone heard from his parents?" Janice asked. "Their mansion is close to your place, Becca. Any sign of life there?"

Becca shook her head. "Except for the cleaning lady and groundskeeper, no one's been there since they went to Europe. Sam hasn't been there once in the ten years since he left. All I can say is, the man sure doesn't want to be found," she muttered. "I guess we may have to do this thing without him." She turned to Sari. "So, what've you got for us?"

Sari took out her notes, her eyes intent on the page, and started to read. At some point, while Becca hadn't been paying attention, her younger sister had developed almost as passionate an interest in Samuel Montford as Becca had. Sari had filled her in on the previous report.

"After his wife and son were killed in Boston," she began now, "with his affairs tied up so that his family would be comfortable but unable to obtain the balance of the Montford fortune, Samuel packed up the few belongings that mattered to him." Sari paused. Swallowed hard. "A scarf Clara had given him, the baby's blanket she'd knitted—and then he left Boston.''

''Did he have relatives someplace he was going to stay with?'' Betty asked.

Sari shook her head, looking around at them. ''He joined a wagon train heading west,'' she said, ''apparently preferring to face the dangers of the wild than live in a society that put skin color above human kindness and goodness and love.''

''He must have been petrified, a man from his social class joining ranks with the poor and desperate people traveling west,'' Rose said. ''Most of the people on those wagon trains had nothing more to their names than they could carry, you know.''

Yeah, they all knew. But no one bothered to tell Rose that.

''In one of the journals I read, written by someone traveling with him, it said that danger didn't scare Sam—that's what they called him, though in Boston he'd always been Samuel,'' Sari continued. ''He said his life was worth nothing, so losing it would mean nothing. Apparently, whenever there was a dangerous mission or job to do along the way, Samuel Montford always volunteered.''

Janice squeezed more lemon juice into her glass of tea. ''It's scary what tragedy can do to a person....''

Remembering their own family's loss just a couple of years before, the women fell silent. Even Rose. To Becca's relief, the waitress appeared then, one of the many college students who found work at the diner. She carried a big tray full of salads of every variety—

grilled chicken, Caesar, chef, fried chicken—and for Rose, a sampler with egg salad, tuna salad and a small scoop of fruit salad on a single piece of romaine lettuce. With no garnishes. Rose couldn't see the point of having something on her plate she couldn't eat.

"So Sam obviously made it west," Betty said when they were all enjoying their selections.

"Yeah." Sari forked a chunk of fried chicken and lettuce into her mouth, referring to her notes as she chewed. A moment later she began again. "With the help of several Southwest Indian tribes, Samuel slowly healed. Over the next few years, he traveled from tribe to tribe in the New Mexico and Arizona territories..."

"The Indian tribes all have their own cultures," Rose interrupted, a smudge of egg salad on the corner of her lip.

Sari nodded, chewed and swallowed quickly. "Yes, but many of the Arizona tribes borrowed from one another's religions, incorporated one another's ceremonies. Dances, songs, even certain rituals were shared among them. And Samuel learned from each one. But he contributed, too. He told them stories, entertained them. And if nothing else, he was a reliable pair of strong arms whenever anyone was in need."

Just like Will, Becca caught herself thinking. She'd never realized how totally consumed she was by the man she'd married. All her thoughts invariably returned to him.

And she was determined not to think about him.

"With loving care—" Sari's gaze met and held Becca's "—and time, Samuel found his way back to life again."

"Did he marry an Indian woman?" Janice asked, picking at her Caesar salad.

"No." Sari shook her head, shoveling in bites as fast as she could. Becca had rediscovered her appetite, too. "Shortly before his twenty-ninth birthday—sometime in the early 1870s—a group of white people came to the Indian village where Samuel was living. They were a Christian sect bent on civilizing what they saw as the poor Indian savages, intending to teach them Christianity and culture."

"That's right." Rose nodded. "The government had turned over the task of educating the Indians to the churches," she said with her usual confident tone. "You know, there was an Indian boy at school with us." She leaned in, lowering her voice to a near-whisper. "Lenore had a crush on him. I think she—"

"Mother!" Becca interrupted.

"Well, I'm sure she—"

"Mother—"

"Yes." Rose lifted her napkin to her mouth. "Well, anyway, the boy told us about how his tribe had first been introduced to our culture."

Sari smiled. "While the missionaries of Montford's day managed to sway a few natives in their direction, for the most part the 'savages' listened with interest, but not with commitment—"

"She did do it with him," Rose interrupted again. "The white man's religion had no impact on them," Sari continued, ignoring Rose. "They weren't swayed from who they were and what they believed to be true."

"That boy wasn't going to be swayed, either," Rose said when Sari stopped for another bite. "He got what he wanted and then bade Lenore adios—"

Sari broke in. "One of the missionary women did sway the heart of Sam Montford," she said.

She suddenly had all the Naylor women's attention. "Elizabeth Campbell had weathered her own share of life's pain but, as Samuel put it, she'd learned to endure and 'wore peace like a mantle.'"

Becca wondered if that was how she could win back her husband. By finding some peace to wear.

"Samuel was apparently attracted to that sense of peace, and then to Lizzie Campbell herself," Sari continued. Not one of them was eating.

"Before she left with her group, he asked her to marry him."

Even Betty was waiting attentively, no longer taking notes. "She accepted."

"I knew that," Rose told them all. "Lizzie is the mother of Samuel's children."

The restaurant's manager, the pregnant daughter of one of the men Becca had graduated from high school with, came to check on them. A few minutes later, their waitress was back, offering dessert. They all declined in favor of more to drink.

Except for Sari. She asked for both.

"Is that all you've got?" Betty asked Sari once the younger woman had taken their order.

"No." Sari shook her head. "Lizzie stayed behind with Samuel when her group moved on, but he was no longer content just to drift. He wanted a home again."

Becca's heart went out to the town's founder. She'd never expected her quest to unearth the life of Samuel Montford would affect her so personally.

"He wanted children," Sari murmured.

He wanted exactly what she and Will had always wanted.

"But whenever he considered returning to Boston with his new bride, a bride he knew his family would approve of, he'd start to suffocate. That was the word he used in his journal—suffocate. He couldn't make himself go back there, couldn't live in a society that had rules where its heart should have been."

"Can I have some of that?" Rose asked as the waitress delivered Sari's hot fudge brownie cake with ice cream.

Sari cut off a chunk, lifted it onto a saucer and passed it to Rose.

"With the dilemma heavy on his mind, Samuel went into the desert with a couple of his Hopi friends and came back with a new lease on life. He'd discovered a small abandoned settlement—probably a camp left behind by settlers heading west—and had suddenly known what to do. Montford money was going to be put to good use."

"That settlement was Shelter Valley," Becca guessed, caught up in the tale.

"It was." Sari nodded. She'd started in on her dessert, but the ice cream was melting on her plate. "Lizzie and Samuel began long weeks of letter-writing, ordering and waiting, but within a year, they had their home built, as well as several others, and some of the people he'd sent for had already arrived. He'd founded a town. And he named it for the haven it was to all those who had pure hearts and were willing to work hard to obtain a good life." Sari finished reading with a flourish.

Haven. That was exactly how the town felt to Becca. Was why she'd never once been tempted to leave. Until recently.

Capping her pen, Betty reached for the bill. It was her week to pay. Janice picked up her purse.

"Wait," Becca said, more sharply then she'd intended. Four sets of eyes were drawn to her taut face. "I have something to tell you."

Sari's eyes softened, though they were filled with worry, too. She knew what Becca was about to say.

"What?" Rose asked urgently. Her mother had never given up hope that Becca might one day come up with something juicy Rose could pass along.

"You need help with another committee?" Janice asked when Becca hesitated. "I've got a little extra time I can spare you."

The offer brought tears to Becca's eyes. "No, thanks, not at the moment, but I'll remember that," she told her sister. "Actually, it's just that—"

"What?" Rose demanded, leaning forward so far she was almost out of her seat.

"I'm pregnant."

Mouths open, Janice and Betty stared at her. Rose gasped, sank back into her seat.

"You are?" her mother whispered, one hand to her chest.

Becca nodded.

"You're sure?" Rose asked.

Becca glanced at Sari and then back at their mother. "Completely."

"How far along?" Betty asked, her voice as soft as Rose's had been.

"Just passed my first trimester." She gazed down at the table, brushing off crumbs with her fingers. Afraid of their reaction, their possible doubts, considering her age.

Shocked silence hung for a moment while the women digested her news. Becca wished Will were there with her.

"Thank God!" Janice broke the silence with words that were more a release of held breath than actual words. Becca looked up. Janice was crying—and grinning so hard it must have hurt.

So were Betty and Rose.

"CONGRATULATIONS, OLD MAN!"

"It's about time, you son of a gun!"

"Congratulations, sir."

The number of well-wishers took Will completely unawares early Thursday morning as he entered the plush meeting room in the administrative offices at Montford. He made his way through the group and assumed his seat at the head of the table.

He smiled at his colleagues, then at his personal secretary as she brought him a freshly brewed cup of Colombian coffee. His mind had been on the finance meeting about to take place. Not on his personal life.

Although he should have been prepared. Becca had told her mother about the baby the day before. It wouldn't have taken Rose twenty-four hours to let the entire town know the news.

"Thanks, all of you," he said, hiding behind his coffee cup. He took a sip, and scalded his tongue. Damn.

"How's Becca feeling?" Dr. Sherman Long, dean of Montford and Will's right-hand man, asked him.

"Fine." If you didn't count how tired she was.

Will spread out his papers. John Strickland was in town; they had a meeting in an hour and he didn't want to be late.

"When's she due?" Associate Dean Dr. Linda Morgan asked.

"Early October."

"Have you started decorating the nursery yet?"

Nursery? Hell, no. Hadn't even occurred to him. He and Becca would have to decide which room they were going to give up. The guest room? But then where would people sleep when they came to stay? His office? Hers?

"Not yet," he said, and then, noticing the looks of surprise facing him from around the table—due, at least in part, to his lack of evident excitement—he knew he'd have to put forth some real effort. "Give us a break, guys," he said, smiling at them, allowing himself to feel, for just a moment, a bit of the very real joy that lurked deep inside him whenever he thought of the coming baby. "We're just getting used to the idea ourselves. We can wait a week or two before setting up a college fund."

A college fund. He'd been working with parents for years as they established funds for their children's education. Odd, after all this time, to think of himself on the other end.

So many things to consider. So many changes.

Had Becca thought about college funds? A nursery?

Somehow he was fairly certain that she had.

AFTER MEETING with the expansion committee, another meeting that began with a shower of felicitations, Will and John Strickland headed out for a round of golf. It had been only a month since their last game, yet so much had happened to him in this quiet little town that Will felt like an entirely different man. An older man.

His shot was still on, though. He found comfort in that.

"So after twenty years, you finally get lucky," John cajoled as Will entered in his birdie on a par four. Along with John's one over par. "Must've been something I said."

"Yeah," Will grunted, rocking his weight from foot to foot as he lined up his next drive. It was a measly par three. He wanted to be on the green in one shot.

He made that and the putt in one, as well. And ended up with the best round of golf he'd ever shot. He could have been on the PGA tour playing like that.

Walking to the clubhouse, golf bags slung on their shoulders, the two men discussed John's swing and whether the light breeze blowing across the desert could have affected a drive or two.

"You know," John said, his voice different, quieter, "tell me to mind my own business if you want, but it seemed to me you were far more driven out there than that ball was."

Was he? Will shrugged. But he had to admit it had felt damn good to send that little white ball sailing.

And to turn his energies to something he understood.

"I never would've noticed five years ago, but after the accident, you know, you live on a different level, become aware of things—of feelings—you'd never realized were floating around before."

Will nodded. In the last month he'd learned a few things about himself. He'd existed on a superficial plane and hadn't even known it. He'd always believed that growing up in Shelter Valley had been one of his biggest blessings, that the town offered him all he needed to live a happy productive life. But lately he'd begun to wonder if maybe he hadn't been *too* sheltered. If growing up in the valley had somehow robbed him of the chance to test himself. For the first time, life was testing him, and he had no idea of his ability to pass muster.

He'd always thought he adored Becca. But his love for her had never been tested, either.

CHAPTER EIGHT

WITH THE SPRING SEMESTER coming to a close—and graduation drawing near—Will's schedule picked up considerably. From teas to formal awards dinners, he was in demand, it seemed, every waking minute of every day those last few weeks in April. Many of the occasions required that Becca accompany him.

These were bittersweet times. Times he both welcomed and dreaded. Being with Becca was difficult these days. The rules had all changed, but he'd been unable to figure out the new parameters. And yet, sometimes when he was out in public with his wife, things seemed exactly as they'd always been. He could count on Becca. They functioned well together, read each other's signals easily. A united front.

"You almost ready?" he called, coming in from work and heading straight toward their bedroom. It was the last Friday in April, just a little more than two weeks since his golf game with John.

They'd been invited to an encore performance of a multimedia production at the university, put on jointly by Montford's Dance, Theater and Music departments. Will had been asked to say a few words before the award-winning play began. People had been calling for weeks, seeking tickets to it.

After the play, he and Becca were hosting a private party at the university for the cast and crew, the faculty and all the visiting dignitaries.

Instead of finding his wife finishing her preparations for the evening as he'd fully expected, he found her curled up in bed, sound asleep.

Will stopped immediately, alarm shooting through him. Had something happened? Was there a problem with her blood pressure? With the baby?

"Becca?" he said softly.

Other than the steady rise and fall of her breathing, she didn't move. Surely if she was ill, she wouldn't be lying there so peacefully.

She'd been writing grants all week, preparing presentations for her Save the Youth funding drive. But other than Wednesday, when the town-council meeting had lasted until ten o'clock, she'd been in bed before nine every night. And she was still tired, despite that.

Glancing at his watch, Will wished he didn't have to wake her.

And yet, just the fact that she was fast asleep before seven in the evening was unsettling to him. He knew that pregnancy was physically exhausting. But Becca had always been able to get by with very little sleep. Her energy always outlasted his.

Her fatigue was scaring him.

He crept closer to the bed. "Becca?"

"Mmm?" She rolled over, but didn't wake up. The covers dropped away from her shoulders.

Another sensation shot through Will, rendering him

weak and needful. What he felt was desire. Red-hot desire. Becca had obviously crawled into bed in the middle of getting ready for the evening. She was topless, her burgeoning breasts a gloriously welcome sight. Feasting his eyes on them, Will swallowed.

He should wake her. Turn away. Stick to the business at hand. The business of seeing his wife safely through this pregnancy. Period. He stared, instead. And fantasized. Remembering her softness, the way her nipples hardened into peaks that he'd take into his mouth. Suckle.

He hadn't had sex in more than six weeks. Far longer than he'd ever gone before. And she was his wife, dammit. The only woman he'd been with in his entire life.

With no conscious thought, no permission sought or granted, even from himself, Will reached out with both hands, taking those breasts into his palms, covering them, caressing them.

"Will?" Becca's voice was groggy with sleep. Her eyes, when they opened and met his, were filled with desire—and questions.

Feeling like a first-class jerk, he stepped back from the bed, turning his head away from his wife's beauty.

"It's time to go," he said, grabbing the clothes she'd laid out on the divan and handing them to her.

"What time is it?"

She still sounded half-asleep. And confused.

"Six-thirty."

He should leave the room. Wait for her in the kitchen. He had to close all the blinds, anyway, turn on the outside lights and the lamp in the living room they always left on when they went out for the evening.

"We have time..." Hesitant invitation colored her words.

Will stood frozen, his throbbing body demanding one thing, his mind another.

He heard the covers rustling behind him and waited, poised, for Becca to approach him. Or had she merely moved over, making room for him to join her?

"Dr. Anderson said we should..."

Hating himself for the pleading he heard in her voice, Will swung around. It made him sick to think he'd reduced his strong vibrant wife to begging.

Dark hair tousled, she lay in the middle of their king-size bed, completely open to his gaze, completely nude except for the tiny scrap of lace panties.

"Becca..." He didn't know what to say. Couldn't think for the desire burning through him. God, he needed to sink himself so deeply inside her that he consumed her. And she him.

He could tell by the seriousness of her gaze that she understood his doubts. He suspected she had some major doubts of her own.

"Making love might help," she said softly.

She was so open, so trusting, as she lay there exposed to him, while he stood above her, a stiff-necked prig in a suit and tie.

And yet...

"What I want right now has nothing to do with love." He had to be honest with her.

He could sense the impact of his words as they slammed into her, almost as though he'd actually struck her. Sitting up, she hugged her knees to her breasts, pulling up the covers—as closed to him now as she'd been open a moment before.

"You don't love me?" she whispered, dry-eyed but trembling.

How did he explain something he didn't understand himself?

"I—"

"Tell me, dammit!" she cried. "Has the love completely died?"

"I don't know."

"Uuuoooo." The pained sound, almost an animal's howl, sliced through him.

The pool of tears gathering in Becca's eyes began to fall silently down her face, forcing Will into action.

"I don't know what I feel, Becca." He tried to be clear when nothing was clear at all. "I don't know what I've ever felt."

He'd hoped to comfort her in a way, to let her know that this wasn't just about the abortion. The words only seemed to make her feel worse. She stared at him wordlessly, pain written on her face.

"I've never before asked myself what I felt. I just knew from junior high that I was going to marry you and so I did."

"I know our parents encouraged our relationship, but there was no shotgun involved, Will," Becca said bitterly. "You make it sound like we live in some medieval age with arranged marriages."

"Of course I don't mean it like that," he said, frustrated, hurting, sorry beyond anything else that he was hurting her.

"It wasn't like you had to marry me to get me into bed," she reminded him. Will's body flared again at the memory. He and Becca had been far too young when they'd first explored their powerful desire for each other. But after keeping constant company since they were twelve years old, seventeen had seemed ancient.

Wiping Becca's tears, Will held her head gently between his hands. "I never had to make a choice, either, Bec. I never *tested* what I felt for you. Never examined it. Never questioned myself about it."

She stared up at him, her blue eyes searching. "Your feelings for me are being tested now, aren't they."

Determined to be honest with her, he nodded slowly.

Becca climbed out of bed and gathered her bra and other things. "Just be aware that inside, where it counts, I am the same woman now that I've always been, Will." Telling him she'd be ready in five minutes, she slipped into their bathroom and shut the door.

Will stood there, hands in his pockets, wishing he could take some comfort from her words. As he looked back over their years together, the memories fading with the pain of the present, he wondered if he'd ever known the woman Becca was inside. Or had he merely seen what he'd expected to see and looked no further?

"THEY'VE HAD A LEAD on Tory," Christine Evans told Phyllis Langford as her friend arrived at her apartment on the first Saturday in May. The two women lived in the same complex and had taken to having their weekend meals together.

Dropping the bag of Mexican takeout on the table, Phyllis grabbed both of Christine's hands. "Where is she?" she asked. And then immediately, "Is she okay?"

Christine, with tears in her eyes, pulled her hands away as imperceptibly as she could and nodded. "She was seen a couple of weeks ago in Florida."

"Was she alone?"

"No." Christine's gaze dropped, then lifted again. "But according to the hotel clerk who recognized her from the photo, she looked good. No obvious bruises."

"So he found her again," Phyllis said. She turned away, busying herself with the food she'd brought. Food was a comfort to Phyllis, evidenced by her somewhat plump figure.

"The man with her fit Bruce's description," Christine confirmed.

"You've got a private detective searching for her, a man who was referred to you by an FBI agent, and the maniac still finds her first."

Christine shrugged. Tory wouldn't be surprised by

that fact at all. Bruce Taylor was obsessed with Christine's beautiful younger sister. "Their divorce didn't keep him away from her. The restraining order didn't. Why should her running away have made any difference?"

Unwrapping tacos, taking the lids off a container of salsa and refried beans, bringing out little bags of chips, Phyllis set the table.

"Bruce is beyond obsessed," Christine went on. "Thanks to his parents' money and the fact that his father has been buying off various officials for years, Bruce has lived his whole life above the law. His entire life he's been coddled by his mother. And his father—who virtually ignored him for years because he was too busy being important and making money—compensated for his neglect by giving Bruce everything he could possibly want. Everything money could buy, that is. *No* is meaningless to him. And apparently, so is everything else—except Tory."

And Christine had encouraged her sister to marry the man. She'd never stop feeling guilty about that, even though she hadn't known what Bruce really was until much later. She'd believed that Tory, at least, was going to escape before permanent damage was done.

"As long as I live, I'll never understand the workings of the mind of an abuser," Phyllis said, sinking into one of the two chairs in the tiny breakfast nook. "He scours the earth for her, and then, when he has her, he beats her up. Wouldn't you figure he'd be nice to Tory? Try to convince her to stay with him?"

Biting her lip, forcing herself to hold back tears she'd given up shedding years before, Christine nodded. A psychology professor, Phyllis knew all the analytical studies of abuse, but that wasn't what she was referring to. Her friend was questioning something much deeper than science—the human soul. And how one could be so damaged. Christine had given up wondering about that.

"Instead, he sees everyone she looks at or speaks to as a threat—someone who might take her away from him—and he has to punish her. If he could only get her to quit looking or speaking, he'd be home free." Christine said the bitter words aloud, but she was barely conscious of being in the room. She sank into the empty chair across from Phyllis, elbows on her knees, and leaned forward, staring at the swirled gray pattern in the tiled floor, afraid the smell of food would make her sick.

"Along with his father's fortune, there's a huge number of employees to do his bidding, to hunt Tory down. And considering all the officials the old man's paid off over the years, there's an unending supply of connections, too." Christine sighed. "He says if he can't have her, no one else will," she told her friend, feeling as helpless as she had most of her life. Somehow she had to be strong for once. Had to step in and do something for Tory.

Phyllis got up and began to rub Christine's back. Christine almost flinched at the contact, willing herself to remember that Phyllis was her friend. That her touch was safe.

"What are you going to do when you find her?" Phyllis asked.

Christine noticed that Phyllis hadn't said *if,* and was grateful. After all, a couple of weeks was a long time. Anything could have happened between then and now.

"I'm taking her to Arizona with me," Christine said. "He'd never expect that. He has no idea where I'm going, would never think to look for me at a school that isn't Ivy League and would never expect her to be with me, anyway. He knows I'm terrified of him. Besides, Shelter Valley is hardly big enough to be noteworthy."

"And small towns have their own laws," Phyllis added, sounding as though she approved of Christine's plan. "Bruce's contacts won't have power there."

That was exactly what Christine was planning on. Tory was the only thing that made living bearable. And she'd gotten Tory into this mess. Somehow she'd get her out of it.

Phyllis dug into her tacos, and after a few more minutes, Christine joined her. She'd learned a long time ago to shut herself down when things were too overwhelming to endure. Shut down and cope. And pretend. She'd perfected the art of pretending.

"So," Phyllis said later as the two women sat curled up on opposite ends of Christine's couch, cappuccinos in their hands. "You plan to help Tory."

Wary at her friend's tone, Christine stared into her cup. "Absolutely." She sincerely hoped Phyllis wouldn't try to talk her out of it. Nothing was going to stop her this time. Nothing.

"Without professional assistance."

Hadn't Phyllis heard anything she'd been saying all these months? Professionals had no power. They spouted textbooks and laws. Christine could do that with the rest of them.

"I'm doing this, Phyllis," she said. Christine had given in all her life. She wasn't giving in this time. Her life had to stand for something. At least once.

"I know that," Phyllis said, her tone softening as Christine's hardened. "I'm not trying to discourage you."

Christine glanced up, a little shocked by the sisterly love she saw in Phyllis's eyes. She still wasn't used to the fact that there was someone in her life who was on her side. Wasn't sure she'd ever be used to that. Or able to trust it completely, either. Phyllis could change; her mood, her feelings, could change. It happened all the time.

"Helping Tory isn't just a matter of keeping her physically safe," Phyllis continued softly. "Even more than the bruises on her body, the bruises you won't be able to see are the ones that will need tending."

Christine nodded. Who better than she to help her sister through that particular hell?

"So how do you expect to be able to get Tory to open up when you can't open up yourself?"

The walls flew up, surrounding Christine in a comforting and secure world.

"I don't know what you're talking about," she said resolutely.

"Of course you do."

Hands trembling, Christine set down her cup before she spilled hot coffee on herself.

"You forget, Christine, I'm not only your friend, I'm a professional. I recognize the signs."

Wrapping her arms around herself, Christine soundlessly hummed a little tune. Birds were singing and the sun was shining.

"Who was he?" Phyllis asked, her voice sounding far, far off. Christine was glad her friend hadn't moved any closer. She'd have had to run then, and she wasn't sure her legs would carry her.

She should never have let her walls down with Phyllis, not for even a moment. She'd never done it before. She should have known better. But she was just so damn tired. And lonely. She'd been a fool to think she could have even a semblance of a normal life. No matter how far she ran, how much she pretended and retreated and hid, she was still Christine Evans, the girl who'd been having sex, unwillingly, since she was thirteen years old.

"Was it Bruce?" Phyllis persisted softly. "Did he hit you, too?"

Christine's bitter laugh didn't resemble her normal sounds at all. "Bruce didn't need to hit me," she said. "He knew I was terrified of him."

"He did, though, didn't he?" Phyllis asked quietly.

Because Bruce's blows meant nothing to her, Christine nodded.

Phyllis didn't move. "Did he rape you, too?"

Christine shook her head. Though, by the time she'd met Bruce, it wouldn't have mattered much if he had. She almost wished he'd taken an interest in her. Then he might've left Tory alone.

"But someone did," Phyllis said, her tone leaving no room for denial.

Christine stared straight ahead, trying desperately to hear her little tune. She'd let Phyllis in too far, couldn't seem to push her back out.

"Who was it, Christine?"

Birds were singing. The sun was shining.

"Who did this to you?" Phyllis was angry.

Frightened, Christine looked at her friend, wondering if now was the time Phyllis would change, when her feelings for Christine would change. She almost hoped it was. She knew how to deal with every negative emotion life had to offer. It was Phyllis's love she couldn't handle.

Phyllis had tears in her eyes, her hands clenched in her lap.

"Who was it, sweetie?" she asked. And then, "Let me help you."

It was raining, big, painful drops that dug at her skin as they landed their cruel blows.

"I'm not going anywhere, Christine." Once again Phyllis's voice came from far away. "I'll be right here with you every step of the way."

The birds were all dead on the floor. Killed by the rain.

"Tell me who he was."

"My stepfather."

CHAPTER NINE

BECCA WAS LATE. She had a meeting with the mayor in half an hour. Because he'd be up for reelection the following year, the weasel had finally volunteered some city funds for Save the Youth. And now Becca couldn't get her skirt zipped up.

Damn.

Letting her arms fall to her sides, she rested them for a moment before reaching behind her to start tugging again. And grunting. The damn thing wouldn't budge.

Unable to decide whether to stamp her foot or cry, she did both. She didn't have time for this.

"Can I help?"

Startled, because she'd thought she was home alone, Becca turned away as Will approached. "No, I'll get it," she said. Bad enough that she couldn't fit into any of her clothes. She didn't need him witnessing the indignity.

"You're going to break your arms, Bec," he said, approaching her as she backed away. He followed as she backed herself into a corner of their room.

"It's stuck," she said.

Turning her gently, he yanked at the fabric, drawing it together enough to get the skirt zipped.

"You need some new clothes, honey," he said, not a trace of humor in his voice.

Becca nodded, turning around again, embarrassed, although she didn't know why. It wasn't as though she didn't have a perfectly acceptable reason for gaining the extra weight.

With the pads of his thumbs, Will dried the tears that had spilled onto her cheeks.

"We can go to the mall in Phoenix tonight, if you'd like, and buy you a whole new wardrobe."

She wanted to refuse. To say that she'd take care of it herself. But she missed Will so much—too much to turn down the chance to spend an entire evening in his company.

"If you're sure you aren't too busy," she said, slipping into her pumps.

Will grabbed the money clip he'd left on his dresser—obviously what he'd come back for—and slid it into his pocket. "It's Monday of finals week, so no one's got time for the president," he joked. "Can you be ready by five?"

Becca nodded, already wondering if she'd made a mistake by agreeing to the trip. The way things were going, the sooner she learned to be happy without Will, the better.

"Bec?" he asked, stopping in the doorway.

"Yeah?"

"I'm looking forward to it."

God help her, she was, too.

THE HEADACHE STARTED while she was still in her meeting with Mayor Smith. He was coughing up some funds—or rather, agreeing not to put a stop on the allocation—but it was going to be "soft" money. Which meant a one-time payment, not a yearly budget as she'd requested. Luckily, she'd written all those grant proposals two weeks before and had verbal promises of enough hard money—money that would be replenished every year—to get the program off the ground in time for summer vacation. She should know by the end of the week.

When she left Mayor Smith's office, her head was pounding, making it difficult to think. Making her sick to her stomach for the first time in almost a month. She was just hitting her four-month mark. Morning sickness was supposed to be finished now. They'd been in for a doctor's visit the week before, and although Dr. Anderson had warned her to get more rest, she'd said the next trimester should be easier.

Apparently someone needed to tell her baby that.

Slumped in her car in the parking lot, Becca tried to decide what she should do next. In twenty minutes she had a meeting with a group of citizens who wanted more traffic lights out by a new housing development being built on the perimeter of Shelter Valley. She wasn't sure she'd be able to hold her head up that long.

Resting against the soft leather seatback, she tried to relax. Loosened the top button of her blouse and undid the button on her skirt beneath the jacket.

The tension was getting to her, that was all.

She'd been thinking about the nursery all weekend. She wanted bright primary colors that would work for either a girl or a boy. Lots of rainbows and clouds and stars. She wanted the furniture to be in light wood, and the carpet to be off-white. She wanted a changing table, a bassinet, a crib and a cradle that she could move from room to room. No playpens. Lots of those little sleepers and disposable diapers. She'd only need a few bottles, as she was planning to breast-feed. She'd need a rocking chair for that. And so she could hear the baby at all times, a monitor system, too.

However, she didn't know where she was going to put any of it. Not because she wasn't willing to give up her office—she was, in a second. Or the guest room, although that was a little small for what she had in mind. No, she just wasn't sure there was any point in decorating a room in that house. Would she even be living there after she had the baby?

Her thoughts weren't helping. Reaching to turn on the ignition, Becca grabbed her right arm, instead. It was completely numb. Shaking her arm, thinking it had fallen asleep, she couldn't feel it tingle. Couldn't feel anything at all.

Her face felt odd, too. Like she'd just come from the dentist and been shot full of novocaine. As she sat there, trying not to panic, she lost her peripheral vision. She was going to pass out—die—and no one would even know.

Somehow, in spite of the fact that her head felt like it was splitting in two, Becca managed, with her left hand, to get her cell phone out of her satchel and to punch in the couple of numbers that would speed dial Will's private line.

"Will?" she cried as soon as he answered.

"Becca! What's wrong?" His voice was strong, reassuring. And full of alarm.

She wanted to tell him what was wrong, but couldn't figure it out for herself. Her arm was numb— would that do it? She was having trouble hearing her own thoughts through the excruciating pain in her head. Giving up trying to see, she'd lain back with her eyes closed. It took everything she had to hold the phone to her ear.

"Becca?" He spoke with urgency. "Where are you?"

"Mayor's office," she said, breathless. And then, to save time, "The parking lot."

She was shivering. And sweating. Needed to lie down.

"I'm on my way."

She heard Will's words from a distance as her body slid sideways over the console. The pain in her head had reached a crescendo, and she didn't think she could take much more. Death would be a welcome alternative.

AFRAID TO WASTE time with the clinic in Shelter Valley, especially since he had no idea what was wrong with Becca, Will called an ambulance from his office and had the paramedics meet him at the mayor's office. He pulled in just as they did, but made it to Becca first.

She was conscious. Barely.

"What happened, Bec? Where does it hurt?" he asked, climbing into the car from the passenger side and cradling her head against his body.

"My head." Her words were slurred. "Blinding me."

His throat closed up. He'd been expecting the problem to be with the pregnancy. He wasn't prepared for anything else.

The paramedics left him no choice but to release her as they lifted Becca away from him and onto a waiting stretcher.

"My arm was numb. It isn't anymore," he heard her tell the young blue-suited men.

"Her pressure's high," one of them reported to the other.

They were on a radio and then on the road to the hospital in Phoenix before Will had time to do anything more than get into his car to follow them. A crowd had gathered outside the mayor's office. People were clamoring to find out what was wrong, but for once, Will ignored them all. He couldn't let that ambulance out of his sight.

Dr. Anderson met them at the doors of the emergency room, barking questions as she walked alongside the stretcher. So intent was she that she didn't even acknowledge Will as he followed them through doors that were marked Patients and Personnel Only.

Becca saw him, though. Her eyes were pinned on

him, begging him to make everything okay. She was frightened.

So was he.

Her voice trembled as she answered the doctor's questions.

The first thing they did was give Becca something to get her blood pressure down. And then Dr. Anderson checked her and the baby thoroughly.

"Everything's fine there," she reported, and though her expression softened, she still looked concerned. "But I'd wager a guess that you aren't getting the extra rest I recommended."

She called for a specialist, who ordered a set of neurological tests. Dr. Anderson assured them that nothing would be done to harm the baby.

"What do you think is wrong?" Will asked Dr. Anderson as they wheeled Becca away for an MRI. He had to know what to expect.

The doctor, sitting on a stool in the examining room, wrote a couple of things on Becca's chart. "My guess is that we're just dealing with a migraine...."

They were about the finest words he'd ever heard.

"Becca's never suffered from migraines before, but pregnancy can bring them on like this. The high blood pressure didn't help."

Leaning against the wall, weak now that the immediate danger had passed, Will asked, "How high was it?" He'd seen Becca an hour and a half before she'd called. She'd seemed fine then. There'd been no signs....

"Not alarmingly so, but enough to complicate things if a migraine was present, anyway."

"And the numbness? A migraine causes that, too?"

"It can, yes," Dr. Anderson said, rising. "We're running the tests just to make sure."

Will wouldn't let the doctor go. "So you think she's going to be all right," he said.

She smiled at him, laid a hand on his arm. "I do—as long as she gets enough rest." Holding open the door of the examining room, she motioned Will through. "You can wait right out here for her," she said. "There's coffee and a vending machine down the hall. She shouldn't be long."

Panic set in as he watched the doctor's disappearing back.

"Dr. Anderson?" he called, chasing after her.

"Yes?" She turned, her eyes warm with reassurance.

"How long until we know for sure?"

"I've called in a radiologist," she said. "We'll know before you leave here today."

SHE WAS GOING to be fine. Becca was perfectly all right. Normal. The baby was normal. Everything was fine.

Will repeated the words to himself over and over as he drove his car back to Shelter Valley, his wife asleep in the passenger seat. They'd given her something for the headache, a prescription for blood-pressure medication and told him she'd probably sleep most of the day.

But as Will saw her so lifeless on the seat beside him, he couldn't shake the fear that had been strangling him since her phone call that morning.

What in hell had he been thinking, encouraging her, a woman of forty-two, to put her body through the trauma of childbirth? Had he been mad? Today it was a migraine. And there'd been her high blood pressure. Something that, in itself, could create life-threatening problems in the future. Not that Dr. Anderson thought they had to worry, but it could happen.

They'd checked her kidney function in the blood-work they'd done, too. Everything was fine there, as well, but the fact that they were checking at all frightened him. It meant the possibility existed that something could have been wrong.

As Will slowed for the Shelter Valley exit, Becca stirred, but settled back down without waking. She looked so vulnerable there beside him, not at all the strong vivacious woman he knew her to be.

That thought raised the vision of how he'd seen her in the parking lot, huddled over her console, limp and racked with pain.

And he knew that if anything happened to her, if something did indeed go more wrong than it had today, it was going to be his fault. He should have listened to her when she'd talked about terminating her pregnancy. He'd been so shocked, so staggered to find that the woman he'd always considered the consummate mother no longer wanted to be one, that he hadn't heard everything else she'd told him. He should have examined the option more closely.

Consumed by guilt, he carried his sleeping wife into their house.

THE NEXT MORNING Becca was relieved to wake up feeling her old self again. She'd slept a little later than usual, due, no doubt, to the medication she'd taken the day before. But the headache was gone and, other than the discomfort of wearing another skirt that was too tight, she was raring to go. Will, thankfully, had already left for the university. If he'd been home, she was sure he'd have nagged her to take the day off.

Becca couldn't afford to lose another day if she didn't have to.

Swallowing her new blood-pressure pills along with her vitamins, just as Dr. Anderson had instructed, and promising herself a nap before her business dinner—the rescheduled traffic-light meeting—she left the house with a list of things to do.

And had to face at least half-a-dozen expressions of concern and good wishes—from her neighbors, from various people as she walked across campus—before she reached her first destination. Because of the crowd in the mayor's parking lot, Will had made a few calls the night before, letting people know how she was. Rose had taken care of the rest.

She found Randi in her office in the Women's Athletic Department at the university. Just in from a meeting with the soccer coach, she was dressed in a pair of athletic shorts and a cutoff T-shirt. She looked gorgeous, with her tanned skin and long legs that seemed to go on forever.

"Hey, sis!" She jumped up from her chair full of energy as always. "How're you feeling? Have a seat," she said, guiding Becca to a chair.

"I'm feeling fine," Becca told her, resisting the urge to stand back up. "I'm not an invalid!" she said with a laugh.

"You wouldn't get that impression talking to Will last night."

"I know," Becca said. "I was only awake long enough to have some dinner, but it was enough time for him to drive me crazy."

Randi sat down in her chair, propping a white-sneakered foot on her desk. "It's kind of sweet, how much he cares."

Becca had thought so, too, until it had dawned on her that his concern was for the baby. And because it was his responsibility as her husband, as the father of her child, to take care of her. It had nothing to do with love.

Will wasn't sure he felt that for Becca. He'd said so. The knowledge was always there, in the back of her mind—her heart—haunting her.

Not that she expected Randi to understand that. The thirty-year-old had never had a truly serious relationship in her life.

"I need some help," she told Randi now, pulling out a notebook from her satchel.

Looking at the notebook—a Becca trademark—Randi grinned. "I figured with the semester ending and summer vacation looming, you'd be hitting me up," she joked. "Which committee do you have me pegged for?"

Becca smiled. She loved her family, her life in Shelter Valley. Everyone was always so willing to help out.

"I'm setting up a series of programs for Save the Youth," she said, thumbing through the pages of ideas and possible directors until she got to Randi's page.

"You got the funding?" Randi asked, excited.

"Mayor Smith came up with enough to get us started," she said. "And I'm expecting to hear about hard funding by the end of the week. Once that's in place we won't have to go through this every year."

"You are amazing, woman!" Randi grinned.

Becca didn't know about that. She just knew she had to keep going. "I'd like to set up some sort of athletic program," she continued.

"What kind of program? Intramural? Competitive? Or just classes? And what sports?"

"I was planning to leave that up to you."

Randi sat back with a thump. "Oh."

"I'd like you to direct the program, if you would."

"*Direct* it? We're talking a huge time commitment here."

"You'll have a budget." Becca named the figure. She really wanted Randi to do this, not *just* because she was perfect for the program and Becca knew she could rely on her completely, but because she thought Randi would enjoy the job.

Being single, Randi always helped Becca during the summer months, volunteering on some project or other. Finally Becca could give her something that she'd really like doing.

"Can I lasso some of my students who are staying in town for the summer to help out?"

"Of course. It's your program."

"Okay," Randi said, and then in all seriousness, "on one condition."

Becca froze in the process of putting her notebook away. "What?" she asked. Randi had never put qualifications on her help before.

"That you let all of us around you do the work on this thing, at least for the summer." Randi paused, as though looking for Becca's reaction.

Becca remained silent. How could she tell her well-meaning sister-in-law that she'd just made her feel like a horse put out to pasture?

"Promise me you'll slow down a little, Becca."

"I'm planning to get more rest," she said, compromising. "I'm scheduling a nap each day."

"*Scheduling* one?" Randi snorted. "Why do you do this to yourself, Becca? Why can't you just take some time off?"

"Because I have to know that I can do it all." She had no idea where the words came from. Was shocked to hear them. Even more stunned to realize they were the truth.

"Why is that so important?" Randi asked softly. "Don't you already know, Bec, that you run this entire town? And that everybody knows it?"

"It's who I am," Becca said, searching inside her-self for answers she'd only just discovered she needed. "My whole life has been spent *doing,* being a person other people can rely on. I'm scared to death I won't be that person anymore."

Her foot back on the floor, Randi sat forward, el-bows on her knees. "We're talking about more than the town, aren't we?"

She supposed they were. "I'm afraid of losing my-self."

"Why? Because of the baby?"

"Maybe." But she didn't think so. Not in that sense. "Maybe because my husband's no longer in love with me."

"Will's coming around already, Becca."

Perhaps. Perhaps not. Becca couldn't bear to tell Randi—or anyone—about the conversation she and Will had had the night of the play.

"I'm scared to love this baby too much in case I lose it," she whispered, tears gathering in her eyes. "And if everything goes okay, I'm scared I won't have the energy to keep up with my baby."

Still leaning forward, Randi reached over and grabbed Becca's hands, holding them silently. There were no words of assurance she could possibly offer; Becca knew that. No way Randi could promise her that everything would turn out all right.

But it still helped, having Randi close, feeling the wealth of her caring.

"I love you," Randi said.

"I love you, too." Becca smiled at her sister-in-law through her tears.

Somehow that was going to have to be enough. The love of her family. Of her friends. The support of Shelter Valley. One way or another, they'd all have to help her see this through.

CHAPTER TEN

IRONICALLY, TODD WAS SITTING in Will's office Tuesday morning when the phone call came. Todd, dwarfing the leather chair, had come to request scholarship alternatives for Stacy Truitt. The young woman wanted to continue her graduate studies at Montford, but couldn't afford to.

And because Todd was sitting there so casually in his khakis and polo shirt, one ankle resting on the opposite knee, because he was asking so boldly, Will had felt relieved. There couldn't possibly be anything going on between them if Todd was willing to champion the girl so openly.

The ringing phone startled both of them. Will's business calls were screened by his very efficient secretary. Becca called on his private line.

He knew, as soon as he picked up, why Freda had put the call through. She knew he was waiting to hear from the private investigator.

"What have you got?" He spoke into the receiver, uncomfortably aware of his friend sitting across from him. He hoped this would be the evidence that would clear Todd's name. Hoped they'd soon be laughing about the vagaries of students, grudges and unwarranted complaints.

"...all the proof you need," the man was saying. "Dates, times, records of meetings at the girl's apartment, a dinner in Phoenix, a night at a resort in Tucson..."

Will felt his heart pound as the investigator continued to give him a very professional rundown of a ruined life. Of several ruined lives.

He avoided looking at Todd, couldn't bring himself to see the man he'd known all his life while listening to repeated episodes of Todd's adultery.

"I know you didn't ask for them, but I've got pictures in case you need them," the man said.

Pictures. Just thinking of what they'd portray made Will sick. And confused. What in hell was the world coming to?

As though compelled by his sense of horror, he looked at Todd then. And could barely control the anger that rose inside him as he saw Todd sitting there, appearing so nonchalant, so guiltless while he came begging on his young lover's behalf.

What about Martha, dammit? How could Todd do this to her? How could he go home to her, climb into bed with her, knowing what he'd done? What he was still doing?

How could Todd face him, the man who'd trusted him, the man who'd stood up for him at his and Martha's wedding?

How could he possibly think he'd get away with this? Especially in Shelter Valley. The town where everyone watched out for their own, where family still mattered, where right and wrong were still based on eternal truths.

Todd was leafing through a golf magazine that had been sitting on a corner of Will's desk. He stopped at the ad for a new aluminum putter that Will was intending to buy.

"You've done a very thorough job and I thank you." Will took special care to be pleasant as he spoke into the phone. After all, it wasn't the man's fault he was bearing such disappointing news. "Be sure you add the film and developing costs to your bill."

Todd glanced at him as Will hung up. "Important call?" he asked. His curiosity wasn't surprising, since Will had barely spoken a word during the entire conversation.

"You might say that," he said now, scrambling for a way to do this, a way that wasn't completely distasteful.

And then determined there wasn't one.

"I now have indisputable proof that you're having an affair with Stacy Truitt," he said baldly.

Todd dropped the magazine. It lay on the floor, unretrieved and folded open. He stared at Will, his lips tight, thoughts chasing themselves across his face. He expressed none of them.

Oddly enough, his silence bothered Will most of all. Where was the boy he'd learned to play baseball with? The man he'd held when his mother had died during their sophomore year of college? The man who'd cried when his first daughter was born? The man who'd been Will's rock when his own sons and daughters weren't.

"Why?" Will finally asked.

Todd continued to stare at him, a nerve in his cheek the only detectable movement in his entire body.

"It's over, my friend," Will said. "It's all going to come out."

Todd nodded. His eyes were overflowing with emotion, and yet there was nothing about the man that was sagging or defeated. Or even regretful.

"What about Martha?" Will asked, angry again. "How could you do this to her?"

Todd still said nothing.

"Don't you care at all?"

Will's voice was hard, his hand clenched into a fist on his desk. For the first time in his life, he wanted to hit a man. To smash Todd's face until he felt some compunction, until he knew what it was to hurt. Until he was at least sorry.

"Of course I care." There was no doubting the truth of Todd's words when his silence finally ended.

"Then why did you do it?"

"She makes me feel something I've never felt before." As sappy as Todd's words sounded, his delivery wasn't. He wasn't defending himself, wasn't really even explaining himself. He was just stating facts.

Will rubbed his fist with his other hand. "Lust'll do that to you."

"It's not about lust," Todd said. "She's like...an angel, sent to earth specially to speak to me."

Todd was losing him. There was absolutely nothing heavenly about adultery.

"She sees value in me that no one's ever seen before. Makes me see value in myself that I didn't even know was there."

"*Martha* values you, man. She's given her entire life to loving you, caring for your children, making a home that you'd be comfortable in, tending to your needs."

"I know," Todd said, bowing his head. "That's what makes this so hard. But I love Stacy so much I can't fathom a life without her."

"You used to love Martha, too."

Todd shook his head. "I still do, but I was never *in love* with her," Todd admitted, shocking him.

"Sure you were," Will said automatically. "You're just caught up in some midlife crisis and not thinking straight." Will sought desperately for an example, some point in their lives when Todd had shown how enamored he was of his wife. He thought back to their wedding day.

And couldn't honestly remember a look on Todd's face, a gesture, a word, that indicated his devotion. The best way to describe Todd, he decided as his memory turned traitor on him, was *content*.

"Open your eyes, man," Todd said. "I was never in love with Martha like you were with Becca."

Suddenly Will's eyes *were* open. Wide. *Like you were with Becca.* But was he?

And how could he insist that his friend feel something that he wasn't sure *he'd* ever felt? Had they both been victims of Shelter Valley? Settling for a life the town provided because it was expected of them?

"Becca would be coming over, and you'd light up like a baseball diamond at night," Todd said almost bitterly. "There was a life that only existed when the two of you were in a room together. It was like you were connected on some wavelength no one else could hear, and it was sickening to witness, believe me," Todd said.

"You and Martha never had that?" Will asked, his mind reeling at the picture Todd had drawn. Could it be true? Had he and Becca really been that way?

Were they still connected—even if only by a thread?

Or was the picture just a skewed painting created from the memory of a middle-aged man who was trying to justify an affair with a girl young enough to be his daughter?

"Martha and I were friends," Todd said. "We *are* friends. There's just never been any real passion between us. On either side."

Will found that hard to believe, too. Todd and Martha had had their share of nights in the dorm room, nights when Will had been asked to find someplace else to sleep. Nights he'd gone to Becca's apartment and hardly slept at all.

"Where do you think this is going, Todd?" Will asked. "Stacy may be here another year or two, but then she's gone. Have you thought of the future at all? Taken into account everything you've risked?"

The man was going to lose his job. Didn't that matter to him?

"I was hoping we'd have time for her to finish her studies here," Todd said. It was clear that he'd given the matter quite a bit of thought. "A Montford education means a lot to her. It meant a lot to me. I know what it could do for her." He paused, lifted his hands and let them fall. "But we're both prepared for it to all come crashing to an end sooner than we'd planned."

"You're going to end it, then? Stop seeing her and hope that Martha will be able to forgive you?"

Will couldn't believe how badly he wanted that to be the case. How much he'd like to find a way for Todd to get his job back at some point. And hoped that Todd's family would not be irreparably hurt by his mistake.

"End it?" Todd frowned. "Of course not!" He leaned forward. "Haven't you heard a word I've said, Will? Stacy is my life."

"Then what—"

"We knew we might have to leave here before she was finished with school," Todd explained. "We're both prepared for that eventuality. I just hadn't expected it to happen so soon."

Speechless, Will just sat there. It was his turn to stare. Obviously he wouldn't even have to worry about firing Todd. The man was planning to walk away from a prestigious position at a prestigious college—one he'd worked his whole life to obtain—without looking back. Incredible.

"Where will you go?" he finally asked. "What will you do?"

"Get a divorce, marry Stacy," Todd said. "I won't have any problem getting some kind of teaching job. And if that doesn't work, I can always get my license, do counseling."

"Where?" Will asked again. Not because it mattered, but because he needed something tangible in order to grasp what was happening.

"Somewhere back East," Todd said. Obviously that, too, had already been discussed. "If Stacy can't finish up at Montford, I want her at an Ivy League school."

Anything for Stacy.

Was this love? The willingness to lay down one's entire life for another?

"What about the kids?"

Todd stared at his hands. When he raised his eyes, they were glistening. "I'm going to miss them like hell," he admitted softly.

Just not enough, apparently, to make him stay.

"By next year we'll be settled and I'll send for them for the summer."

The man had gone stark raving mad. Or maybe *he* had. No one was who he'd thought, not anymore. Todd having an affair, leaving his job, his wife, his family. Becca, willing to consider aborting the child they'd waited two decades to have, not sure she wanted to be a mother anymore. His own doubts about his part in Becca's decision, the fears that had been plaguing him since her migraine. Doubts about decisions he himself had fallen into rather than chosen. The town he'd always loved maybe sheltering him too much all these years, robbing him of the necessary tests of his mettle, of life, rather than providing space for him to grow.

Nothing was making sense anymore.

"WHAT ARE YOU doing?"

Becca started, swinging around to face Will in the doorway of her home office Tuesday evening.

"Thinking," she said.

"Standing in the middle of the room?"

"I was thinking about rearranging it."

"Not by yourself, I hope. That desk's heavy."

"No." Becca shook her head. "I wasn't going to do it myself."

"I thought you liked your desk by the window," he continued, coming fully into the room. He was still wearing the dress slacks, shirt and tie he'd worn to work, though, in deference to the Arizona May heat, he'd removed his jacket the second he'd left his office at the university. He looked so good to Becca, tall, solid, reassuring.

And sexy as hell.

"I do love my desk there," she said now. "But we might have to move it out of this room."

He frowned. "Why? Where would you put it?"

Shrugging, Becca looked at him. "That's my problem. I don't know."

"Then why—"

"We need a nursery, Will," she interrupted, tired

of all the games they were playing. Tired of their being nice to each other on the surface when they were tearing each other up inside. "Can you think of any other room we could use as a nursery?"

"My office?" But he didn't sound particularly enamored of the idea.

"Your office is bigger. This room is more practical," she said, only because it was true. "Besides, it's closer to our bedroom."

He thought for a moment. Walked around the room, as though contemplating. "The crib would look nice over there," he said, pointing to the alcove across from the window.

Becca nodded. "That's what I thought. And the changing table over there." She pointed to the adjacent wall.

"Right." He went over to the spot and stood there. "It can't be by the window. I don't want him throwing something through it or kicking the glass."

"Or rolling off," she agreed, her stomach tightening as she envisioned all kinds of possible mishaps.

"Todd resigned today," he announced suddenly.

"What?" Becca asked, moving over to stand beside him, as though his nearness could make the blow easier to bear. Or *her* nearness could somehow give him the comfort she knew he must need. "What happened?"

"The private investigator came up with the goods," he said. His eyes were clouded, his face contorted with grief.

Becca ached for her husband. Todd had been his best friend for as long as she'd known him.

"What did Todd say?"

As Becca listened to the story, her heart turned slowly to ice. If Todd could fall so completely out of love, couldn't Will? Was this where they were heading?

Love really wasn't strong enough to conquer all, was it.

"Has he told Martha?" she whispered when he finally fell silent.

"He's going to do it tonight."

"How soon will he leave?"

"Almost immediately," Will told her, drawing a finger down the side of her face. "With the semester ending, there's no reason for either of them to stay."

"No reason, except for his wife and four kids."

Pulling Becca into his arms, Will held her against him. "I know, baby, I know," he said, the pain in his voice undisguised.

He held her for several minutes and Becca gradually sank into him. She hadn't realized how completely starved she was for the contact. Not just sexually, though there was definitely that, but for the security and comfort of Will's arms around her.

Too soon, just as she felt his body responding to her nearness, he pulled away. Circling her desk, he stood behind it. "We could move this into my office," he said, completely ignoring what had just happened. "Like you said, it's a much bigger room. We could both work in there."

Trying to understand, to give him time, trying not to feel hurt by his withdrawal, Becca thought about his suggestion. Was thrilled that he'd even offered. "It might work," she said.

If they were both still living in the house by then.

She'd always been a little lonely working back here in her office—had felt cut off from the rest of the house. From him.

"We probably won't be using the office at the same time in the beginning, anyway," he said, looking around the room again.

Becca chuckled. "I have a feeling neither one of us will be using it a lot in the beginning. Ever try concentrating on three hours of sleep?"

His brown eyes warm, concerned, he asked, "You really think it'll be that bad?"

"At first, yes." She hoped that was all the bad it would be, that the reality wouldn't be worse than that. She could pull all-nighters when she was twenty; at forty-two her brain stopped working without at least a few hours of uninterrupted sleep every night.

And yet, as she cradled the tiny life inside her, a joyful glow spread throughout Becca's body, invigorating her. If she could carry this baby to term, deliver him and bring him home, she knew she would find the energy to care for him.

"Becca, there's something I've been wanting to talk to you about," Will said, returning her thoughts to the present—to him. He was leaning against her desk, his feet crossed in front of him.

Becca turned cold. "Is this something I need to sit down for?"

Running a finger thoughtfully along his lower lip, he shook his head.

Somehow that didn't reassure her.

"I've been doing a lot of thinking," he began. Becca sat in the armchair she usually used for reading. She'd unbuttoned her skirt when she'd come home, and as she sat, the zipper slid down, as well.

"Thinking I should have done weeks ago," he continued.

Dry-mouthed, Becca nodded.

"I couldn't understand, still can't, actually, how—medical considerations aside—you wouldn't want this baby."

"I know." She was having a hard time believing it herself. Except when the panic hit.

But they'd already been through this. Did they have to do it again? Was he never going to get over it?

"Because of that," Will began again, speaking slowly, "I don't think I gave proper consideration to the physical concerns."

"What physical concerns?" she asked, frowning. He didn't want her getting fat? Didn't want to give up his office? None of that sounded like Will at all.

"Medical ones."

Becca's heart began to pound. He and Dr. Anderson had been alone when they'd wheeled Becca down for that MRI. Did he know something she didn't?

"What is it?" she asked. "What's wrong?"

God, don't take this baby from me. Please don't take this baby from me now.

"Nothing," Will said. He stood up, came over to crouch beside her chair. "But yesterday scared the hell out of me, Bec," he admitted. "It showed me quite clearly what you'd been talking about—the dangers of taking on something this momentous at your age."

"Did Dr. Anderson tell you something she didn't tell me?" Becca barely got the words past the fear that was choking her.

"No!" He brushed her hair back gently. "It's nothing like that. You're fine. The doctor still believes you can deliver this baby without a hitch."

Head aching, she tried to read in his eyes what he wasn't telling her. "Then why—"

"I just want you to know that if you still want to terminate this pregnancy, I'll support your decision."

She stared at him, trying desperately to remain calm, but her face felt numb, her skin chilled. Had he deserted her so completely now that he didn't even want her baby?

"It's too late," she whispered, devastated and afraid that the words referred to far more than the fate of her pregnancy.

"Too late?" he asked, frowning, seeming completely unaware of the effect his words were having. Did he actually think she cared so little? Perhaps he was right; perhaps he really didn't know her.

"I'm going on seventeen weeks," she stated conversationally. "Unless the mother's life is in imminent danger, they won't terminate after twelve."

Becca wasn't sure whether the brief burst of feeling that crossed his expression was relief, joy or disappointment. It came and went so quickly.

She sat there looking at him, trying to understand him—and failing hopelessly. It occurred to her again that perhaps he *didn't* know her anymore. But perhaps she didn't know him, either.

It was a frightening thought. One she wasn't prepared to deal with. She had no idea where that left them. Or their baby.

CHAPTER ELEVEN

AFTER LUNCH with their sisters and mother on Wednesday, Becca and Sari went shopping for the maternity clothes Becca and Will had missed buying on Monday. After adding the salad to the baby already taking up residence beneath her waistband, Becca couldn't wait any longer.

"Mom was in rare form today," Sari said as the two women perused the racks in an upscale maternity shop in Phoenix. "I didn't think she was ever going to stop laughing when she told that stupid chicken-crossing-the-road joke."

Becca grinned, adding a jumper she didn't think she'd buy to the other things she was carrying over one arm. "She's happy about the baby."

"Yeah," Sari said, her face softening. "She's happiest because she knows you've wanted one for so long."

"I was surprised she hadn't heard about Todd and Martha yet," Becca said, handing her growing pile to the salesclerk waiting to assist her. She'd told her sister about their friends on the way into Phoenix.

"For Martha's sake, I'm glad," Sari said. "I'd die if anything happened between Bob and me, especially if the whole world found out."

Becca refused to discuss this; it was too dark. Too frightening.

"What do you think?" she asked, instead, holding up another dress for inspection. It had quickly become apparent when they'd entered the shop that she'd have to give up suits for the duration of her pregnancy. Maternity clothes didn't seem to come in suits.

Sari wrinkled her nose. "A little young. Maybe you'd better get someone else to write Samuel's script," Sari said, apparently not distracted from the subject of Martha.

"No." Becca shook her head. "I'm not going to take anything else away from Martha." She'd already given the matter some thought. "I'll keep a close watch, and if she shows any signs of being over-whelmed or not wanting to do it, I can always get one of the theater people at the university to write something. But Martha was really looking forward to doing this, and it may be a diversion for her."

Sari pulled out a denim jumper, saw the embroidered butterflies on the front pocket and put it back. "Will there be enough time for someone from Theater to do it? This is the tenth of May—less than two months till the Fourth of July."

"There'll be time," Becca said, wondering if she'd have to go with slacks for the duration. None of these dresses seemed right for a woman in her forties. But with temperatures reaching 120, a summer pregnancy was going to be bad enough—but wearing slacks would be suicide. "The kids aren't out of school until the first week of June. They're only going to have three weeks to put this thing together, so it'll have to be basic, anyway. Besides, the scriptwriter can be there with the kids—like a work in progress. Betty's write-up for the paper will be pretty comprehensive.''

Drifting over to another rack, Sari found a nondescript black dress that might do. ''We should have all our research wrapped up by next week,'' she said.

Becca nodded. She'd been thinking a lot about Samuel Montford these past few days. The first—and the fourth. Cassie, ex-wife of the current Sam, had been back in town for several years. Had made quite a name for herself in veterinary science...

''Mrs. Parsons! How are you?'' Turning, Becca saw little Kaylee Holmes, the daughter of Karen and Dick Holmes, yet another couple Becca had graduated from high school with. The family had moved to Phoenix several years before.

Kaylee wasn't so little anymore. ''Kaylee!'' she said, shocked to see the girl's very distended stomach. ''I don't have to ask how you've been! I didn't even know you were married.''

Kaylee grinned. ''I'm not.''

''Oh.'' Becca was a little nonplussed by Kaylee's cheer. In her day an unwed pregnant woman would have been embarrassed by her condition, saddened by it—shamed, even. She wasn't entirely sure which of the two worlds was better.

''So what are you doing here?'' Kaylee rushed into the awkward silence. ''Shopping for a gift for someone?''

''Yes,'' Becca said in unison with Sari's ''No.''

Kaylee frowned in confusion. "You are or you aren't?"

"Becca's pregnant," Sari chanted, her voice filled with all the pride and joy Becca should have been expressing. "She's in the middle of her fourth month."

"Ohhh." Kaylee drew out the word, then began to move off toward another part of the store. "Well, I hope everything goes okay for you."

"Yeah," Becca called, turning back to her shopping, "you, too." She hadn't missed the fact that Kaylee hadn't offered her congratulations. Only a doubtful wish that everything would be all right.

She tried to concentrate on the clothes in front of her, tried to find something appropriate for her age— but spent the next few minutes forcing herself not to cry.

"You okay?" Sari finally ventured to ask.

"No, I'm not okay," Becca snapped, then burst into tears. "I'm a freak, Sari," she said, hiding behind a tall rack of dresses while she made an effort to compose herself. "Look at these clothes. None of them are right for me, and you know why?" She didn't wait for Sari to respond before continuing. "Because I'm too old for this. These clothes are fashioned for kids Kaylee's age. What in *hell* do I think I'm doing, pretending I belong here?"

"It—"

"Did you see the way she looked at me?" Becca interrupted her sister. "Like I was something gross?"

"She did not. She was just surprised," Sari said.

"I changed Kaylee's diapers at the day care!"

"Aunt Beth was pregnant with Joe when she was changing Suzie's diapers." Suzie was their second cousin on their mother's side. Their aunt's first grand-child.

"When it comes to pregnancy, my peers are *kids,* Sari. I have no business doing this. It's like I'm an old lady trying to recapture my youth." Becca just couldn't get over the feeling that she was gatecrashing a party where she didn't belong. And the fear that as soon as the fates spotted her, they'd kick her out. The fear that something would happen to her baby, that she'd miscarry, that the baby was never meant to be.

"You have every reason to do this, Rebecca Par-sons," Sari said, only lowering her voice when she noticed another shopper glancing in their direction. "God gave you this baby, this little soul, to nurture and bring into the world. If He thinks you're the right woman for the task, then that's just how it is and you'd better straighten up and do your job."

Becca wasn't as certain of that as Sari. Her sister had turned to religion as a way to deal with her grief after Tanya was killed by the drunk driver two sum-mers before. She saw God's hand in everything as a result.

And yet, as Becca stood there fiddling with a hanger in an attempt not to look at her sister, she had to admit there was some truth to Sari's words.

"You do think I belong here?" she asked softly, daring a peek over at Sari. "In this world of mothers and babies?"

Sari's eyes were filled with tears—and love and happiness, too. "I'm sure of it," she said, giving Becca's hand a squeeze. "Now let's go find you some decent clothes so Junior isn't humiliated by an old hag of a mother who's running around naked."

WILL LIKED her new clothes.

"You don't think I'll look ridiculous in them?" Becca asked after dinner that night. They'd just finished the dishes and she'd asked Will to wait a minute before he disappeared into his office for the evening. She needed his opinion. After all, they made a lot of public appearances together.

"I think you'll look beautiful."

The air in the kitchen was charged as their eyes met, held, spoke things they wouldn't allow themselves to say.

Becca swallowed. "You don't think they're too young? I haven't worn jumpers in years."

"Maybe you should have."

Not sure what he meant by that remark—was it a compliment or a dig at the way she'd changed? Becca gathered up the maternity clothes and started folding and returning them to the bag. But she couldn't erase the brief glimpse she'd had of Will's desire for her. Or the answering inferno she felt in herself. They'd been making love since they were seventeen years old. In all that time, they'd never gone more than a week without it, and usually they reached for each other several times a week. They were now going on four months.

Becca was deathly afraid of the way that fact changed their future.

"I had lunch with my mom and sisters today," she said as she folded. He was still standing there. And she wanted to keep him with her as long as she could.

"It's Wednesday. Right," he said as though only just remembering. "How are they?"

"Good." Sari was great. Her sister had a new strength, a strength she'd never had, even before Tanya's death. "We're wrapping up the Samuel Montford biography."

Will came over to the table and sat down. "Tell me about him."

Becca looked at him silently for a moment, wondering why he'd stayed with her when almost every night for the past few months he'd escaped to his office as soon as the dishes were done. She was afraid to hope that he missed her as much as she missed him. Desperately. Afraid to trust that somehow they'd find a way back to each other.

"I really feel a kinship with him." She started slowly, speaking of a subject that meant a lot to her and was without pitfalls. Leaving the rest of the clothes piled on one end of the table, she sat down across from Will. "Samuel Montford suffered and survived emotionally painful things, but his spirit remained intact, and that gives me strength."

"How so?" He leaned forward, his interest plainly visible.

She told him about Samuel's early hardships, his broken dreams, lost family, broken heart. The way he'd responded by giving years of his life to helping Indian tribes, whose lands, whose very way of life, were being stolen from them. She described what Samuel had learned from the tribes, lessons about family, community, responsibility. Finally she told Will how Samuel had met the missionary woman, fallen in love again.

Will listened intently, asking pertinent questions. Until that last bit. He looked a little skeptical when it came to Samuel's second foray into love.

"Samuel knew, even before he and Lizzie moved to Shelter Valley, that the town's major enterprise was going to be a university that rivaled his beloved Harvard."

Will nodded. "He founded the university, of course," he said. As the current president, he certainly knew the school's history. "Inspired by those Indian tribes' strengths, their values—though not their religions, per se—the university began with what, these days, we'd call a mission statement. The students at Montford were not only to learn knowledge and skills from textbooks and classes, but from the example of the people who taught them. They were to learn the importance of honor, of wisdom and strength, of acceptance and peace. The value in retaining an open mind…"

Will had been reciting almost by rote, but his voice slowly faded.

"I'd forgotten that," he said softly, looking inward as his fingers tapped the kitchen table.

Becca sent up a tiny silent prayer.

"Did you know that he wrote that mission statement in memory of Clara and their lost son?" she asked him.

Will shook his head.

"And in honor of Lizzie and the children they had together. He wanted to change the world."

"I've never heard that."

"The best thing about all this..." Becca's voice was passionate as she tried to communicate with her husband indirectly, since that was the only way she seemed to be able to reach him. "The best thing is, he really believed he *could* change the world. Even after all his disappointments, he didn't give up."

Will nodded. His head still bent, he glanced up at her.

Nervous to push any further, Becca sat back. "Did you know that most of his instructors were his scholarly companions from Boston?"

"I didn't," Will said, his face relaxing into an interested smile. "It's a shame so much of this information became lost or obscure."

Becca nodded. "I know, but Samuel was adamant about being remembered for his legacy, especially the university, and not for his private life. Besides, each generation is so caught up in its own concerns. It's too easy to forget what previous generations achieved. History becomes simplified—like reading just the headlines, instead of getting the details."

Will nodded respectfully. "I agree. So what do we know about those friends of his?"

"Apparently he wrote to them and was quite humbled by the numbers who were willing to leave their old lives behind and move west to help him with his venture.''

"That was quite a sacrifice in those days."

"He paid them more than generously, of course," Becca inserted. "He was nothing if not realistic."

"Still," Will said, his elbows on the table, "it's amazing that even now, more than a hundred years later, Samuel's philosophy is maintained, not only by how rigorously we select our faculty, but by the meetings and retreats we attend before the beginning of every semester. Meetings that continue to instill Samuel's values—even if we've forgotten exactly how we came by those values."

"And a code of ethics, for both students and faculty that's still enforced."

"It's kind of humbling to see what a huge impact one man can make," Will murmured.

"And encouraging to know that conviction and strength really do exist, and that sometimes they're enough to conquer whatever the world hands out."

Will smiled at her and Becca's insides melted. Taking a deep breath, she placed one hand over his on the table.

"I want you to know, Will, that I'm glad I didn't go through with the abortion." Though difficult to say, those words were also the truth. "No matter what the cost."

He shook his head. "Not at the cost of your life."

He spoke with such vehemence Becca was left in no doubt that her life still meant something to him.

But it would, because he was a compassionate man. It didn't necessarily follow that he was still in love with her or wanted to stay married.

"I'm grateful you told me that, though," he continued.

Peace settled over her. "I'm out of the doghouse, then? At least on that score?"

"I have to be honest with you, Becca." He pulled his hand away. "Because that's one thing we've always been with each other..."

Becca's stomach started to hurt. She wished she'd never begun this conversation.

"It isn't the rightness or wrongness that eats at me. It's the fact that I've always seen us as sharing the same life—one life—with the same goals and dreams—"

"We do!"

He shook his head. "I'm not sure I ever knew your dreams, Bec," he said sadly. "For that matter, I'm not sure I knew my own. This whole situation, with you not sure you even wanted a baby when I thought that was the one thing that mattered to you—it's opened my eyes to the fact that I don't really know you."

Tears gathered in her eyes. She didn't want to cry. Refused to cry. But she couldn't help it. "I'm sorry."

"No, Bec, you did nothing wrong," he said, looking her straight in the eye. "This is my fault."

But she still lost.

"Sometimes I wonder if maybe I just had this image in my mind of what my life was destined to be, of who you were, of what we wanted—but that's all it was. An image. I never dug deep enough to find reality. Maybe even to know that it existed.''

Scary as the thought was, Becca could understand what he was saying. "Kind of like that movie where everyone was living in a TV sitcom and didn't know they weren't real?''

"Exactly.''

Becca ached badly. For herself. For him, too. She could feel his struggle almost as well as she could feel her own. The confusion. And, on her part, the fear.

"So where do we go from here?'' she whispered.

"I guess to bed, and then to tomorrow morning.''

"One day at a time.''

"Right.''

"For how long?''

"I don't know, Bec,'' he said, his eyes sadder than she'd ever seen them. "I wish to God I did.''

CHRISTINE EVANS called Will on Friday. They'd already had several conversations by phone.

"I'm sorry to bother you, Dr. Parsons,'' she said as soon as Freda put her through.

"It's no bother,'' Will said, feeling an unusual fondness for the woman. "We're expecting you here in another couple of weeks.''

He paused, but when Christine remained silent, continued. "Have you got all your arrangements made, or is there something we can help you with?'' he asked. Christine's arrival on campus was something he figured he could handle. Something he could control in a life that had become very difficult.

"That's what I'm calling about," she said hesitantly. Almost as though she was planning to back out.

He hoped not. Christine Evans was perfect for Montford. She was a breath of fresh air, a trip to younger days, easier times. She was his twenty-year-old idealized memory of Becca personified.

"I'm afraid I've been held up longer than I'd anticipated," Christine went on.

"So you still intend to come?" Will asked, getting right to the point.

"Oh, yes, Dr. Parsons," she said. There was no mistaking her enthusiasm—a reaction he hadn't heard from her previously. She'd been so contained it was almost intimidating. "This position is the best thing that's happened to me in a long time. It's just that I have some family obligations this summer, and I'm not sure how long they're going to take."

"Your sister?"

"How'd you know?" Her voice was sharp.

"In your interviews you stated that your only family was a sister."

"Oh," she said. "Yes, I forgot that."

"Is she having some sort of problem?" Will asked, although he knew he probably shouldn't. But if someone in Shelter Valley could help her, he'd be remiss not to find that out.

"Nothing that won't take care of itself," she assured him vaguely. "Is there anything you need me to do from here?'' she asked. ''Any reading, other than the school manual you've already given me, any paperwork, lesson plans, whatever? You'll let me know?''

Will chuckled, appreciating her work ethic, happy that she was still so committed to joining them. ''You wouldn't happen to have a spare psychology professor hanging around, would you?''

He'd been reading résumés for Todd's possible replacement all morning. So far, all he'd gained was a headache.

And he had a Rotary luncheon to attend in Phoenix, fund-raising for Montford.

''If you're serious, I might have,'' she said, surprising him.

''Well, if you might have, I'm serious.'' And suddenly he was. Very serious. Todd Moore was going to be difficult to replace. No matter what other faults he had, Todd was a gifted teacher.

''Let me talk to a friend of mine, see if she's interested,'' Christine said.

''Is she at Boston College with you?''

''Yes.''

Will had a flash of Becca, sitting at their kitchen table the other night, her maternity clothes spread around her, telling him how Samuel Montford's friends had stood beside him, coming en masse from the East Coast to support his effort. Which reminded him—he'd have to commission an official history of Montford's life for the university.

''I'd like to have your friend's name, if I may,'' he

said. "I'll pass it along to Freda so she'll be sure to put her through if she calls."

"It's Phyllis. Dr. Phyllis Langford."

Christine's voice warmed as she said the name.

"She's a good friend?"

"Yes, she is."

Remembering the shadows in Christine's eyes, Will was glad to know that his reserved new English professor had a friend.

He was interested in speaking with this Dr. Phyllis Langford. She must be a very special person.

CHAPTER TWELVE

MARTHA TOOK the news of her husband's infidelity far better than Becca would have. The two women were having coffee at the diner on Friday of the following week—the meeting place at Martha's request—while they went over the list of kids who'd already signed up for theater in Save the Youth's summer session. They were doing things a little backward, assigning parts before the script was written, but Martha wanted to make the parts fit the people who were playing them.

Some read well. Some didn't. Some memorized well. Some didn't. She could write the script accordingly. And the kids came away feeling good about themselves and their abilities.

"Mother gave her Montford report to Betty during lunch on Wednesday," Becca told Martha. "She worked on the descendants, and her report was the last one. Betty said to tell you she'd have everything to you by Sunday."

Martha nodded. "That gives me a couple of weeks before the kids are out of school and ready to—"

Mary Blount, the town librarian, stopped at their table, interrupting Martha. "I was so sorry to hear about you and Todd."

"I know," Martha said, her unlined face still youthful looking.

"What about you and the kids? Is there anything we can do?"

"We'll be fine," she said, smiling sadly, "but thanks."

As Mary left—and other curious friends and acquaintances continued to send surreptitious glances their way—Martha didn't fall apart. She didn't shake with rage. She merely returned to the pages in front of her.

While Becca admired Martha's stiff upper lip, she hurt for her, too. Martha didn't deserve this.

Dressed in her usual jeans and blouse, her friend looked just as she had the million other times they'd met in town. Even after four kids, Martha still had a decent figure, wore her makeup tastefully, kept her short hair fashionably styled, although the color did tend to change every year or so.

"We can go somewhere else if you'd like," Becca offered. "My house would be good. Will's out—he's meeting with the architect for the new building today."

Martha shook her head. "I intend to stay right here and get this over with," she said. "Besides, it actually kind of helps—knowing that everyone cares, I mean. I've never been more glad than I am right now that I live in Shelter Valley." A tear lingered on Martha's lashes before she brushed it away.

"I could kill Todd," Becca said, burning up for her friend.

"It's not all his fault."

"How can you say that?"

Looking up, Martha didn't blink as she said, "Twenty years with no magic is a really long time."

Becca didn't know what to say.

"I hate him for what he's done, but I can almost understand how it happened," Martha said. Becca's heart went out to her anew as she met her friend's devastated gaze.

"We got married for the wrong reasons," Martha said softly, curling the corner of one of the pages in front of her. "We did it because it was what everyone, including us, expected. You know how Shelter Valley is—you grow up knowing that your ultimate goal is marriage and children."

Becca nodded. It had taken her twenty years to grow out of that expectation. At least the children part of it.

"My marriage to Todd was convenient, you know?" Martha said. "You and Will were getting married. Todd and I were great friends. It was easy, the next step in our life plan. We sort of...fell into marriage."

Becca's nerves started to tense as she listened. Wasn't this exactly what Will was telling her about *their* marriage?

"But I still can't believe Todd did this," Martha said, shaking her head again. "He's humiliated me, has the whole town thinking I'm not enough of a woman to keep my man. It's not fair to the kids." She stopped, took a sip of her coffee in a rather obvious attempt to compose herself. "We were best friends. I trusted him."

"You didn't have any idea he was having an affair?"

"None," Martha said, tears brimming a second time. "That's what hurts the most, you know? The lack of trust. If he'd only come to me, told me, instead of going to her behind my back..."

"He doesn't deserve your tears," Becca snapped. She'd have liked about ten minutes with her pal Todd right then.

"I know."

Martha looked up several moments later, her face more relaxed. She'd obviously won the battle with her emotions, for the time being, anyway. "You know," she said, "all I wanted was what you and Will have always had, Bec, and I never had that with Todd. I wanted the fireworks, the stars. I wanted my heart to jump, my eyes to light up, just because someone walked into a room—the way yours do when Will comes in."

"My eyes don't light up," Becca said, embarrassed. And a little frightened, too. Was she really that far gone? She couldn't be. Because if she was, she'd never survive when Will walked out of her life.

"Yeah, they do," Martha assured her. "They always have. His do, too, when he looks at you."

Becca pondered that, a part of her pleased, hopeful. But just a very small part. If Will's eyes lit up, it must be out of habit. How could it be out of love when the man didn't even *know* if he loved her?

She couldn't think about that now.

If she and Martha stayed there much longer, Becca was going to have to order something to eat, even though she'd already had both breakfast and lunch. She seemed to be hungry all the time these days.

"I'm also angry that Todd's off having fun while I'm still home all day, taking care of his kids. The jerk." She made an ugly face.

Becca chuckled. "You got the kids. They're life's real reward."

"Yeah." Martha's face warmed, a bit of the light she'd described moments ago in her eyes. "And now you're finally going to have one, too," she said, looking down at the new plaid maternity jumper Becca was wearing. "I can't tell you how happy I am for you, Bec."

A bit teary-eyed, Becca smiled at her friend. In spite of everything, she was happy, too. At least about the baby...

Their waitress, a young woman neither of them knew, came to ask if they'd like refills on their beverages, and both women ordered desserts, as well. Martha figured she owed herself a treat.

"Now that we've got the hard funding for Save the Youth, I'd like to plan on doing a play every Fourth of July as part of Shelter Valley's annual celebration, and maybe a Christmas show, too, kind of an after-school thing," Becca told Martha while they waited. "How'd you like to sign on as theater project director?"

"I'd love to," Martha said. She smiled, though her

eyes were still dulled from the painful week she'd had. "Look at you, hitting up a poor girl when she's low."

"I'll be able to pay you," Becca said. She knew Martha had to be a little concerned about money. The kids would be fine. Todd would support them, and Martha, too, for a while. But Martha, who'd quit college to have Todd's baby, would eventually have to find a way to support herself. Unless she went to work in the cactus-jelly factory just outside town or waited tables, Shelter Valley had very little to offer.

"Thank you," Martha said softly, tears brimming in her eyes again.

"Becca! Martha! I didn't know you two were going to be here."

Becca turned, her heart jumping just like Martha said it did, when she recognized Will's voice behind her. He was with someone Becca had never seen before. His new architect friend, she suspected.

The two men joined them at the table, and Will introduced John Strickland. As the four of them passed two full hours sitting there in the diner talking and laughing, Becca wondered if maybe that wasn't an appreciative glint she saw in Martha's eyes. John Strickland was a very charming man. He was also sensitive, a man who'd suffered and known loss, who recognized it in others.

Becca wanted to hug him for building up Martha's self-confidence. Even if he didn't know he was doing it.

It was just the way Becca had always heard. When

a door closes, a window is opened. Maybe this was Martha's window.

And maybe she'd have a window, too, if her door closed.

She just hoped she'd be able to fit through the framework when it did.

GRADUATION CAME. The population of Shelter Valley swelled, as it always did this time of year, with parents, friends and relatives of the graduates. For these last few weeks of the school year, there was at least an hour's wait at the diner, whatever the time of day, and the two local hotels, both by the highway, were full.

Becca, the perfect president's wife, was as much a credit to Will as ever as they made appearances at parties, dinners, alumni fund-raisers. Other than those appearances, doctor's appointments and in bed at night, Will rarely saw her those next few weeks. Getting her Save the Youth program up and running was taking the majority of Becca's time.

Phyllis Langford, it turned out, was interested in the psychology professorship. She called, sent her materials and, at the request of the Psychology Department, flew out the last week of May for an intensive set of interviews. She received a unanimous vote and was offered the position before she left town.

During his interview with her, Will found her to be not only a well-educated applicant worthy of hire, but a sensitive listener, as well. She seemed to hear things that weren't actually expressed. Things people felt but didn't say. He was sure she'd be a real asset to the university.

Without his even asking, she'd reassured him that Christine was fine—and greatly looking forward to living in Arizona.

She also explained her own reasons for wanting to make such a drastic move. Not only was it a step up for her professionally, as Todd's position was more senior than the job Phyllis currently held, but she knew it was time to make a break from Boston—and the ex-husband she found difficult to let go of completely. She was looking to Shelter Valley for a fresh start. A new life.

Will figured she was looking in the right place.

The first Saturday in June, with the university between sessions, he and Becca went into Phoenix to pick out nursery furniture. The job was surprisingly easy as Becca knew exactly what she wanted and they both liked the same things. Even down to the rocker she chose for the nursery.

"We should have one for the family room, too," Will said, testing the chair for himself. His feet on the footstool, his body cushioned by the soft leather, he could fall asleep in it—perfect, he decided, for when he was taking his middle-of-the-night sleepless-baby turns.

Becca gave him an odd look when he said something of the sort to her, and he realized that his thoughts had carried him someplace he hadn't yet decided to be. Into the future. Still living with Becca.

Her eyes filling with tentative hope, she silently

asked him if he'd made a decision, if he'd figured out whether he was in love with her, or if their life together was really just a sham.

He couldn't give her an answer. An answer he needed just as badly as she did.

And still, in that silent communication they'd been sharing since they were banned from passing notes in junior high, she let him know that his time was running out. He'd better come up with something, or she was going to take his choices away from him.

It was the first time he realized that he wasn't the only one who could end their marriage.

BECCA LAY uncharacteristically awake that night. She didn't feel sick. Didn't have any physical aches, no sharp pains—no numbness, either. Her stomach just felt odd. Like she had little champagne bubbles trapped there.

She'd been having this strange indigestion, or whatever it was, for most of the week.

Will, sleeping restlessly beside her, turned his head. She closed her eyes, hoping that if he awoke, he'd think she was asleep. She couldn't face any intimate conversation just then—and intimate was all it could be, with the two of them lying side by side in the bed they'd shared for almost twenty years.

They hadn't both been awake in that bed at the same time in months. Every night Will waited until she was asleep before climbing in beside her, and whoever woke first in the morning didn't linger long enough for the other to wake up.

Hearing his deep, regular breathing, Becca relaxed, her eyes popping open again. Will was facing her, his strong features softened with sleep. She took advantage of the rare opportunity to study him, to look her fill, to stare avidly at the man she'd been in love with forever.

Will mumbled in his sleep. And moved. A leg. An arm. Once, just his hand along the mattress. But with every restless move, her body felt another jolt of heat. She wanted him so desperately. Needed to feel those hands on her body, wanting her.

Becca turned over, pulling the covers carefully over her shoulders, staving off the shivers that were coursing through her body. She wished she was wearing more than the thin silk sleeveless gown she'd pulled on in deference to the one-hundred-degree weather they'd been having.

And remembered how he used to tell her that no matter how many times he touched her breasts, their softness still amazed him.

Becca started to cry, slow tears that trailed quietly down her cheeks.

Back in those early days, in spite of their harried schedules, they'd had sex twice a day. So how was Will managing with nothing for more than four months? An image of Todd crept into her mind. *He* hadn't needed his wife to find sexual satisfaction.

Becca was scared to death that Will might have found someone else, too. Especially after her talk with Martha, who'd had no idea that Todd had been fooling around.

Could Will be fooling around on her? Was that the real reason they hadn't made love for so long?

Will moved again, resettled himself, and desire for her husband consumed Becca, in spite of her fears.

A sob escaped before she even knew it was coming. Throwing back the covers, she started to sit up, to escape the bed that was far too crowded.

"Becca?" Will's hand shot out, grabbing her arm. "You okay?" he asked sleepily. He might be only half-conscious, but his grip was strong.

"Fine," she said quite normally, considering, and then ruined the effect with a big sniffle.

"What's wrong?" he asked, sitting up and switching on the bedside lamp in one movement. He turned her to face him. "Are you ill?"

Becca shook her head. She couldn't look at him. This was so humiliating. Here she was, in bed with her husband, wanting him. And there *he* was, in the same bed, not wanting her.

"You had a bad dream?" he asked.

She shook her head again. She felt so helpless, so hopeless, as though nothing mattered. And yet everything did.

Pulling her up against his body, clothed only in a pair of cotton boxers, Will spoke to her softly, offering one meaningless reassurance after another. He shifted, bringing his lower body into contact with her—and Becca began to cry again.

"It's about this afternoon, isn't it," he said.

She knew immediately what he meant. That mostly wordless conversation over the rocking chair. His confusion over who they were, who they were going to be. The day had been ruined after that. Luckily all they'd had left to do was pay the bill and make arrangements for everything to be delivered the following week.

"I'm not going to desert you, Bec. You know that, don't you?" he asked.

She shrugged, her shoulders moving against his bare chest. His arms were around her, his hands clasped across her stomach. His chin rested on the top of her head.

"It's not really even about you, not completely," he said. "It's about me—about being blind and shallow. It's like I went to sleep at twenty and woke up and I was forty-two."

So who was the man she'd shared those twenty years with, if not him? Becca wouldn't ask him, wasn't sure it even mattered.

"Talk to me, Bec," he pleaded.

And because she didn't know what else to do, because he'd always been the one she went to when the world rocked too far on its axis, she did.

"Will, if I ask you something, do you promise to answer honestly, no matter how painful that answer might be?"

He swallowed. "Yes."

"Have you ever slept with anyone else?"

"No." He waited a moment, while the silence in the room filled with tension. "Have you?"

"Of course not." Becca licked her lips, tasting the salt of her tears. "Do you want to?"

"No."

"You're sure about that?" He'd never lied to her before.

"Yes."

"Have you ever had fantasies of being with someone else?"

"Of course," he answered, still holding her. "Every man does. I kind of figured every woman does, too." His voice was calm, comforting. But she was beyond comfort. "Don't they?"

"I don't know," Becca said. She couldn't think about that now. "Probably."

He grew still. "Do you want to sleep with someone else, Bec?"

The tears started again, welling silently. "No."

She could feel the sudden tension drain out of him. And hated his being so sure of her when she was sure of nothing at all.

The room was so quiet she could hear Will's breathing. And her own. Until she thought she was going to scream. Or lose her mind. She'd never known anything could hurt this much.

She had to ask. "Do you?"

"No." He didn't even hesitate and Becca started to relax a little.

"How can you be certain?" She didn't know why she had to push him, other than that she couldn't get Martha's pain-filled eyes out of her mind.

"Because if I was ever going to want another woman, it would've been the new English professor I hired, and I'm not the least bit tempted."

Becca's world crumbled.

"You're interested in one of your teachers?" She couldn't imagine a worse nightmare.

"No!" he said, chuckling. "Didn't I just say I'm not?"

"But you like her."

He turned Becca then, tenderly, until he was looking into her eyes, his face mere inches away.

"Only because she reminds me so much of you."

She couldn't trust him anymore. Couldn't believe what he was telling her. "You want her."

Her fear, her overflowing, hormonally unbalanced emotions, bubbled up from inside.

"I do not want her, Rebecca," he said, never more convincing in his life. His eyes were steady, full of frustration, but steady. Unwavering.

However, according to Will, Todd had been perfectly steady, too, when he'd come begging, requesting money for Stacy. Apparently if the girl was young enough, beautiful enough, a man would do anything for her.

"She wears her hair the way you used to when we were in college, held back in those barrette things and long, almost to her hips."

"I thought you liked my hair shorter."

"I do!" Will sighed, his brows furrowed as his frustration built. "She just reminds me of a simpler time. A time when no answers were necessary because I didn't know there were any questions."

"What else about her reminds you of me?"

"Her intelligence. You've always been my equal or more in any debate."

And they'd had some good ones.

Becca leaned back against him, tired, wishing for oblivion to take her away from her whole confusing life. At least until she had enough strength to make sense of it.

"But mostly," Will continued when she just wanted the whole conversation to be over, "it's her eyes."

He'd been close enough to notice her eyes?

"They're blue like yours," he said, hurting her even more, "but what really reminded me of you— of the way you are now, not twenty years ago—was the shadows in them. I wish I could take the shadows out of your eyes, Bec."

There was no mistaking the sincere, intense note of caring in his voice. No doubting which woman he was with at that moment. And really no doubting his fidelity. Whether she believed him about the occupants of his dreams or not, she knew that Will had never been unfaithful to her.

At least not yet.

"Please make love to me," she whispered.

His hands splayed possessively across her belly. "I'm still not sure...."

"I know we have problems, Will," she said in a rush. "I'm not dumb enough to think that sex will wipe them away. But it might help."

"I want you, Becca, so badly I ache with it most nights, but—"

"I won't hold you to anything," she promised him. "I just want to feel your body naked against mine again. To know that I'm the woman you want in your arms when you cry out in satisfaction."

"You've always been the woman I want in my arms."

CHAPTER THIRTEEN

WILL'S STRUGGLE was unlike any he'd known before. His body was on fire for the woman in his arms. After months of sleeping beside her, of denying himself what had always been his for the taking, he was ready to explode with need.

And yet...

"Our lovemaking has always meant more than just sex." He attempted to explain himself to her. "From the very first, it was a commitment—a promise for tomorrow."

Becca didn't say anything. Just nodded, her hair tickling his chest.

"I'm not going to make promises I might not be able to keep. Especially not to you."

"I appreciate that, Will. But don't you see, if we both agree that there are no promises attached—"

"What was that?" Will interrupted her to stare down at his hand, where it lay across her belly.

"Shh," Becca said.

It came again, very faintly. A light tap against her abdomen. From inside her abdomen.

"It's him!" Will said, his voice filled with wonder, with awe.

Becca giggled. "Or her."

He continued to look at her belly, though there was no way he was removing his hand.

"Can you feel it?" he whispered. Could the child really hear him, like some of the books said?

"Of course I can feel it," she whispered back. He could hear the smile in her voice.

"Does it hurt?"

"No, but I gather it might later on." She stopped as one more little nudge bumped against his hand. "Right now it just kind of tickles."

They waited silently for another five minutes, but their baby had apparently decided he was finished entertaining his parents. Will still couldn't bring himself to break his contact with Becca. With the moment.

Softly, slowly, he ran his hand over her belly—up to her rib cage, down to her hips.

Driven by the need to get closer to her, to the miracle they'd created together, he drew up her gown, lifting it until he had access to her bare belly. He caressed it again, side to side, top to bottom, her soft skin igniting the fires he was trying so hard to quench.

All he was going to do was touch her. It had been so damn long since he'd touched her. Just her belly. His baby. No more.

Just her belly. His palm trailed over it again, feeling the goose bumps as she responded to him. Becca lay perfectly still against him, almost as though she was holding her breath.

Continuing its caressing motion, his palm slid up to her ribs again.

Looking down, he caught a glimpse of the silky

white triangle of her panties. He knew what velvety treasure lay beneath them. Knew exactly where to touch her, how to touch her, to have her squirming beneath him, crying out his name as though he were king of her universe.

His palm slipped. Up. Encountering the underside of her breast. It was heavy against the side of his finger. And soft. So soft.

Will, groaning, slid his hand over that breast, cupping it. Just her breast. He'd only touch her breast. It had been so long.

Breasts. Not just one, but two. His hand slid over to cup her other breast, squeezing softly, possessing. And before he knew what was happening, his other hand had followed the first, until both her breasts were captive to him.

Becca's nipples hardened in his palms, tight buds poking at him. She liked him to run his fingers lightly over the center of that hardness.

So he did. Just briefly. For a moment. No more.

Teasing the tips of her breasts made her writhe.

That silky white triangle was like a flag, blazoning, capturing his attention, bringing his gaze back to it over and over again.

But he wasn't going to do any more than look at it. No matter how badly he wanted to rip those panties off his wife's body, no matter how eagerly she invited him, how badly she wanted him, he wasn't going to do it.

He just wasn't.

But he could play with her breasts. He was already

there, anyway. She felt so good, so right, naked beneath his palms. Kind of like coming home. And she, pushing her nipples more firmly into his palms, was enjoying herself, too.

They always talked while they were making love. From that very first night, when she'd been nervous and he, so awkwardly rushed and needy, had been trying to take his time with her, they'd made love verbally, as well as physically.

But tonight, neither one of them said a word. They weren't making love.

As Becca started to quiet in his arms, her lower body not quieting at all as it issued the familiar invitation, Will teased her nipples again. She wanted him to. She was telling him she wanted him to.

So he did.

He was in actual pain, strained to the point of near agony, but he wasn't going to give in to it. He lay back, propped against the pillows, taking Becca with him. And was very careful not to move his lower body—or to let hers touch it, either.

A man could only stand so much.

Tilting her head, Becca gazed up at him, her blue eyes languorous with a passion he'd missed more than he'd realized. She licked her open lips, and he lowered his mouth to cover them. They'd looked so incomplete, so needy.

She was hot and moist and tasted just like he'd known she would. Like Becca. God, he'd missed that taste.

He'd just kiss her. That would be the compromise. Nothing more.

"Mmm," he groaned. Hearing his own voice surprised him. They weren't speaking. Weren't making love.

Little sounds were coming from Becca's throat. Hungry, wanton sounds. Sounds he'd never heard before.

Will kissed her harder, covering her mouth completely, insatiably, mating his tongue with hers.

The guttural sounds from her throat were driving him mad. Making him do things he'd never done before, or at least not in the same way.

Stop! his mind yelled at her as he pulled her down beneath him, riding her wildly through their clothes, his penis down between her legs. She was making him insane.

The friction of his frantic movements rode his boxers down. He continued moving against her until, growing impatient, he reached down and pushed them to his knees.

His penis was free. Hard and heavy and free.

Without thought, Will stopped at the triangle between Becca's legs, pulling it to one side—just enough for him to find her moist opening and plunge himself inside.

She was climaxing by the time he completed his first thrust. He climaxed on his second.

It was the most incredible experience he'd ever had in his life.

And he hated himself for what he'd done.

SHE'D BEEN WRONG. She'd told Will that their making love wouldn't have to change anything—except that it might help. It did change things. But not for the better.

If anything, Will was more distant from her than ever. They were having sex often, nightly when they could manage it, but they weren't making love anymore. For Will, adding sex to the equation only made his struggle worse. Becca could see that.

She just didn't know what she could do to help him.

Rehearsals for the Fourth of July play, *The Hero,* were in full swing. The whole town seemed to be contributing as the teenagers brought Samuel Montford's history to life. Parents were involved in set- and costume-making, merchants were donating supplies. A musical score had been written and the Save the Youth music program was participating, as well.

Becca stopped in for rehearsal on the third Tuesday in June and was gratified to see how well everything was coming together. She watched the scene that depicted the discovery of gold in Shelter Valley just a couple of years after Samuel and Lizzie had settled there, and the corruption resulting from that discovery.

There'd been an influx of prospectors and gold-miners who brought with them the greed and mistrust that accompanied many of the stakes in the Old West. The boys playing the prospectors were better than good, bringing the scene to such life Becca felt a shiver.

Martha's oldest daughter, Ellen, was on stage in the next scene, playing Grace Montford—Samuel's granddaughter—who fell in love with George Smith—Mayor Smith's father—an avaricious and crafty man who came to town, planning to make a fortune of his own. Though a handsome and superficially charming man, George Smith was empty inside. Grace married him, shared with him her portion of the Montford inheritance. Coming to Shelter Valley had paid off for him. And the town had been paying for it ever since.

Becca knew the rest of that story. Leaving the auditorium for her next stop—Sari's house, to see how her sister was doing with the costumes she was sewing—she remembered what her mother had told them about old George. Had he squandered Grace's inheritance, the town of Shelter Valley might have been better off. But he hadn't, of course. With his cold heart and calculating mind, he settled alongside the other Montford heirs and became a patriarch in his own right. The Smiths had always been a thorn in the side of the townspeople.

"You're not looking too good," Sari said, greeting her at the door.

"Other than this heat, I'm perfectly fine," Becca said, dropping into a chair in Sari's family room, soaking up the divine air-conditioned coolness while Sari went back to work at the cutting table she'd set up. "I saw Dr. Anderson just last week and everything's fine. I'm getting enough rest, I'm eating well. Baby's growing according to the charts." Used to

Sari's honesty—a right she'd gained through sister-hood—Becca was surprised at her own defensiveness.

"I wasn't talking about your physical state, Bec," Sari said softly when Becca had finished. "You don't look happy."

Becca drooped, all the fire draining out of her. She watched Sari cut pieces from a bolt of brown fabric, told herself to get up and help. But at five and a half months pregnant in the Arizona heat, she just didn't have the energy to move. The trek across town had done her in.

"I'm not happy," she announced baldly.

"Because of Will?" Sari stopped cutting and glanced up.

Becca looked around her at the furnishings that were more comfortable than fashionable, the sewing paraphernalia sitting on Sari's table, the books and other objects on the ledge between the family room and the kitchen. All things that meant something to Sari. The house was clean, but it looked lived in. Like a home.

Her own house just looked clean.

Her eyes rested on the picture of Tanya on the man-tel over the fireplace. Taken just a couple of weeks before Tanya died, it showed the sixteen-year-old grinning at the camera as if she owned the world.

Sari's only child. Lost to her. And Sari had the courage to live, anyway.

Becca had been so frightened of losing her child that she'd contemplated not giving birth to it. That way her baby could never be taken from her.

"It's more than that," she admitted, although if she could talk to Will, really talk to him, she'd feel a lot better.

Sari was cutting fabric again.

"I've been thinking a lot about why I was going to have that abortion," Becca admitted. "Maybe because Will needs answers so badly, I don't know, but I've been trying to figure out what was really prompting me to do something that seemed so out of character to the people who know me best."

"And?"

"I was afraid to have the baby."

"Yeah," Sari said, unpinning the pattern she was using and placing it on another part of the material for repinning. "From the medical report you received, you had reason to be afraid."

Becca shook her head. "I don't think it was just that," she said, only now realizing it, as she voiced thoughts that had been haphazardly running through her mind.

Raising her head, pins between her teeth, Sari mumbled, "Then what?"

"I think I was afraid to have it because I knew I'd never survive losing it." Becca looked at Tanya's picture again. "Chances of me miscarrying were higher than if I'd been younger or had a baby before. Birth defects are still a distinct possibility. And if we make it through all of that...well then, the danger really begins. Then my baby goes out into the world and a million other things can befall him."

Hearing Becca's anguish, Sari dropped the pins and

the scissors, and came over to kneel beside Becca. Putting her head in her sister's lap, she rubbed Becca's leg.

"I'm nothing but a coward," Becca confessed.

"Being aware of the dangers doesn't make you a coward, Bec," she said. "It makes you human!"

Sari was so strong, Becca loved her more than she'd ever thought possible. Stroking Sari's hair, she thought about letting it go at that. But she and Sari had always been honest with each other.

"Not if I choose the easy way out so I don't have to deal with them."

"But you didn't!" Sari said. "You made the choice to have this baby."

But would she have if it hadn't been for Will? If she hadn't known how much her choice was hurting him?

"And look what you do for Shelter Valley!" Sari said, her voice earnest. "You're no coward, Bec. You stand up to Mayor Smith and you—"

"George Smith can't hurt me," Becca broke in, shaking her head. "This town has always been my haven. And I've been wondering lately if Shelter Valley's maybe too *much* of a haven for me," she said slowly. "A safe haven..."

"What do you mean? There's nothing wrong with living in a safe place."

"There is when it keeps me safe from the trials and tribulations of the world."

Which was exactly what Will had said.

"It's safer than the big cities, that's true," Sari

said, "but that doesn't always keep terrible things from happening here."

As they both knew. Tanya had been killed two miles from home.

"Besides," Sari continued, laying her head back down, "living in a small town like this, a relatively safe, secure place, isn't a bad decision. More of a smart one."

Becca shook her head. "Not if you're choosing to live here because you're running away."

Sari was quiet, the weight of her head on Becca's lap a comfort.

"Loving Will has always been safe and easy, too," Becca whispered. "But now it's not, and I'm afraid to do that, too."

"To love him?"

Becca's throat tightened with the tears she was fighting. "Yeah," she said, her voice quavering. "He's not sure about so many things. I really shocked him with wanting the abortion—and now I'm afraid to trust my heart to him, afraid I'll do something else that will destroy his affection for me..."

Sari hugged Becca's legs as Becca's voice trailed off.

"I'm even..." Becca started and then stopped as tears got in the way again. "I'm even more afraid of losing him."

The room was silent for a time, the air conditioner's steady hum the only sound.

Becca's hand stayed busy, smoothing Sari's hair behind her ear. The motion was almost therapeutic.

"Lately things haven't been getting better with us. We seem sort of...stalled, and I spend all my time thinking about where we went wrong. I can't just keep waiting for him, Sari, knowing there's a chance that when all is said and done, he'll be gone."

"Life doesn't come with any guarantees, sis," Sari said sadly.

"I know." *Will says that, too.*

Both women were silent, comforting each other with their presence as the minutes passed.

"Bec?" Sari asked softly after a time.

"Yeah?"

"Will you do something with me?"

Sari sounded nervous, a little scared. Which scared Becca.

"Of course," she said, instilling confidence where she felt none. "What?"

"Promise you won't make a big deal of it—not at first, anyway?"

"I promise." Becca took a deep breath, bracing herself.

Sari stood, urging her out of her chair. "Come on."

Following her sister through the house and back to the master bedroom, she asked, "Where're we going?" But the question was mostly rhetorical. She didn't really expect an answer.

Heart pumping, stomach churning a little, Becca allowed herself to be pulled along. Her mind raced ahead, wondering what was in store, arming herself. Had Sari decided it was time to get rid of Tanya's things? The ones she kept in a box on her bedroom shelf?

"Okay," Sari said, stopping as they reached the bathroom. She opened a cupboard, took out a familiar-looking box. "Here," she said, handing it to Becca.

Staring down at the home pregnancy test, Becca wondered for a second if her sister had lost her mind. Becca's pregnancy was already confirmed. And more than obvious. Why would—

"I want you to tell me how to use this," Sari said, her voice shaking, "and then wait with me until I know."

"Until…" Becca looked up. "You?" she asked, tears springing to her eyes.

Sari wouldn't meet her gaze. "I don't know," she said tensely. And Becca remembered her promise not to make a big deal of things. Instantly she understood why. If Sari was wrong…

"Okay, it's really very simple," she said confidently, as though they were baking bread, as though the outcome was no more important than a loaf of bread. She opened the box, showed Sari the simple steps and sent her off.

And spent the next couple of minutes praying harder than she probably ever had.

Sari's face was pinched and white when she opened the bathroom door a couple of minutes later.

"I don't think I can handle the wait," she said, and burst into tears.

Pulling her sister into her arms, Becca sat with her

on the end of the bed. "What if I'm wrong?" Sari cried. "I've gotten my hopes up, even though I knew I shouldn't. I just can't seem to help it."

"Does Bob know?" Becca asked. Her brother-in-law loved kids as much as Will did.

"No." Sari shook her head. "Not until I'm sure. I don't want to disappoint him."

Becca thought back over the many similar tests she'd taken in the past twenty years, the times she'd cried herself to sleep on the bathroom floor when the result had been negative. She could certainly understand Sari's reaction. And her fear.

"How late are you?"

"Two months."

"You've been keeping this to yourself for over a month?"

Sari nodded. "Seemed kind of silly to get everyone worked up when it was probably just my nerves freaking out on me," Sari said. "Bob and I have been trying ever since we had Tanya, and nothing's ever happened. Why should now be any different?"

Given her own situation, Becca had no answer to that. "Maybe the scarring from your problems with Tanya's birth has thinned enough to allow fertilization."

"Does scarring do that?" Sari asked, sniffing.

Becca thought about it. "I don't know," she said. "But it might." Because Sari was listening and Becca was grateful for the distraction the topic was offering her younger sister, Becca went on to outline a couple of incidents she'd heard about involving scars that had changed over the years. Her college roommate who'd cut her hand washing a glass. A friend of their mother's who'd been burned.

"Oh, Bec," Sari interrupted her suddenly. "I want this soooo badly..." Her voice broke and she started to cry again.

Recognizing that Sari's tears were, at least in part, a release of the tension she'd endured for the past month, Becca just kept an arm around her and let her cry.

"Aren't you a little bit afraid? Of being pregnant?" she asked when Sari finally quieted.

"No," Sari said, shaking her head. "Not yet, anyway. Right now, I just want this so badly it's all I can think about."

"Even after losing Tanya?" Becca asked. Losing her niece had terrified her, had affected her feelings for the child growing inside her.

Slipping to the floor at her sister's feet, Sari took both of Becca's hands in hers. "I *had* Tanya, Bec," she said, her eyes filled with an odd peace and glowing with love. "Those were the best sixteen years of my life. I'd do them over in a heartbeat."

Afraid to finally know, to have her hopes crushed, Sari refused to check the test when the time was up. Becca rationalized until she was out of breath, and yet Sari did nothing but stare at the bathroom door with worried eyes.

"You want me to do it?" Becca finally asked.

"I just don't want the answer to be no."

''There are no guarantees in life, sis,'' Becca repeated Sari's words back to her as she stood up.

Sari grabbed her hand, holding her back. ''Just
don't tell me the second you walk in the door,'' Sari
said. ''That way, if the answer's no, I still get a few
seconds to hope...''

Becca nodded and went into the bathroom. One
glance, and she started to cry. Sari needn't have worried; Becca couldn't speak if she'd wanted to. She
couldn't get a single word out.

''Becca?'' Sari called, her voice filled with trepidation.

Composing herself as best she could, Becca turned
toward the door, walked straight to Sari and threw her
arms around her.

''Congratulations, Mommy,'' she whispered, and
broke down completely.

CHAPTER FOURTEEN

BECCA'S NEXT APPOINTMENT with Dr. Anderson, on Thursday, the second-last week in June, was another positive one. At five and a half months, she was still progressing normally. Her blood pressure had even fallen into the normal range.

"How long can sexual activity continue?" Will asked the doctor as she measured Becca's protruding stomach.

Feeling herself blush, Becca wished he'd picked a better time to ask such a question. But she held her breath, anyway, waiting for the answer. She was starting to live for those moments of closeness with Will. As long as they were connecting—even in these silent sexual interludes—she had hope. Besides, Will's tenderness during those nocturnal forays was sustaining her.

"As long as everything proceeds normally, you should be able to continue intercourse into the last month," the doctor answered after writing measurements down on Becca's chart.

Before they left, Becca told Dr. Anderson about Sari's good news, asking if she had room for one more patient. Up to this point, her sister had been seeing a general practitioner in Shelter Valley, but with an "over forty" pregnancy, she'd agreed to Becca's pleas to switch to a specialist in Phoenix. Will jumped in, too, telling the doctor about the child Sari had lost, how important this new pregnancy was to Sari and Bob—to all of them. The doctor smilingly agreed to fit Sari in.

Then Dr. Anderson spoke with them about several tests she wanted to run on Becca—some of them optional—and told Becca to make appointments for those they chose to pursue.

She and Will discussed those tests during the drive back to Shelter Valley. They'd both done a lot of reading on the subject.

"I don't think you need the amniocentesis, Bec," Will said as soon as they were out of city traffic. "It's painful, and even if it tells us there's some kind of defect, we're going to have the baby, anyway."

He was silent for a moment, then said, "Aren't we?"

He wasn't sure of her anymore. But how could she blame him when she was having so many doubts herself? This was an answer she knew for certain, however.

"Of course we are." She'd determined that when she'd opted not to terminate her pregnancy.

"We need the ultrasound, though, and all the bloodwork, plus the diabetes test," Will said.

"I agree."

"Do we want to know the sex of the baby?"

"I don't." Becca had already given that some

thought. She wanted to do this the old-fashioned way. To be surprised. "Unless you do?"

She wasn't sure of him, either.

"No, I'm happy to wait," he said.

They drove in silence for a while. "Still no calls on the baby furniture?" Will asked about five miles down the road.

"Nope." Becca shook her head. "Other than to say it was back-ordered. I haven't heard from them since."

"I'll give them a call tomorrow."

"Thanks."

Until they knew when the furniture was coming, Becca was still using her office as an office. No point impinging on Will's space until she had to.

Another ten miles whizzed by. Becca could smell Will's aftershave. It made her look forward to that night, when the lights were out. When they'd said their good-nights and he reached for her across their big silent bed.

"We should probably look into signing up for those childbirth classes the doctor mentioned," Will said.

Becca nodded. "I'll call tomorrow."

THE BABY'S FURNITURE finally arrived, three weeks late, on the last Thursday in June. Becca, just home from the day care when the delivery company had called to say they'd be there within the hour, had phoned the high school for help moving her office furniture out of the nursery. Within fifteen minutes she'd had ten boys from Save the Youth on her door-step. She ordered pizza for all of them.

By the time Will got back from the state Higher Education Administration luncheon he'd been attending in Phoenix, the work was done. His home had a nursery.

"The furniture looks great, just like we envisioned," he told Becca, standing beside her in the doorway of the room. "But the walls sure look bare, don't they?"

"I was thinking the same thing," she said. "What do you think—wallpaper, paint or just some colorful balloon appliqués? Fabric ones," she added. "Maybe with sequins."

"I'll bet we could hire some of the kids who've been working on *The Hero* sets to come over and paint."

Becca nodded. "And then put up some appliqués?"

"Sure." Glancing around, Will shrugged. "Are they something we can just go buy?"

"Probably." Becca walked farther into the room. "But what I'd really like to do is make them," she admitted, a little embarrassed. Busy with her civic and charitable duties, she'd never really been the home-making type. An occasional afghan was all she ever managed.

Will's face was relaxed; he seemed pleased by her suggestion. "Will you have the time?" he asked. "I sure don't want you overextending yourself."

Warmed by his concern, Becca smiled. "I have a

feeling that by the end of the summer I'm going to have more time to sit and sew than I know what to do with.''

ALMOST AS IF BY DESIGN, they both turned away from the nursery and moved down the hall, through the formal living room, to Will's office on the other side of the house. Will left long enough to exchange his suit for some gym shorts and a T-shirt, and with little disagreement, he moved furniture around until they were both satisfied. They each had a personal workspace, enough privacy for phone conversations taking place at the same time, and the room still looked coolly elegant.

While Becca rearranged her files, Will sat down at his desk, intending to get through the day's mail. And found himself watching Becca, instead. There were still some things he could predict. The way she kept her pens lined up in a desk drawer, instead of in a holder on top of the desk. Her preference for index cards, rather than notebooks.

He knew that she preferred baths to showers, that Cheerios was her favorite cereal. That the only chocolate she liked was Hershey's milk chocolate. None of that fancy stuff for Becca. He knew lots of little things about her.

He just didn't know what she wanted out of life.

''How much thought have you given in, say, the past ten years, to my goals in life?'' His words dropped into the silence that had fallen.

''What?'' Becca looked up, perplexed.

Will repeated the question, his tone not accusatory, just curious.

"Well," she said, frowning. "I guess not much." She looked over at him, her eyes filled with apology. "I guess, when I think about it, I'm not really even sure what they are, other than to do well with Montford—and to have a baby, of course."

"Things anyone in town could tell you," he replied, still not with accusation. But with sadness.

"You've given thought to my goals?" Becca asked softly.

"No." He shook his head. "And that's the point."

He debated telling her something and decided to do it. "Sari called the other night after you were asleep," he said.

"Which night?"

"The day she found out about the baby."

"Oh. You should have woken me."

"She called to talk to me, Becca. She told me why you wanted the abortion, about being afraid of loving and losing."

Becca stared down at her desk. "I'd rather she hadn't done that."

"It's nothing to be ashamed of."

"Being a coward is definitely worthy of shame," she told him, her voice tinged with disgust.

"You didn't do it, honey."

Becca made no response. Will had the feeling she wasn't being easy on herself.

"What's happened to us, Bec? I had no idea you

were afraid of anything. I'd have said, if anyone could handle this, it was you."

"I don't know what happened." She shook her head. "Maybe we got lazy."

He nodded, picking up a pen only to throw it down again. "The relationship I thought was so close was merely drifting along, existing out of habit?"

Had the love he'd felt for her all these years been merely a habit, too? Something he was *supposed* to feel, programmed to feel? An emotion that lacked depth, maybe wasn't quite real?

"I thought we were close, too," she said, her voice low, defeated. "But it was all just going along with the flow, doing what was expected of us, wasn't it? We didn't really know each other at all."

No! His mind immediately dismissed her words. Yet weren't they exactly what he'd been wondering himself?

"So where do we go from here?" he asked.

Becca pushed away the files she'd been sorting through. "I don't know," she said. "I guess we have to figure out why this happened. Do we just not care enough? Or were we too comfortable, taking each other for granted?"

He nodded, thinking she made good sense. He just wasn't sure where to find those answers. "Maybe it goes deeper than that," he offered, thinking out loud. "Maybe we first need to decide, individually, what it is we want out of life."

She looked across at him, her features reflecting her pain. "I guess we do."

Which left them right back where they'd started. Traveling through a rocky relationship with no clear destination in mind.

WILL WASN'T BIG on celebrations, especially the day-long-and-into-the-night kind. Maybe if he'd been able to melt into the crowd, to be anonymous, affairs like this wouldn't be so bad—but he didn't think so. Crowds and endless hours of making merry exhausted him. They always had.

But this year, accompanying Becca to Shelter Valley's Fourth of July festivities, he discovered that the day wasn't as bad as usual. In the first place, he was taking a long hard look at the town he'd always simply accepted and finding many things he liked. And in his spare time, he was too busy keeping an eye on his wife to be bothered by all the people scurrying around him.

Dressed in deference to her position, she was wearing one of her dark-colored maternity dresses and pumps. He'd done his darnedest to get her to dress more comfortably. Was even wearing shorts and sandals himself to help her out, but she'd have none of it. At least the dress was sleeveless. And the pumps were low-heeled.

Watching her with her constituents, smiling, finding something nice to say to everyone—and knowing that she meant everything she said—made him proud of her. Her presence seemed to be magic as she smoothed away worried frowns, solved problems at booths that weren't set up according to plan, found ice when a delivery wasn't made, designed a make-shift table skirt out of a table runner when one went missing, filled in when a worker didn't show up. Witnessing it all, running errands for her, filling in at the balloon booth when the helium tank was delivered late, he found it hard to recognize this woman as the one he'd discussed with Sari a couple of weeks before. The woman who considered herself a coward.

The woman who was afraid to love in case she lost.

This Becca, the one who could handle anything and make it look easy, was the woman he'd always known. The one he'd always thought he loved.

"You okay?" he asked her when he'd finished with the balloons and sought her out.

She was manning the Shelter Valley Information booth while the mayor's secretary ran to the portable bathrooms set up on the outer edge of the town square. "I'm fine," she said, smiling at him.

She looked happy. And tired.

"Don't overdo things, Bec," he warned. Not just for the baby's sake. Or even just for her physical health. But for her peace of mind, as well. He knew now how much she feared losing this baby. He was going to do everything in his power to see that didn't happen.

"I won't."

"Yes, you will." He stood his ground. "You've been running nonstop since six o'clock this morning, and it's 110 degrees out here."

"I've been in the trailer a lot," she told him. The town had an air-conditioned mobile office and first-aid center stationed in the middle of the carnival. "They've got Krispy Kremes in there." The glazed doughnuts were made in Phoenix and were becoming world-renowned for their sinful sweetness.

"Your face is flushed."

"Quit nagging."

He leaned his hands on the table, shoving his face directly in front of hers. "I'll make a deal with you." She smelled damn good—inciting a brief flash of her moving silently on top of him the night before.

"What deal?"

"I'll quit nagging if you'll agree to go home for at least an hour this afternoon and have a nap."

She frowned, stacking brochures that were already in neat rows. "I have to be here for the unveiling of Samuel," she said.

The statue, still in its crate, was holding the place of honor in the middle of the town square.

Another council member waved as he passed the booth. Becca waved back.

"That's not until four o'clock," Will said. "I promise to have you back by then." And before she could protest further, he added, "Don't worry about the play. Martha's got everything under control, and it doesn't start until seven, anyway, so if there's a last-minute problem, you'll be back in plenty of time to fix it."

Becca's face wore a saucy grin when she looked up at him. "Did you know John Strickland's in town for the holiday?"

"No." But he was damn glad to hear it.

"He's helping Martha move the sets."

Rose walked by, a foot-and-a-half-tall Follies hat on her head, the perfect complement to the red silk flapper dress she was wearing. She was busy talking to the ladies on either side of her and didn't even notice Becca and Will.

"She's looking good." Will smiled.

"With two babies on the way, she's happier than she's been in years," Becca agreed, smiling, too.

But Will wasn't going to be sidetracked. "Is it a deal?"

"You'll come with me?" Becca asked.

"Yes."

Will was kind of pleased that it mattered. He'd intended to stay with her, anyway, to make sure she did indeed get some sleep. He had reading he could catch up on while she rested.

"Okay."

RELAXED AND GLOWING from the success of Samuel's unveiling, in spite of the absence of all three of the living Montfords, Becca looked beautiful to Will as she slid into her seat beside him just before the curtain rose on *The Hero*. Wearing a sleeveless denim jumper and tennis shoes, she could have passed for one of the students about to perform. Except for the belly.

That made her Will's.

"They're ready to go backstage," she whispered. "Martha's running around like crazy, but the props are in position and all the kids know their lines. They're really excited."

They weren't the only ones. She could barely sit still.

Glancing down at her, Will placed her hand on his thigh. He could feel her warmth through the thin cotton of his shorts. She'd redone her hair, too, drawn it back on both sides with small silver combs.

This entire production rested on her shoulders. If it was a bomb, not only would she face tonight's disappointment, it wouldn't bode well for her Save the Youth program, either. Yet she didn't seem fazed by that.

There was no tenseness around her mouth. No strain in her eyes, worry lines around her brows. She was just plain excited.

Which was exactly what he would have expected of her. If the play was a bomb, Becca would find a way for the bomb to explode with dollar bills.

And yet—despite her strength, her resourcefulness—she was terrified to have a baby. Terrified to the point of almost robbing herself of something she needed more than anything else in life. Becca the powerful, Becca the weak; he could hardly believe the two women were one.

"I wish we could've gotten hold of Sam Montford IV," she whispered to Will. "Dammit, he should've been here."

"When's he ever done what he should?" Will whispered back. The man had been unfaithful to his young wife, then abandoned her to face the tragedy he'd left behind. Why, after almost ten years, did Becca think they needed him here? He'd not only betrayed his wife, he'd deserted Shelter Valley. Although he hadn't told Becca, Will had been rather glad she hadn't been able to track the man down.

AS THE CURTAIN ROSE on the portable stage they'd built beside Samuel's statue, Will put his arm around Becca and pulled her close.

Thanks to the outdoor misting system the town had had set up around the temporary seating, Becca could snuggle into Will's side without getting too hot. Or making him too hot, either. Sari and Bob were sitting on her other side, and they were doing the same thing, with Bob's arm around Sari, her head on his shoulder.

Becca envied them their happiness.

She'd seen Randi in the audience as she hurried in. Will's younger sister was sitting with a group of her friends from the college. Janice and Betty were there, too, with their husbands and kids. And Rose and her friends. They all waved at her, giving her a thumbs-up for luck.

Becca and Sari both cried when Samuel's Clara and baby boy were murdered.

"I'm sure glad we don't live in a time that would condone such behavior," Will leaned over to whisper. And in spite of the sad story, Becca felt a little smile inside as he confirmed what she would automatically have assumed six months ago—that her husband was compassionate. Not just judgmental.

Becca tensed as Samuel began his dangerous trek across the plains.

Will rubbed her shoulder. "You okay?" he whispered for at least the tenth time that day.

"Fine," she whispered back. And for that moment, her answer was true. She was completely absorbed in the play, its characters as real to her as people she knew.

Even Will was sitting rigidly when gold fever hit Shelter Valley, bringing violence and greed into Samuel's little town. And then in the late 1880s another tragedy struck. The second-born child of Samuel and Lizzie—a daughter, Elizabeth—disappeared. At fourteen, she'd been spending a lot of that summer off wandering on her own, according to her mother's diary. And one day she just didn't come home. Samuel spent the rest of his life searching for his beloved little girl, but she'd vanished without a trace.

The town—even Lizzie—eventually accepted the fact that she'd had some kind of accident and eventually been consumed by unforgiving desert life.

"What do you think it could have been?" the teenager up on stage whispered, conveying the stark terror and grief Lizzie must have felt back then.

The old sheriff shrugged sorrowfully. "A mountain lion perhaps, coming down for water," he told the girl's distraught mother.

Lizzie nodded in resignation, and Becca could hardly stand to watch.

"Or maybe a javelina," the sheriff said.

Thinking of the 450-pound wild pigs that roamed the desert—even now—Becca shivered, tears streaming down her face. Will squeezed her hand with his free one, pulling her more snugly into his side.

"Want to go?" he whispered.

Yes. But she couldn't. Becca shook her head.

Samuel Montford went to his grave believing that his little Elizabeth was still alive.

CHAPTER FIFTEEN

WITH THE FOURTH OF JULY behind them and her Save the Youth program such a rousing success, Becca had more time on her hands. Time to worry. To think. To rest.

John Strickland was in town for most of July, and when Will wasn't occupied with other university responsibilities, John kept him busy with plans and meetings—and on the golf course, as well.

"I'm going to shoot six under par by the end of the summer if it's the last thing I do," Will said one morning on his way out for a round of golf with John.

Becca waved him off from her half-reclining position on the leather sofa in their peaceful, window-enclosed family room. Sewing sequins to a silky appliqué, she pondered Will's parting remark. She'd had no idea he felt such passion for his performance on the golf course. She'd known he enjoyed the game, of course. How could she not, considering the number of times a year he played? She'd just never realized his actual score was important to him. Or what under par meant, for that matter.

Was it the first time he'd ever mentioned it? Or had she just never listened before?

Becca had a terrible feeling it was the latter.

The time they had free that summer, they spent in
the company of others. With Sari and Bob, Randi and
her friends, sometimes John. Sometimes Martha,
who—other than receiving a generous check every
two weeks from someplace in Connecticut—had not
heard from her estranged husband at all. When Becca
and Will were alone, their conversations were too
fraught with pitfalls that neither of them understood.

They spoke little.

Becca made sure she did any business she needed
to do while Will was out of the house, leaving his
office to him when he was home.

Which also helped keep them apart.

On the first Monday in August, in her seventh
month of pregnancy, she and Will drove to Phoenix
for an ultrasound. They were also picking up Todd's
replacement, Phyllis Langford, from the airport while
they were in town. During the drive, Becca questioned Will about the new psychology professor. Anything to take her mind off the upcoming ultrasound.

"She seems a very down-to-earth, dependable type
of woman," Will told her. "Highly intelligent."

Sounded as though Phyllis was someone Becca
would like. Right now, though, she liked the excuse
of not thinking about what lay ahead even better.
"Describe her appearance."

"Red hair, a bit overweight, medium height,
dresses tastefully. Pretty."

They still had a few miles to go. Thank God.

"She's not married?"

Of course she wasn't; she was coming alone.

"No," Will said patiently.

"Has she ever been married?"

He shot her a sideways glance. "Yes, Bec, she has, though my teachers' love lives aren't part of the interview process. She simply happened to tell me in conversation."

"She's coming from Boston College, you said?"

"That's right."

They were getting far too close to the clinic for Becca's comfort. She could hardly breathe.

"Is that her alma mater?"

"No. She graduated from Yale."

Will made a left turn, and they were only a few streets away from the ultrasound place. *Please, God, let my baby be all right. Let them find both heart ventricles, all the valves and organs—everything they need to find.*

"How old did you say she was?" Becca asked.

Will reached over and held her hand. "I didn't, but I'd guess she's about thirty-four."

"Just a bit older than Randi."

"Mmm-hmm."

"And she's never had any children?"

"Not that I know of." Holding the wheel steady with his knee, he signaled a lane change, clasping her hand all the while.

Becca wondered if Phyllis wanted children as badly as *she* had. If she ever felt the helplessly empty feeling so deep inside you couldn't reach in and pull it out.

"Just think, Bec, we're going to get to see our baby today," Will said softly.

"Yeah." *And that's exactly what I'm afraid of.* There were so many things they checked for. So many things that could be wrong.

"We'll get to see his little fingers and toes, see his face."

"Yeah." *It might be a her.*

"Dr. Anderson's been keeping such a close watch on things, we know he's growing exactly on course, that his heart is extremely healthy."

Her stomach relaxed just a little. Will had seen through her sudden intense interest in a woman she'd never even met. "Yeah."

"He's kicking hard enough to tell us his parts work."

With one hand splayed across her belly, Becca smiled. "Yeah." And then, "Will?"

He glanced over, brows raised in question.

"Thanks."

As HE'D predicted, the ultrasound of Parsons, Jr., as Will had taken to thinking of his offspring, indicated that everything was just fine. The measurements were as they should be. All limbs and organs were present and functioning. He, Becca and the ultrasound technician had counted ten fingers and ten toes.

He and Becca had counted them again several times that week—whenever they showed the video of the ultrasound to one or another of their loved ones.

They still didn't know the sex of the baby—by

their choice, mostly—but Jr. hadn't cooperated, either. It didn't matter to Will; he was a daddy. At almost thirty-two weeks along, Parsons, Jr. was pretty much a fully developed baby—just needed some growing time.

The phone rang as he was leaving his office on Tuesday, a week after he'd taken Becca into Phoenix. His secretary had already gone for the day.

"Parsons," he said, catching it on the third ring.

"Dr. Parsons?"

Instantly recognizing the voice, he sat back in his chair. "Yes, Christine," he said. "I've been waiting to hear from you. How are things with your sister?"

He still wished he knew what "things" were. Phyllis Langford, upon her arrival the week before, had confirmed that Christine's delay was due to her younger sister, but beyond that, she'd been no more forthcoming than Christine.

"She's doing okay," Christine said, her voice sounding more animated than he'd ever heard it. And yet, it was still oddly infused with caution, as though that was as much a part of her nature as breathing. "She had some trouble with an ex-husband, but now she's back here. She'll be moving out to Arizona with me. We've already shipped our stuff, and I'm just calling to let you know we're on our way out," she said.

Will grabbed a pen. "I'll be at the airport myself to pick you up," he said. "When does your flight get in?"

"We're not flying," she told him. "I decided to drive out, so I'll have my car with me."

That would take her another five days at least. Five days he couldn't really afford to give her. But he would.

There was just something about her.

"Fine," he said, but had to add, "Be careful."

"Always," Christine said. Somehow he knew her response was more a promise than a platitude.

WHISTLING AS HE LEFT the quiet campus that afternoon, Will looked around him at the big old buildings, the green lawns with benches and tables that would be crowded with students in another few weeks. Shelter Valley grew from a population of three thousand to almost ten thousand when school was in full session. The white latticework gazebos were mostly deserted now, but soon couples would be huddled together there, stealing kisses between classes. The cement-mounted porch swings, located throughout Montford's campus, would be moving again, rather than hanging lifeless as they were now. Groups of students would be lounging on the grass, studying, campaigning, planning, complaining, telling jokes. The occasional tired kid might be found sleeping there, too.

His step picking up, Will hurried toward his car. God, he loved this place. Looked forward to the day when Parsons, Jr. would be one of the students out on that great expanse of lawn.

Work was due to begin on the new classroom

building the second week of September, in time for students to participate in the official ground-breaking ceremony.

The building would be a weathered old man by the time Parsons, Jr. attended Montford.

So would Will.

Too buoyed up to get lost in life's tangled realities, Will drove through downtown Shelter Valley on his way home, waving to friends and acquaintances who recognized his car as he passed by.

On a whim, he pulled into an angled parking spot along the curb outside Weber's department store. The old edifice still sported a green-and-white-striped awning, just as it had in days gone by. The floors were wooden and they creaked, something Will remembered from his childhood. That and the clean, chalky smell he'd found so exciting as a little boy. A bell over the door rang as he went inside.

"Will! How the heck are ya?" Jim Weber called out to him from behind the counter. The great-grandson of the store's founder, Jim had graduated with Randi.

"Doing well, Jim," he said cheerfully. "How about yourself?"

"Fine." Jim nodded. "Business is good. I saw Becca the other day," he continued, coming around the counter to follow Will down one aisle of the old store toward the clothing department in back. "She's looking great."

Yeah, she was, if Will said so himself. Which he didn't. "Thanks."

Jim said something else, and Will nodded although he hadn't heard the remark. He was too preoccupied with his own situation, his own emotional state. It still wasn't clear where he and Becca were headed, not clear which of his feelings about Becca were real and which merely creations his mind had formed in her image.

With a small wave, he kept on walking when Jim stopped to help another customer.

It didn't take him long to find what he'd come in for. Weber's wasn't that big. Martha and Sari were giving Becca a shower the following month, so Parsons, Jr. would have plenty of things to wear. But Will didn't want to wait that long for his baby to have some clothes hanging in the closet. Its emptiness was too eerie when he walked in to the nursery late at night on his way to bed.

Settling on two of the tiniest outfits he'd ever seen—triple-checking to make sure they really were for normal, newborn babies—he chose one in green and one in purple. They'd be fine no matter which sex Parsons, Jr. turned out to be.

There might as well be some things in the drawers, too, he thought, and picked up several little packages of T-shirts. Paying for his purchases, accepting Jim's smiling congratulations once again, Will left the store a relatively happy man. If the past few days were any indication, Becca would have dinner waiting for him, and he was anxious to get home to it. To her.

Even if he did have to retreat to his office alone as soon as the dishes were finished…

HE'D BEEN IN HIS OFFICE for more than an hour, engrossed in the financial plan on his computer in front of him, when Becca slipped into the room. With a brief distracted smile in her direction, he continued with his work. She'd obviously left something she needed on her desk.

Becca didn't go to her desk. She sat on the sofa across from him—on the *edge* of the sofa, which had to be hard, considering how much extra weight she was carrying in front these days.

He looked up from the screen.

"I have to talk to you," she said.

"Sure." He turned the computer screen away. "You need my help with something?"

"You might say that." Becca wet her lips, her hands clasped in her lap.

Will waited, happy to be patient with her. At this point, whatever Becca required, he was there to provide. He owed her that.

It also made him feel good to help her. Was even, though he wouldn't admit it to anyone but himself, a little gratifying to know that she needed him.

She took a deep breath, gazing at him steadily, her brow creased, her eyes almost—was that apology he read there? Pity?

What the—

"Will, I want you to move out."

She wanted him to—

"What?" He must have heard her wrong.

"I want you to move out."

"Out of this office?" he asked, his mind a jumbled mass of confusion.

"No." She shook her head.

Somehow he hadn't thought so. But nothing else made any sense.

"Out of this house."

"I own this house." It was the only thing he could think of to say.

"We both own it," she reminded him gently.

"Right." We, as in the two of them together. "So?"

"I want you to move out."

She'd said it again. Almost as though she *meant* the incredible, unbelievably painful words.

He wanted to go to her. To touch her. To connect with the woman who'd been a part of his life forever. But she was almost a stranger as she sat there so composed.

So unafraid.

While his life was crumbling around him.

"Why?"

"I think we both need you to."

"I don't need it." There. She was wrong. They could end this nonsense.

"I think you do." Her face was filled with many things. She still cared about him; he could see it in her eyes. Though he looked, he couldn't find any spite or anger or any of the other negative emotions that could have explained the words she was uttering. What he did see was much more frightening. Conviction.

"Why?" he asked again. He felt completely unprepared. Completely unlike himself.

"We've been drifting for years, Will, going nowhere. You said so yourself."

"Maybe I was wrong."

"I don't think so."

In all honesty, neither did he, but that didn't mean—

"We've talked about this several times over the past few months, but we're still just drifting. Nothing changes."

He opened his mouth to tell her she was wrong. But his conviction didn't match hers.

"You still aren't sure what you want, what you feel," she told him. Her voice wavered, giving Will hope.

"I know I care about you."

"Caring and being in love are two very different things."

"Lots of marriages are based on caring."

"I want love." She paused, then said slowly, "And you aren't even sure you *want* to be married to me."

"What about you?" he asked. "You're almost eight months pregnant, Becca. You shouldn't be here alone." She was terrified of losing him, wasn't sure she could cope by herself. Sari had told him all about it.

"In the big city, I'd agree with you," she said, "but here in Shelter Valley all I have to do is holler and I'd have fifteen people on the doorstep. That's one of the many things that are so great about living in this town."

Okay, but still…

"What if you can't holler? What if you go into labor?"

"Randi has agreed to stay with me for the last month of my pregnancy."

Will slammed back in his chair, feeling as though he'd just been punched. She'd really thought this through; it wasn't some rash decision. She meant it. She wanted him to leave his home. To leave her. She'd already made plans for his replacement.

Desperate, Will searched for anything that could justify his staying right where he was.

"You're trying to push me away because you're afraid of losing me," he blurted, gaining hope when he thought about what he'd just said. It made perfect sense. "Just like you didn't want to love the baby because you were afraid…"

With tears brimming in her eyes, Becca shook her head. "A month ago you might have been right," she said. "But not anymore, Will. A month ago, maybe even a week ago, I would have been too scared to ask you to leave, even though I already knew then that it was the right thing to do. You need some time to yourself, the freedom to figure out what you really want out of life."

"I don't want to move out."

"I know." She smiled, but her lips were trembling. "And I don't particularly want you to go, but even more than that, I don't want you to stay."

Will tried to understand—mostly so he could talk her around. "I just don't get it," he said, frowning.

"Don't you see?" she asked. She stretched her hands out to him, then pulled them back, clenching them together in her lap once again. "If you stay, I'll never know whether you're here because it's expected of you or because you really want to be here."

She had a point. But he was willing to take his chances, anyway. He didn't want to move out.

"I need the time, too," she said, jarring him. "I need to know that my desperation to have you here is because I love you, not because I'm afraid to be without you."

Oh, God. This was bad.

"I'm forty-two years old," she told him, leaning forward as she implored him to understand. "I'm going to be a mother, to have another life dependent on me, and I've got to be strong enough, courageous enough, to handle that. I can't live my life in fear."

He searched desperately for a rebuttal, for reassurances that this wasn't necessary, but she just kept on talking.

"Last week, when we went to have the ultrasound, I ruined what could have been an incredible experience by being afraid, every second, of what that doctor might find. While you were busy rejoicing over every finger and toe, over the little mouth that yawned, I was frantically counting heartbeats." Holding her belly, she continued, "Not to mention the days beforehand that I lost worrying about going to the darn thing—and all for nothing. Those were days I could have enjoyed."

"Everyone worries now and then, Bec," he assured her. He had to say something. To try.

"I need the time," she said again, shaking her head as she looked down at her hands. She raised her eyes to meet his, and he saw tears in them.

"You aren't sure why you married me. Well, I'm not sure why I married you, either."

He wasn't prepared to hear that. Will's stomach felt like lead.

"I was graduating from college, had no clear place to go, was afraid to be alone. We'd been together for years. You were safe. The known quantity."

"It had to be more than that!"

"Maybe. I was young, immature." She shrugged. "It's time I grew up, Will."

She *was* grown up. An entire town relied on her, and she handled it just fine. Hell, she'd grown up long before he had, accepting their barrenness while he'd still been kidding himself that it simply wasn't the right time for them to have a baby. She'd faced the facts.

But looking at her now, he knew it didn't matter what he believed. What mattered was what *she* believed about herself.

That thought hit him squarely in the gut. She was right. He *did* need the time, just as she did. To figure out what *he* believed about himself. What he wanted. Who he was underneath the roles he played. He owed it to her, to himself, to their child.

They deserved to have all of him. Anything less wasn't enough.

"A while ago you said that maybe we each have to decide what we want out of life, and I agree with you," she murmured.

He stared at her, sick at heart, and nodded.

"I don't think we can do that living together. You can't break a habit if you're living it."

"I'll look for a place tomorrow."

Becca stood up laboriously, the effort leaving her short of breath. "Randi's hoping you'll stay at her place. At least until she's ready to move back. It'll give you time to find something you really want."

Time to find something permanent, he read into her words.

This was worse than he'd thought.

With a sick feeling in his gut, Will nodded. "I'll go tomorrow."

CHAPTER SIXTEEN

BECCA LEARNED very quickly what Martha had been talking about when she'd said that Shelter Valley helped her through the initial breakup with Todd. Will wasn't even out of the house before the calls started coming. Randi had told a couple of people at work that she could be reached at Becca's house, and that was all it took for word to spread, like a raging fire, all over town.

But in spite of all the support, she missed Will desperately. That first night she didn't even try to go to bed. Just sat in his recliner in the family room and hoped she'd fall asleep without realizing it. Probably because she was almost eight months pregnant, she did.

The second night, she lay down on the couch, wondering if she could again trick herself into sleep. And found that if she kept the television on, she could.

By the third night, she'd pulled bedding out to the family room.

"Aren't you feeling well?" Randi asked, jumping up to take the blankets and pillow from Becca. "The couch back helps support you, maybe?"

"Maybe." Becca hadn't really thought about it, but

yes, she supposed it did. Now that she didn't have Will's back to prop her belly against.

Randi spread a sheet on the oversize leather couch, tucking it around the cushions. "Are you having pains? Should we call the doctor?"

"No." Becca handed Randi one end of the blanket. "Not unless you think she could treat pains of the heart."

Randi stopped, blanket held in midair. "You're missing Will that much?"

Nodding, Becca bent to smooth the blanket over the sheet, trying to hide evidence of the ready tears. "I've never slept in our bed without him at night."

"Never?" Randi asked, shocked. "What about the time he went to Washington to receive that commendation... Oh wait, you went with him, of course." She smoothed her end of the blanket. "What about that conference he went to in Omaha? You stayed here to run the huge second-hand sale in the town square to raise money for the new clinic."

"I stayed with Sari," Becca said. "Bob was out of town then, too, at a swim meet with Tanya, and we had a couple of girls' nights out."

Randi plopped down on the makeshift bed, pulling a pillow onto her lap. "You've never slept in your bed without him?"

Smiling through teary eyes, Becca shook her head. "Never."

"Have you talked to him?" Randi asked hesitantly.

Becca nodded. "He calls every day to make sure I'm okay."

"He does?" Randi perked up. "So you guys are talking."

"No." Becca wished they were. She badly needed to know what Will was thinking, to share with him the discoveries she was making. She wasn't happy, but she was still sane. That had to count for something. "His calls are always quick," she told Randi. "Just asks if I'm okay and says he has to go."

School would be starting soon. She knew he was busy. But too busy to talk to his wife?

"So," Randi said slowly, "you planning to sleep on the couch for the rest of your life?"

Becca lowered herself beside her sister-in-law, unhappier than she'd ever been, but determined to hold on. "If I have to."

"You, uh, think this is permanent, then?" Randi asked, picking at the pillow.

Becca heard the sorrow in Randi's voice. Felt an answering pain in her own heart. "I don't know."

EXHAUSTED AND FEELING every day of his forty-two years, Will dragged his aching body in from a game of racquetball. It was his first Saturday afternoon of living alone, and he wanted nothing more than to crawl into bed and sleep for...well, forever, maybe. He should never have challenged the head of the Math Department to a game. The man was ten years younger than he was.

But what had hurt worse than the killing he'd taken on the court had been the pitying glances the other man had sent his way when he thought Will wasn't looking. God, he hated pity.

Almost as much as he hated living in Randi's house.

The answering-machine light was blinking as he rounded the corner into the kitchen. Pushing the button out of duty—he owed it to Randi to get her messages to her—he listened with half an ear as he filled a tall glass with ice from the bag in the freezer, then topped it with water from the jug in his sister's refrigerator.

Good thing he wasn't hungry. Water and ice were about all Randi had plenty of. Unless you counted the wheaty, grainy bar things his sister seemed to live on. She had a whole cupboardful of those. And fifteen boxes of cereal. His sister was a nut.

Four messages later Will was sitting at the kitchen table, leaning back in his chair, the water almost gone. He was going to have to get up and get some more. Eventually. When his thirst won out over his exhaustion.

"Will? It's Becca."

He sat up straight. Set his glass on the table. She'd introduced herself. He knew her voice, dammit.

"We've left it pretty late for childbirth classes, but we can still get into one if we start this week. There's an opening at the clinic here. Call me if you're interested." *Click.*

In two seconds flat, Will had speed-dialed his home number. He paced the kitchen floor as the phone rang, stomach tense. He was only slightly disappointed when he got his own answering machine. Maybe that was best for now. He and Becca using machines to do their conversing.

He agreed to her suggestion and hung up.

THE FOLLOWING SATURDAY Martha called to invite Becca to attend the Little League state championships being held right there in Shelter Valley. For the fourth year in a row Shelter Valley's preteens had made it to the final rounds. Martha's youngest son, Tim, was pitching for his team of nine- and ten-year-olds.

Still recuperating from her first childbirth class two evenings before, Becca wasn't inclined to accept. She was exhausted, physically, but spiritually, too. She'd thought the classes would bring her and Will closer. That being there with him would rekindle the silent closeness they'd shared all summer. Instead, they'd been like strangers. Polite. Distant.

Aside from the conversation necessitated by what they were doing, they didn't speak at all.

By the time she'd been asked to lie down, her big belly almost reaching Will's shoulder when he sat on the floor beside her, she'd been wallowing in humiliation.

"The game starts at five-thirty. How about if I pick you up at five?" Martha said. "We can get a hot dog before play starts."

Catching a glimpse of herself in the bathroom mirror as she walked past, mobile phone in hand, Becca reconsidered her decision. Her hair was a mess, sticking up at odd angles, she wore no makeup and had on a pair of her husband's sweats, cut off into shorts, with a balloon of a T-shirt on top. The colors didn't even match.

"I'll be ready," she told her well-meaning friend.

Martha knew what she was going through. Had probably even guessed that ever since Randi left that morning, Becca had been wandering listlessly around the house, wondering where she'd gone wrong. She'd spent the greater part of the morning in her bedroom, lying on her bed, wetting Will's pillow with tears she'd promised herself she wouldn't shed.

BECCA RAN INTO Phyllis Langford at the Little League game. She'd spent no small amount of time with Phyllis over the past couple of weeks, since it was a traditional responsibility of the president's wife to help introduce new hires and their families into Shelter Valley life. And regardless of whether she and Will were living in the same house, she was still his wife.

Due to Becca's precarious situation, she and Phyllis had grown close more quickly than would ordinarily have happened. Whether it was her training or simply a natural sensitivity, Phyllis was a good listener. A caring, objective, sensible listener.

She, too, was still aching for her ex-husband and could understand Becca's own circumstances without being told too much about them.

"Phyllis! What are you doing here?" Becca asked as the woman opened a lawn chair next to Becca and Martha's. Martha was currently making a run for more bottled water for the team, but would be returning shortly. Her oldest daughter, Ellen, was manning the snack truck, and her two other kids, both girls, were at an end-of-summer swim and slumber party.

"You can't go anywhere this week without hearing about Shelter Valley's chances in the playoffs," Phyllis was saying. "I figured, what better way to jump into town life? I grew up watching my brothers play Little League. I've always loved it. Besides," she added in an undertone, "I love the little house you helped me find, but the walls don't make great company. I can't wait until Christine arrives."

Phyllis's gentle humor was a relief, considering Becca's current state of mind. "I'm glad you're here," Becca told her. "You can explain this darn game to me."

"Sure. I'll tell you everything you want to know."

Martha came back then, and Becca had an uneasy moment when she realized just who Phyllis was in Martha's life—her soon-to-be ex-husband's replacement at the university—but the two women had already met earlier in the month, and Martha smiled a welcome.

"It's good to see you," she told Phyllis, followed by an apologetic grin at Becca. "Remember my cousin Jenny? She used to visit for a week every summer when we were little."

"The one from Nantucket?" Becca asked.

Martha nodded. "Yeah. She just called on my cell while I was at the store. Her husband's in Phoenix on business. She heard about my breakup with Todd, and they rented a car and are on their way out to see me this evening. I'll have to be home by seven.''

Sensing her friend's need to have some time with her family, Becca turned to Phyllis. "Okay, I've been ditched. Would you mind giving an old pregnant woman a lift home?"

"I can take you," Martha insisted.

"Forget it! You go visit with your family. I'll be fine."

"I'll be glad to drive her home," Phyllis told Martha.

After another five minutes of arguing—five minutes during which Martha stopped at least three times to turn toward the field and yell at the top of her lungs—she finally gave in. Becca and Phyllis were going to go hijack Sari, since Bob was at a Rotary Club meeting that evening, and go out for dessert after the game. Phyllis would then take Becca home.

Satisfied that Becca would be doing something other than hanging around at home, Martha finally sat down. But was soon on her feet again. First to swear at the ump, who, in Martha's opinion, wasn't smart enough to have graduated from kindergarten, then to tell her son to keep his eye on the ball, and the third time to make sure the boy on third base knew to run into home. In spite of the fact that his little legs were carrying him as fast as they could—and making damn good time—Martha's words were on his behind the whole way in.

"I guess when you're a parent you have to play the game, too," Phyllis said, grinning.

Hearing her, Martha turned around, made a face and went right back to yelling. Apparently the ump had made another bad call.

Listening to Martha's hoarse yelling, Becca thought about Phyllis's words. Parents lined both sides of the ball field. Very few were sitting calmly in their seats. Some were coaching, as Martha was. Some just cheering. Some were drying children's tears, helping Ellen at the concession, keeping score, planning after-the-game celebrations. They were all actively engaged. Martha was the oldest one there.

As a parent you had to play the game.

Becca would be fifty-two when her child was ten. Ten years older than Martha was right now.

Fifty-two and playing Little League.

IN TOWN SATURDAY EVENING, looking for something besides grainy bars to eat, Will grabbed a take-out burger at the diner and then, munching as he drove, stopped off at the grocery store. He hit the frozen-food section first.

"I was so sorry to hear about you and Becca, William. Perhaps you should just do whatever she wants you to do you can go home. Whatever's making her objectionable probably won't last, anyway. It's her condition, you know."

Turning from the case, with an armload of frozen pizzas, Will saw Mrs. Huckaby, his old Sunday-school teacher, behind him.

"Yes, ma'am," he mumbled, turning back. *The old biddy.* A whole lot she knew. He *had* done what

Becca said. Which was why he was living at his sister's little house, rather than the spacious home he'd had built a few years ago.

Wheeling the cart quickly down the aisles, he came to a halt and backed up when he passed the water. There was still a lot of it in Randi's pantry, but he should replace what he was using.

"Will! I was so sorry to hear about you and Becca."

The voice was feminine again—and behind him. But it wasn't his Sunday-school teacher.

"Thanks, Thelma," he said brusquely. He might be baching it, but he didn't need help from the town tramp.

"I'd love to have you over for dinner," she crooned, noticing the forty frozen dinners he'd stacked in the cart.

"Thanks, Thelma, but I already have plans."

"I can see that," she said, taking the hint with a smile as she looked again, pointedly, at his cart. "Well, if you ever decide to find out what a *real* woman's like…"

"I may just take you up on that," he said as she walked away, knowing he wouldn't consider it for a second. Thelma was well-known in town, and basically harmless. She was too obvious to do any real damage.

Several ten-gallon water jugs heavier, the cart was a little harder to push, but Will was determined not to repeat this experience anytime soon. He intended to load up, get out and not come back.

He had only one more stop to make before he was done. Potato chips. And beer. He'd run into an old buddy from high school, Duane Konch, at a comedy club in Phoenix the night before. Duane was a lawyer, divorced, but doing quite well in Phoenix. He was driving out to Shelter Valley with a couple of buddies for a poker game with Will.

Something Will would never have done at home with Becca. And yet, something he was looking forward to.

He didn't make it as far as the potato chips before he was accosted again. But this time, at least, it was with only a pitying glance—not words. He didn't actually have to stop. Or respond.

One of the sociology professors. Damn. School was starting soon. Could he look forward to pitying glances all day there, too? Did everyone have to know everything? Couldn't his life just fall apart in peace?

He could just imagine what would have happened if he'd brought home one of the women who'd come on to him at the comedy club the night before.

There would've been a race to his front door to tell Becca the news.

Picking up two bags of the chips Becca usually bought, Will paused before putting them in his cart. She usually bought some of that dip stuff to go with the chips. Looking around the aisle, Will didn't see any dip. Or any signs to tell him where the stuff might be. Besides, dip was a women's thing. Men didn't dip.

He started to put the chips in the basket a second

time, then changed his mind again. The chips were a bit bland without dip, as annoying as the stuff was. Looking around one more time, he saw a display of chips that were sour cream and onion. Just what he needed. The dip already in the bag. Must've been made for men whose wives had kicked them out. Picking up four of them, he headed, eyes downcast, to the checkout.

He couldn't take another well-meant condolence, spoken or otherwise. He didn't want somebody to stop him and ask him what he was doing with chips and so much beer, either. Didn't want to answer any more questions, period.

He didn't want anything to get back to Becca.

He wasn't doing anything to hurt her.

But she'd told him to figure out what he wanted. She'd told him to find a home of his own that he really liked.

She expected him to be gone long enough to need a home of his own.

Will grabbed another bag of chips from an end-rack display on his way to the checkout.

Enjoying bachelorhood was what this separation was all about. Wasn't it?

"YOU SHOULD MOVE to Phoenix," Duane told him later that evening as he laid down his cards to Will's winning hand again. They'd been discussing Will's trip to the grocery. "It's the only way to get away from the gossip. The people in this town will remember everything about you till the day you die."

Will knew that. He just wasn't sure moving to Phoenix would be any improvement. Shelter Valley was home. Not just ''home'' as a place to live but ''home'' as something more fundamental—part of his very nature. What kind of man was he to turn his back on it the minute it got ugly, lost its youthful sheen? Or was he the one who'd lost the sheen? He, who was finally seeing the cracks in the sidewalk?

Shelter Valley hadn't been young the day Will was born. The cracks had already been in her sidewalks. As irritating as they were, he was rather fond of them.

''There's a condo for sale near my country club,'' Roger offered. He was the doctor, if Will remembered correctly. Podiatrist. Or was it pediatrician? After four beers, Will wasn't positive.

''It'd be a long drive to work every day,'' he said, offering the deck to Scott for a cut.

The youngest of the four, Scott was a radio announcer in Phoenix. He'd been divorced twice.

''But a short drive on weekends,'' Scott said, grinning. ''Not so far to take a lady home to bed after a night of dancing.''

Will might be feeling a little blurry about things, but he knew he wasn't at that point yet. The point of bringing women home.

Having the guys in, drinking far more than he should, sitting in a room full of smoke and foul language—that was enough of a stretch.

But damn, he thought, looking around the table, his gaze landing on the chips piling up in front of him, this sure was fun.

"Let me know when you're ready to file the papers," Duane said. "I'll save you a bundle."

Staring at his cards, not sure if that was a six or a nine, Will's fun screeched to a halt.

"File the papers?" he asked, trying to enunciate clearly.

"For the divorce," Roger filled in, belching as he helped himself to his fifth beer. The man should be a fat ugly loser the way he was sucking down those beers, not an athletic successful doctor.

After the couple of seconds it took him to compute Roger's words, Will put his beer bottle down on the table so hard beer sloshed out the top. "Who said anything about divorce?"

"You're separated," Scott said cynically, a man well-versed in the realities of broken relationships. "That's just the prelude to when she hits you up for all you've got."

"Becca wouldn't do that. We're just taking some time to be sure the decision we made twenty years ago was the one we wanted to make."

"Uh-huh," all three men said together with knowing grins.

"She didn't want me to leave." Will heard his voice getting louder. "It was the only way for us to get a clear look."

Though he wasn't sure he was seeing any more clearly away from Becca than when he was sleeping right beside her. He still carried her with him everywhere he went.

"That's what they all say," Duane told him. "Take it from a guy who hears about it all day long."

"Becca's different." Was she carrying him with her, too? He suspected she was. Did that say anything about them? He took another swallow of beer as he thought about that.

"Just take my card," Duane said, pulling a business card out of his wallet. "Call me when she hits you with it. Because trust me, man, she will."

"My wife cried a pool of tears after she kicked me out," Roger said. "A month later she came after me for half of everything."

"I held her at a quarter," Duane reminded him.

"And thanks to you, I'm in for ten," Roger said, throwing a couple of chips on the table.

"I'll double you," Will told him, recklessly throwing out chips. He needed another beer, too. To chase the one he was going to down in one gulp just as soon as he won this hand.

He'd better get used to bachelorhood. It might be all he had.

The next day, when Will stumbled out of bed some time after noon, Duane's business card was still sitting right where he'd left it in the middle of the kitchen table.

CHAPTER SEVENTEEN

"GIVE ME SOME EXERCISES to do," Becca asked Randi the last Monday morning in August. After seeing Martha dash around at the Little League tournament on Saturday—and the energy her friend exerted when Shelter Valley knocked in the winning run—Becca knew she had to prepare herself for the years ahead. Starting immediately.

"What kind of exercises?" Randi asked, coming fully into the family room to join Becca on the floor.

"Stay-young-and-energetic ones."

Randi laughed. "I noticed the eye cream on your bathroom counter when I went in for fresh towels," she said. "How long you been using that stuff?"

"One day," Becca admitted sheepishly. "You notice any difference?" She batted her eyes.

"Oh, Bec," Randi said, laughing, "your eyes are beautiful just the way they are."

But Becca was determined. "Still, it doesn't hurt to get in shape. I may not be able to do anything about the aging that comes with forty-two years of living, but I can certainly control what kind of shape my body's in."

Grinning, Randi looked at Becca's huge belly. "I wouldn't be so sure of that if I were you."

But before the morning was over, Randi had taken Becca through an entire series of safe yet effective exercises to help her, not only during the birth but the weight-loss period afterward, as well.

"You do these every morning, keep them up after the baby comes, and you'll live to be a hundred," Randi promised her.

Finally, a promise Becca wanted to hear. If she lived to be a hundred, her baby would be almost old before she died.

THAT NIGHT, alone in her house, Becca reached rock bottom. And nothing happened. She didn't convulse. Or scream. She didn't foam at the mouth or run raging through the rooms like a maniac. She sat quietly on the leather sofa in the family room, doing absolutely nothing, seeing nothing. Feeling nothing.

Nothing mattered. She was completely and utterly alone. Not just in her house, but in her heart.

Glancing at the rocker she and Will had picked out together, she knew, objectively, that seeing it there should hurt. But it was just a chair. Not moving. As lifeless as she.

"I'm okay," she announced to the dust motes collecting on her tables. They didn't stir. "I'm not falling apart."

The room didn't notice at all. Didn't change at all.

Will was gone. They'd been separated for almost two weeks with no sign of reconciliation. She was all alone in the world.

As the time passed, Becca sat there, amazed that

nothing terrible or urgent was happening. She wasn't being carried away by men in white coats; she wasn't dying; she wasn't even crying. She was still sitting calmly in her family room, untouched. As was everything around her.

The bookshelf held the collection of favorites she and Will had gathered over the years—including the book with the torn black binding they'd picked up in a musty old store on a back street in London. It was a collection of world mythology.

Her sofa was clean. She and Will kept it that way. They had a bottle of leather cleaner under the sink in the kitchen. The thick tapestry rug lay with its familiar pattern, images of doves in each corner with a serpent wrapping around most of the piece. You had to really look to see the figures. But she'd looked at it so many times, she saw them immediately.

The television sat silent across the room, part of the home-theater system she'd bought Will for Christmas. It had Surround Sound, a DVD player, a VCR. His stereo components were there, too.

The plants needed dusting, though not watering, thanks to Randi.

They were going to have to get another CD rack soon. Theirs was almost full. The afghan lying along one corner of the back of the love seat had a bump on one side, where it was folded unevenly. She'd fix it.

The walls still looked pretty good, though they hadn't been painted since the house was built. Hmm. Could be they looked so good because she'd only turned on one small lamp, on the end table beside her, when she'd come into the room.

She didn't see any smudges in the entire wall of windows, but then, it was nighttime. Dark outside. The tiny lights in the distance, seen from her vantage point up on the mountain, would hardly cast enough illumination to show smudges.

She was glad. Smudges bothered her, and she didn't have the energy to wash windows.

Becca wondered if she was going to fall asleep sitting there. Not that she felt sleepy, but it was night. She'd feel sleepy eventually. She could always pull the afghan over her if she did.

Of course, she'd have to get up and walk over to the love seat to pick it up. Later. But that would take care of the bump where it was folded unevenly.

Just as she was feeling almost resigned to her numbness, the baby gave her a not-so-gentle nudge. Looking down, Becca watched as a small lump formed against her belly, visible even through the T-shirt she was wearing. It moved slowly across her belly and she followed its progress, both inside and out. She could feel the tiny body part move. She could see it.

"It's okay, little one," she murmured, almost dazed as she watched. "My mind's still here, with all the other things in this room. I'm alert and aware. Believe it or not."

The movement stopped.

Placing her hand over the small lump still poking

out, she rubbed gently. "I'm going to be able to take care of you," she whispered. "I'm sure of it now."

With these words came the first twinge of feeling. Though intense, it lasted only a brief second and was gone.

The lump disappeared.

"It's not that I didn't have enough strength, which was what I feared," she said quickly, still talking out loud. "I just didn't know I had it. It hadn't ever really been tested."

The baby kicked, and feeling returned to Becca in a rush. Big tears welled up in her eyes, slid down her face, as her heart opened up and dark lonely holes filled with peace.

"I'm okay," she whispered. "Whatever comes, I'm going to be okay."

As though digesting the meaning of those momentous words, the baby was still.

"I may not be happy," Becca admitted, half laughing through her tears as she looked down at the mound that hid her baby. "I'll never be completely happy without your daddy." She stopped. Sniffed. Wiped her tears. "I love him so much...."

Her voice broke. "But I'll be okay, no matter what," she said with a shuddering breath.

The baby pushed, and Becca felt his small touch, first inside her and then where he pushed against the hand she had lying across her belly. He was probably only responding to her warmth. Or maybe the limb had already been there. But in Becca's heart, her baby had just reached out to hold her hand.

''I love you.'' She'd never said the words to her baby. Never allowed herself to think them.

And yet, when uttered, they were as natural as the breath that had accompanied them.

''I love you so much,'' she said again, unable to stop the flow that had finally broken free from the dam she'd built around her heart.

''No matter what happens, I'll be here for you.'' She knew that with complete certainty. The doubts were gone, the fears replaced by something much stronger. Something that would see her through. ''If you have a need, I'll meet it,'' she promised softly, caressing her child. ''I love you.''

The source of her strength. It was that simple.

Her child.

Hers and Will's.

A miracle.

BECCA SLEPT in her bed that night. She'd put the couch bedding away and was already curled up before Randi came in from the basketball camp she'd been attending. She awoke briefly when Randi popped her head in to check on her and say good-night. And then drifted off again, holding Will's pillow to her chest.

The bed was big.

But she slept.

PHYLLIS LANGFORD hung up the phone slowly, deliberately, taking great care to make sure it rested completely in the cradle, taking care not to make a sound. Though it wouldn't have mattered if she'd dropped it.

Or screamed. Alone in her pretty little house that Tuesday morning, she was the only one who would have heard.

Christine had been in a car accident. She was going to be okay, Will had assured her—just arriving in Shelter Valley later than she'd planned. Instead of having more than two weeks to get settled before school started, she'd have only a few days. She'd reach town shortly before classes resumed.

Even that was okay. She was going to stay with Phyllis, anyway, at least for a while. Phyllis could get the room ready for her and her sister, Tory, who was coming with her. It wasn't as if she had a lot to do with her spare time.

Still, Phyllis couldn't shake the feeling that something wasn't right. Not one to give in to fits of fancy or an overactive imagination, she still couldn't rid herself of the sense of unreality.

Christine had called Will, which was fine. Expected. But she hadn't called Phyllis.

And that was odd. Very odd.

Shaking her head, telling herself that she needed only to wait until Christine arrived to get her answers, Phyllis grabbed her keys. Will hadn't just talked to her about Christine. He'd asked her a telling question or two about life, as well. And about Becca.

Becca had been confiding in her all along, but this was the first conversation she'd had with Will since the couple's separation.

He'd asked for a clinical definition of love.

She couldn't give it to him. Real love, the kind he

was searching for, was something you believed in or you didn't. It was bigger than proof.

Phyllis headed out to her car, intent on visiting Becca—especially after Will's questions. She'd made a couple of friends very quickly, of whom Becca was the closest. Even if the only thing she could do was keep Becca company while her normal activities were curtailed, that was better than sitting around alone. Worrying.

Dressed in an attractive, tank-style cotton maternity jumper that looked almost cool enough to withstand the 110-degree temperature, Becca invited Phyllis in with a gracious smile and more composure than Phyllis had ever seen her exhibit. She couldn't help wondering if perhaps she was seeing the real woman lurking inside Becca Parsons, the woman who'd been pushed beyond endurance by life's crises.

"I just made a pitcher of fruit smoothies," Becca said. "You want one?"

"Sure." Anything cold and icy sounded great. Pulling her sweaty sleeveless blouse away from her skin, Phyllis followed Becca back to the kitchen. What she'd give to have long beautiful legs like Becca's. To be able to wear short shorts, instead of the knee-length, thigh-hiding things she had on.

She might be younger than Becca, but the other woman definitely had the edge.

"You start teaching in less than three weeks," Becca said, pouring icy pink liquid from a blender into two tall glasses.

"Yeah." Phyllis took both glasses and carried

them to the table while Becca put the leftover smoothie in the freezer. "We have meetings all next week, and then, soon after that, the kids come back. That's the part I look forward to."

Becca joined her at the table. "We've got some great kids here."

"That's what I've heard." Phyllis thought to the weeks ahead with excitement. "I can't wait to be part of it all."

Becca sat back in her chair, her features relaxed as she sipped her drink.

"Did you attend Montford?" Phyllis asked.

"Yeah." Becca nodded. "Best four years of my life."

It was an opening Phyllis couldn't pass up. "You and Will haven't had great years together?"

"Of course we have," Becca said, though her brow was furrowed as she looked down at the imaginary spot she was scraping off the table with one long slim finger. "It's just that we wanted kids so badly." She smiled sadly. "We got married in college and started trying right away, thinking we'd have our first baby before Will started work on his dissertation. We were planning at least half a dozen, all told."

"Wow." A few weeks ago Phyllis would have been floored by such a goal. But after meeting enough of Shelter Valley's citizens, seeing firsthand how they put family first and actually took the time to enjoy their lives, she wasn't quite as shocked. Shelter Valley's straightforward approach to happiness would have seemed naïve to her even six months ago. Now she'd begun to believe in it herself. Despite her failed marriage, she'd had a good experience of family life as a child, and she understood how making family and community a focus, a priority, could create a sense of genuine contentment.

Looking around at Becca's beautiful impeccable home, Phyllis said, "So what happened?"

"We couldn't get pregnant."

Becca's words were simply stated, but her eyes portrayed many years of heartache.

"We tried everything, went through test after test, procedure after procedure, but nothing worked."

Phyllis wiped condensation from her glass. "What was wrong?"

Becca shrugged. "They never found anything, really. Nothing that would have prevented fertilization."

"But you and Will stayed together through it all?"

"We did," Becca said. "He was wonderful to me, understanding, loving, putting up with me when the disappointment became unbearable." She smiled. "He'd take me away to exotic new places, fill my mind with exciting new treasures, keeping me so busy that I'd fall into bed in whatever hotel we were staying at and actually go to sleep."

Trying to put herself in Becca's shoes, to feel what her friend had felt, Phyllis frowned. "So what happened?" she asked again. "Why did you and Will separate once you were finally pregnant?" It seemed that her friends had a dream come true in their midst and should be gloriously happy. Not living in two different homes.

Unless the baby wasn't Will's?

"I don't know," Becca said, her voice wavering. "It's all so crazy, so confusing."

"Is the baby Will's?"

Becca's eyes opened wide. "Of course!"

"Then..."

"I thought I had to have an abortion."

Phyllis couldn't have been more taken aback if Becca had told her she'd had a sex-change operation. There'd been no mistaking the anguish in Becca's eyes when she explained how she'd always wanted a baby.

"Had to have? Why?"

"I'm forty-two years old."

And suddenly Phyllis understood. "You were afraid something would go wrong."

Becca nodded, tears still brimming in her eyes. "I only figured it out myself not so long ago, but I was just afraid, period. Afraid to open myself up to any more love because that meant I also had to open myself up to the possibility of loss. Of being hurt."

Nodding, Phyllis took a sip of her drink before it got too warm. "I can understand that."

"You met my sister, Sari, the night of the Little League championships," Becca said.

"She's pregnant, too," Phyllis said, remembering. Sari was as beautiful as Becca and giddy with happiness. Kind of hard not to be a little jealous of all the blessings these sisters shared. "I don't know when I've ever seen anyone so animated."

"Yeah," Becca said. Her smile faded. "But two years ago you'd have met a different woman entirely. Sari lost her sixteen-year-old daughter in a car accident."

"Oh, my gosh." Phyllis's stomach dropped. "I'm so sorry."

"Me, too." Becca's eyes lowered to the table again and another imaginary speck. "The thing is, I was so busy tending to Sari, I never realized how much Tanya's death was still affecting me. I've been terrified of losing anyone else I love."

"It's debilitating to realize that there are some things we just can't control," Phyllis offered, thinking suddenly of Christine. Her friend had never known the security of control. Had never known a day of peace.

"Will couldn't forgive me for wanting the abortion."

"For moral reasons?" Phyllis asked.

"I don't think it's that," Becca said slowly. "At least, I don't think so anymore."

Phyllis heard the note of doubt.

"You don't blame yourself for considering the idea, I hope."

"I'm trying not to."

"Becca, there are times when abortion may be the only choice. Certain extreme situations…"

Becca glanced up, her eyes filled with doubt. "I know that in my head, but in my heart…"

"I knew a girl once who'd been molested by her stepfather," Phyllis said, thinking of Christine's broken spirit as she'd told her story. Hoping that her friend was truly all right after this latest episode. Needing to see Christine. Angry that something else had happened to her and wishing she could find a way to ensure that Christine never had to suffer again.

"He was usually careful, but one time, when he was particularly drunk, he forgot. She got pregnant."

The sound Becca uttered was heartfelt and desperate.

"She knew she couldn't have that baby. Not only would it ruin her life, her reputation, get her kicked out of high school, not only would it tell her little sister what had been going on, but if she wasn't capable of tending to her stepfather's lusts, he'd turn to her younger sister. This girl had to protect her little sister at all costs."

"Please tell me she had the abortion," Becca said, holding her neck. "How could a teenage girl possibly be expected to bear the child of...of such an unholy union?"

"There wasn't a legal clinic where the girl was living."

"No." Becca's blue eyes were filled with empathetic pain.

"She found a quack who did it for her, but as a result, she'll never be able to have more children."

"How can life be so cruel?" Becca whispered.

Phyllis had asked herself the same thing many times since Christine had confided in her.

"I don't know, Becca, but don't you see? That's why, when we're given a blessing, we can't look at the what-ifs." Phyllis desperately needed to help her new friends find the happiness she felt so sure was waiting for them. "We just have to grab it with both hands and experience it completely for as long as we're blessed with having it."

Smiling through her tears, Becca asked, "Could you please tell that to my husband?"

"You don't think he's willing to be happy?" Phyllis had never had that impression.

"I do," Becca said. "It's just that when I was considering the abortion, it made him feel he didn't know me at all. He was just so shocked. It made him start to question all kinds of things he'd never questioned before. It made me take a good long look at things, too."

"Tough situations have a way of doing that to a person."

"I've found my answers," Becca said with such peace that Phyllis knew something had changed since the last time she'd seen her. "Now I just have to wait until Will finds his." Becca paused. "And pray they're the right ones."

Thinking of the questions Will had asked her earlier that day, Phyllis had to wonder if he'd ever find the answers he was looking for.

Because he wasn't asking the right questions.

CHAPTER EIGHTEEN

JOHN STRICKLAND and Will were out on the golf course the next day, in spite of the more-than-hundred-degree heat. Will's off-white golf shirt clung to him; dust from the course clung to it. His shorts, a dark tan color, were not quite so badly off, but he figured it was only a matter of time. He was sweating like a pig.

And still determined to knock that little white ball clear to Africa. Or as close as he could get. Setting his cleated shoes firmly in the ground in front of the tee, he positioned his body, tested his stance, then positioned again.

"So what's this about you and Becca going to childbirth classes together?" John asked just as Will was preparing to swing. His club hit the ground with a thud.

"Yeah," Will grunted. They'd had their second class the night before, and seeing Becca had only confused Will more. He missed her so damned much—had been almost desperate for the opportunity to touch his wife, if only to place a pillow beneath her swollen body.

Will swung, knocked the ball onto the green within two feet of the pin.

"Good shot," John said, stepping slowly up to the tee. "I'm thinking about moving to Shelter Valley."

Will grinned. Finally some good news. "I'll be damned."

"Yeah," John said, getting off a beautiful shot, as well.

They gathered their golf bags and started the trek toward their golf balls once again.

"This isn't just because you've taken a liking to Martha, is it?" Will asked.

"No," John said, so matter-of-factly Will knew it was the truth. "She's still too raw from the breakup of her marriage, and while we've enjoyed the little bit of time we've spent together, neither one of us is ready for anything more. But I know that soon I'll be ready to settle down again, to have a home and someday a family. I loved my wife deeply, but I think I need to move on now. Who knows? If Martha and I still like each other after her divorce is final, maybe I'll ask her out."

Will was delighted to hear it.

And a bit put out. His friend was on the brink of discovering what he himself was in the process of losing.

"How did you know you loved your wife?"

Settling his heavy bag more firmly on his shoulder, John half turned toward Will. "You're asking *me* that, old man? You've been at this love business a lot longer than I was."

His eye on the little white ball still several yards

ahead of him, Will strode along. "Time means nothing. It's what you do with it that counts."

"What'd you do with your time?"

Will shrugged. "Obviously I didn't pay enough attention to my wife. Funny how you can live with someone for twenty years and not even be sure you know them."

"Keeps life exciting."

Will harrumphed. If this was excitement, he could live an entire lifetime without it.

Another couple of holes, a missed shot, and Will and John took shelter from the sun on a bench beneath a canopy set up for that purpose, sipping water from little paper cups.

"So tell me what you loved about Becca back in college," John said into the silence that had fallen. Midafternoon on a sweltering day, the two men had the back half of the course to themselves.

"Her body, of course." Will gave the expected— and true—response.

"From what I can tell, she's still got that going for her."

Will was kind of proud John had noticed—once he'd suppressed the initial instinctive need to kill any other man who looked at his wife.

"That's it? Her body?" John asked.

"Well…no. Her intelligence really attracted me."

"She lose that somewhere along the way?"

"Of course not."

John nodded. And suddenly Will knew what he was getting at. Focusing more completely, he was surprised to find that there was quite a list of things he appreciated about Becca.

"I love the way she carries her composure with her everywhere she goes. Like she's some kind of damn princess entering the room."

John pulled his five iron out of his bag. Will planned to take the next hole with a seven.

"You can always count on her manners. She knows how to act in any situation," Will said, kind of surprised to realize he'd noticed such a thing. Or that it mattered to him.

John slid his five iron back into his bag.

"I can tell what she's thinking by the look in her eyes."

"I know what you mean," John said quietly, and Will realized the other man was thinking of his deceased wife.

"She's the most unselfish caring person I've ever met."

"Does she make your blood race?" John asked.

The question was a bit personal, but... "Yeah, she turns me on as much now as she did in college. More probably," he added. "She's got experience now."

"Besides sex," John said, giving Will a sideways glance, "does she make your blood race?"

Looking out at the rolling green lawns spread before him, Will thought about that.

"She sure can make me angrier than anyone else I've ever met, if that's what you're asking."

"Yup." John took his seven iron out of his bag. "It was."

"Why?"

John stood. "That's love, man," he said. "They make you crazy, feeling all kinds of things you don't feel with anyone else. It's only because they can make you feel so incredibly good that they can make you feel so incredibly bad."

Will stood, too, pulled out his five iron. "When did you become so smart?" he asked.

John shrugged, set his ball on the tee he'd just pushed into the soft ground and assumed his position.

The game ended in a tie, but Will hadn't been playing his best. He'd been having a hard time concentrating.

"Let me ask you something," he said as they headed out to their respective vehicles in the nearly deserted parking lot.

"Shoot," John muttered, lofting his bag into the trunk of his rental car.

"You've lived in the world—big cities, high-level jobs, faced all kinds of challenges."

John slammed his trunk, leaned back against it, arms folded in front of him. "Yeah."

Will stood beside the car, his bag still slung over his shoulder. "So what do you think you'll find here in Shelter Valley to test a man's mettle?"

"Look at you, man," John said. "You've faced twenty years of disappointment, not being able to give your wife the one thing she truly wanted."

Will didn't need to be reminded of that.

"Guess that would test a man's mettle. Probably more than some white-collar game you could get all wrapped up in, working for some big company in some big city somewhere.''

Will pondered his statement.

"You and Becca are separated, right?" John asked.

Will nodded. John knew that. Hell, the whole damn town knew that.

"What could possibly be more of a test than losing your wife?"

NOT BOTHERING to change out of his sweaty dusty clothes, Will left John in the parking lot of the golf course and drove straight to his brother's house. Greg and his family weren't back yet from their summer home up in northern Arizona, but Will had a key. He only needed access to the attic above the garage, anyway.

Greg and his wife had taken their van, leaving the floor beneath the attic clear for the ladder Will lifted off its hook on the wall. He hadn't been up in Greg's attic for years. Had no idea how hard the package would be to find. He knew only that he'd find it if he had to open every dusty old box up there.

WITH RANDI OFF watching a practice tennis match— and keeping an eye on her new women's tennis coach, as well—Becca had the house to herself again. Wandering from room to room, she regaled her baby with facts about his father, merely sharing the memories as they came to her.

She missed Will so much her body ached. Someday, maybe, she'd be able to get angry with him for what he'd done, for promising to love her forever and then taking it back. She'd heard that anger was a cure for pain.

She'd just didn't *feel* angry yet.

The problem was, she understood. Will was a good man. A great man. The best. Honest. Caring. Responsible.

"He'll make a perfect daddy," she assured her baby.

He could control many things, could make himself do whatever needed to be done. But he couldn't make himself love her.

No one could do that.

He'd stick by his marriage vows. She knew that. Simply because he was Will. But if he didn't love her as she loved him, the marriage would not only be empty, it would be too painful to bear.

"Please don't hate me," she whispered to her sleeping baby. "But I've called an attorney in Tucson. I'm going to file for divorce and release your daddy from an impossible promise he's trying to keep."

Before the tears that threatened could overwhelm her, Becca made herself keep moving. She shuffled blindly into the master bathroom, squirted some bubble bath into the tub, and then maneuvered for another couple of minutes until she was sitting on the side of her huge garden tub, able to turn around far enough to reach the faucet.

With the water running, she peeled off the lightweight maternity dress she'd worn all day, but had to stop to blow her nose before removing the gargantuan underwear she'd had to purchase that summer.

"Stop crying," she demanded as she gazed at her form in the floor-length mirror. "You have to do something besides cry."

Clothes in hand, she wiped fresh tears from her eyes and stepped into her room-size closet to deposit the day's wardrobe in the dirty clothes hamper. Which brought a fresh wave of tears. The hamper never got full anymore.

She thought she heard someone call her name as she came back into the bathroom. She stopped a moment, then chided herself for her folly. Randi would be out for another couple of hours, at least—more if she went for drinks with some of her friends, who'd driven up from Phoenix.

Becca was going to have to get used to being alone.

"Becca?"

Freezing in midstep, Becca listened. "Will?" she called, feeling foolish as her voice echoed in the silent house. Was she so desperate that she was concocting his voice from the sound of water running in her tub?

Becca shook her head, grabbed her robe from the back of the door so she'd have it within reach when she got out of the tub and closed her ears to everything but her own thoughts. Picturing the baby she'd soon be able to hold.

"Becca? Can I come in?"

Spinning around, Becca clutched her long robe in front of her.

Will? She tried to answer him, but no sound came out.

"Becca? Are you all right in there?" he asked, but didn't give her a chance to answer.

His dear, sweet, worried, gorgeous face appeared in the bathroom doorway, to be followed by the grungiest body she'd ever seen. He was covered in dust. His clothes were sweat-stained. His hair, a little grayer at the temples than it had been a few months ago, was mussed and damp with sweat.

"What have you been doing?" she choked out over the emotion clogging her throat. She'd been so lonely tonight. Unbearably lonely. And here he was. Solid and strong. Right here in her bathroom.

"I went to get this," he said slowly, his eyes wide as they took in her mostly naked body.

Becca just continued to stare. He looked so damn good to her. Perfect, standing there, wanting her.

"Guess I should've taken the time to shower, but I've wasted too much time already..."

He glanced down at his golf clothes, and Becca noticed the box he was holding.

"What's that?" she asked, only mildly curious. She was more interested in hearing he'd come back to stay.

Not that he'd come to give her an old dusty box.

"It's for you," he said softly, lifting it toward her.

Suddenly self-conscious, Becca turned and slipped into her robe, knotting it tightly beneath her breasts before turning back to take the package.

He seemed to notice only now that the box was

covered with dust. "Here, let me," he said, brushing it off. He ripped through the tape securing it, too, reached inside and pulled out a little wooden table box.

"Oh…" Becca's voice trailed off as her eyes once again flooded with tears.

Gingerly taking the box from him, she ran her fingers over the frosted-glass top. More than memory than by sight, she read the words inscribed there. *Mommy's treasures.*

"I can't believe it," she whispered, loving the box with her hands, afraid to look up, to find out this moment was a dream born of a desperate imagination.

"Where was it?" She was still staring at the box.

"In Greg's attic."

He'd kept their box.

If this was a dream, she was going to play it out for all it was worth. The lid of the box opened as easily as it had twenty years before. Her fingers found the little card she'd left there. Blinking back tears, Becca read the words Will had written there so many years ago.

As thankful as I am for this baby, I'm even more thankful that you're my wife.

"It's truer now than ever," he said softly, coming forward as she read. He lifted her chin with one finger. "As thankful as I am for this baby," he recited, his voice thick, "I'm much, much more thankful that you're my wife." His eyes, filled with love, held hers.

That one look was all she needed.

Will had returned to her.

Sliding her arms around him as best she could, Becca clutched the box behind his back and sank against the man she loved.

"Welcome home," she whispered, just before his lips descended to claim what had always been his.

He kissed her gently, and Becca rediscovered the taste of him. The taste that had always sent fire raging through her. It was no different this night, and suddenly, too impatient for slow controlled loving, she quickened the kiss, darting her tongue into his mouth, around his lips, needing the passion they'd discovered this summer to quell the pain that had followed.

"I figured out something important," Will broke away long enough to say.

"What's that?" Becca asked, running her hands over his body until she found the erection her belly prevented her hips from finding.

"The love's always been there, Bec."

She stopped, looked up at him.

"It's what kept us together through all the bad times."

"I know."

She reached up, kissed him again.

They were both breathing raggedly when he pulled away. "Guess I need to get cleaned up before I finish this." His hands trailed down inside her robe.

"I happen to have a bath waiting right here..."

It was all the invitation Will needed. Rather than slowing him down, the tub actually helped him in reaching his ultimate goal. The back supported

Becca's heavy body. The porcelain sides supported her legs and gave him something to lean on.

All in all, she figured she'd made the right decision to drown her tears in a bath that night.

While she'd been gazing into frothy bubbles and wishing on stars, her husband, her lover, had appeared to take her to a galaxy all their own. If this was a dream, Becca knew she never wanted to wake up.

The man she'd loved all her life was back where he belonged.

EPILOGUE

BETHANY TANYA PARSONS was born two weeks before classes started that fall. A healthy seven-pound baby girl, she had lusty lungs and no compunction about using them. Before her body was even fully free from her mother's, she was greeting the world.

Her mother came through the birth just fine, with only four hours of labor and a relatively easy delivery. Smiling, a plastic cup of orange juice in her hand while the doctor finished up around her, Becca looked young and beautiful, her eyes glowing with dreams come true.

Her father, on the other hand, lost ten years of his life as he coached and breathed, sweated and prayed. He followed the nurse as Bethany was carried to the scale and weighed, as her mouth was swabbed and her skin wiped clean.

He left her to their expert care only when he heard Becca's voice behind him.

"Sari?" she said into the phone she held to her ear. "You can come over now!"

A pause as Becca's merry eyes glinted. "Yep, already."

And then, "Piece of cake."

"He's right here," she said next, obviously replying to Sari's bombardment of questions. "Oh, he did okay," she said, sending Will a naughty look that he intended to make her pay for the second she was able.

Becca's eyes softened suddenly, filling with tears. "It's a girl, Sar," she said. "We named her after Tanya."

Taking his daughter from the nurse, Will brought her over and placed her on Becca's breast. It occurred to him that he'd lived most of his life for this moment, the moment he'd see Becca's baby.

She was more beautiful than anything he'd ever imagined.

"Love truly does heal all pain," Becca whispered into the phone, but her eyes were for Will alone.

"Thank you," she mouthed to him.

Feeling his eyes fill with unfamiliar tears, Will knew that he was the one who owed all the thanks. He'd been given a second chance at the same life.

And this time around, he knew how much it was worth.

Turn the page for a preview of
MY SISTER, MYSELF
the second book in Tara Taylor Quinn's

SHELTER VALLEY STORIES

Available next month,
wherever Harlequin Books are sold.

CHAPTER ONE

SHE WAS ALMOST THERE.

The Shelter Valley exit, once a two-day drive away, was now just two miles ahead. How had more than thirty hours passed without her being aware? What had she driven by along the way?

Was she going to take the exit? Or wasn't she?

How could she possibly make a decision when she wasn't ready?

If Christine didn't show up to take this job, she'd lose it.

Another green sign whizzed by the passenger window of Tory's new Ford Mustang. *Shelter Valley—1 mile.*

Christine. Tears flowed from Tory's eyes, as they'd been doing for most of the trip, trailing almost unnoticed down her face. *Christine.* So beautiful. So worthy.

What do I do? How do I go on without you?

And then, to herself, *How do I not?*

Tory's life had been spared. That made no sense to her. Justice had not been served.

"What do you want me to do?" she cried to an absent Christine when the silence in the car grew too overwhelming. "Bruce thinks he killed *me*, not you."

Pulling over to the shoulder of the road, Tory barely got her car into park before the sobs broke loose.

Her beloved older sister had only been dead a week.

Tory was all alone. Completely and totally alone for the first time in her godawful life. And she'd thought, after spending two years fleeing a maniacal ex-husband, that it couldn't get any worse.

Her tear-stained face turned toward the sky, she tried, through blurry eyes, to find some guidance from above. Was Christine up there in all that blueness somewhere? Looking out for her? What would her sister want her to do?

There were no answers from above. But straight ahead, there was another green sign with fluorescent white lettering. *Shelter Valley, this exit.*

Twenty-six-year-old Tory Evans had been searching for shelter her entire life. But she'd never found it. Was this time going to be any different?

As long as Bruce thought her dead, she'd be safe from him.

Coming from old New England money, he had widespread influence. His tentacles were everywhere. They'd infiltrated every city, every small town, every hut she'd ever inhabited while trying to evade him. Bruce Taylor had never been denied. His mother, having found him perfect in every way, had refused to allow any kind of discipline in his life—still refused to see that her grown son was less than exemplary, making excuses for him with every infraction. And his father, a shipping magnate, had assuaged the guilt of his neglect with everything money could buy. He'd even bought off someone in the legal system the one time Tory had gone to the law for help regarding Bruce's physical abuse. Somehow the tables had been turned on her, the innuendoes so twisted that Tory had known, even before she'd faced the judge, that she was going to lose.

At thirty, Bruce didn't know the meaning of the word no. He took what he wanted—accepted it as his due. And he wanted Tory. Was obsessed with keeping possession of his ex-wife. The only way to be safe from him was to be dead. To stay dead. And to let Christine live.

It was never going to work.

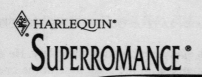

HARLEQUIN®
SUPERROMANCE®

You are now entering

WELCOME
TO
RIVERBEND
POPULATION
8793

Riverbend...the kind of place where everyone knows your name—and your business. Riverbend...home of the River Rats—a group of small-town sons and daughters who've been friends since high school.

The Rats are all grown up now. Living their lives and learning that some days are good and some days aren't—and that you can get through anything as long as you have your friends.

Starting in July 2000, Harlequin Superromance brings you Riverbend—six books about the River Rats and the Midwest town they live in.

BIRTHRIGHT by Judith Arnold (July 2000)
THAT SUMMER THING by Pamela Bauer (August 2000)
HOMECOMING by Laura Abbot (September 2000)
LAST-MINUTE MARRIAGE by Marisa Carroll (October 2000)
A CHRISTMAS LEGACY by Kathryn Shay (November 2000)

Available wherever Harlequin books are sold.

HARLEQUIN®
Makes any time special ™

Three complete novels by *New York Times* bestselling author

Penny Jordan

Marriage of Convenience

Three tales of marriage...in name only

Claire accepted a loveless marriage of convenience to Jay Fraser for the sake of her daughter. Then she discovered that she wanted Jay to be much more than just a father....

Lisa and Joel were at loggerheads over their joint guardianship of her sister's little girls. So Joel's proposal of marriage came as a shock.

Sapphire had divorced Blake when she'd found he'd married her only to acquire her father's farm. Could she even consider remarrying him—even temporarily—to ease her dying father's mind?

Don't miss *Marriage of Convenience*
by master storyteller Penny Jordan.

On sale in November 2000.

HARLEQUIN®
Makes any time special ™

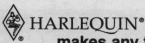

This Christmas, experience
the love, warmth and magic that
only Harlequin can provide with

*Mistletoe
Magic*

a charming collection from

BETTY NEELS
MARGARET WAY REBECCA WINTERS

Available November 2000

HARLEQUIN®
Makes any time special ™

Visit us at www.eHarlequin.com

PHMAGIC

Presenting...

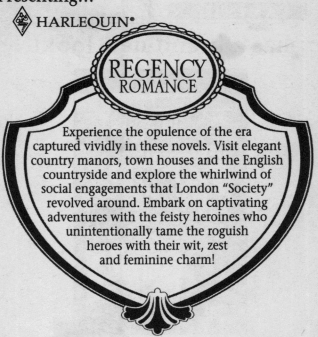

HARLEQUIN®

REGENCY ROMANCE

Experience the opulence of the era captured vividly in these novels. Visit elegant country manors, town houses and the English countryside and explore the whirlwind of social engagements that London "Society" revolved around. Embark on captivating adventures with the feisty heroines who unintentionally tame the roguish heroes with their wit, zest and feminine charm!

Available in October at your favorite retail outlet:

A MOST EXCEPTIONAL QUEST by Sarah Westleigh
DEAR LADY DISDAIN by Paula Marshall
SERENA by Sylvia Andrew
SCANDAL AND MISS SMITH by Julia Byrne

Look for more marriage & mayhem coming in March 2001.

HARLEQUIN®
Makes any time special ™